Her One T

A Novel

Ruchita Misra

HarperCollins *Publishers* India

First published in India by HarperCollins *Publishers* 2023
4th Floor, Tower A, Building No. 10, DLF Cyber City,
DLF Phase II, Gurugram, Haryana—122002
www.harpercollins.co.in

2 4 6 8 10 9 7 5 3 1

Copyright © Ruchita Misra 2023

P-ISBN: 978-93-5699-611-3
E-ISBN: 978-93-5699-612-0

This is a work of fiction and all characters and incidents described in this book are the product of the author's imagination. Any resemblance to actual persons, living or dead, is entirely coincidental.

Ruchita Misra asserts the moral right
to be identified as the author of this work.

All rights reserved. No part of this publication may be reproduced, stored in a retrieval system, or transmitted, in any form or by any means, electronic, mechanical, photocopying, recording or otherwise, without the prior permission of the publishers.

Typeset in 10.5/14 Minion Pro at
Manipal Technologies Limited, Manipal

Printed and bound at
Manipal Technologies Limited, Manipal

MIX
Paper from responsible sources
FSC® C043100

This book is produced from independently certified FSC® paper to ensure responsible forest management.

Her One True Love

Thank you Neena for teaching Shikhar. We love you!

Ruchi

*For Shikhar,
Rishi and Shaurya*

Prologue

Houston Orphanage and Children's Centre, Texas
August 1992

The joyless magnolia walls of the waiting room closed in as guilt, remorse, and despair clutched at my throat.

Steady. Gather yourself. This is no time for emotion.

I looked sideways at the man I called both boss and best friend. He was staring at the boy unblinking, his eyes gleaming. A plan so daring that it seemed impossible had just begun to take shape in my head. If I could pull this off, it would be the perfect solution for everyone. But *could* it work?

'With a *bit* of luck,' my brain replied.

'Are you being honourable—or even fair?' a voice in my head asked, and I immediately shushed it.

I had to do this. No matter what it took. And, with that, in a matter of seconds, for the second time in his life, I altered the fate of that boy.

'Being a parent requires love, not genes,' I leaned towards my friend and mumbled in his ear. I straightened and watched him grow still. The words, as I had hoped, touched a raw nerve.

Uncharacteristically nervous, as he fidgeted with the cuff of his shirt, my friend continued to look at the twelve-year-old boy who was now leaning against a wall a few feet away from us. I followed his gaze. The boy's black shorts were too short and orange T-shirt too big. His clothes hung around him like a shield from the world.

We pulled the boy off the streets just in time. He was setting himself up as a peddler. Mark Smith, the head of the Children's Centre, had briefed us before this meeting. *You know, he has a frightening temper and has been suspended from every school he's been to.*

He was probably the most handsome boy I had ever seen.

He had a mop of curly, dark brown hair, a chiselled nose and eyebrows that were defined in a long, beautiful arc. However, it was his eyes, all at once blue like the summer sky and grey like rain-heavy clouds that had caught my attention when he first walked into the room thirty minutes ago.

I'd have known those anywhere. Those were eyes I had spent the last decade thinking about. Eyes that reminded me of the most beautiful and the most painful time of my life. Eyes I would have given everything to see again.

And here they were.

He doesn't sleep through the night, wakes up screaming and kicking. He bites like a two-year-old.

Once you looked past the beauty of his eyes, what really caught your breath was that they were vacant. Dead.

This is the last time we're taking him back. If he runs away again, we'll let the police put him in juvie.

The boy was tall for his age, an odd mixture of fear and defiance on his face. I looked at the boy's fingers—beautiful and long, like an artist's. Or a pianist's. Right now, they clutched a worn-out Rubik's cube.

Prologue

He can barely read or write. He speaks in broken sentences. But he is clever—scary clever. It's probably a dangerous decision to have anything to do with this boy.

I saw my friend eyeing the cube and knew what would follow. With my friend, I always knew what was coming. I made a living, and a darn good one, from that knowledge.

Despite the steady stream of caveats and warnings from the Centre staff, I could see that the boy had captivated my friend. The machinery in my brain worked faster. Mark crossed his arms and stared first at my friend and then at me, a tad perplexed.

'Rubik's cube,' my friend said.

The boy nodded.

'You like it?'

The boy nodded.

'Are you any good?' my friend asked teasingly. I wondered whether the boy caught the tone because I saw him look up sharply.

'Any good?' my friend prodded again, smiling.

The boy shrugged.

'I have fourteen offices across the world, and I keep one of those on my table in each of them.'

The boy looked at Mark and then again at my friend. He bit his lip.

'Do you think you can solve it faster than me?' my friend asked, and I smiled.

Something flashed in the boy's eyes. A spark. Some life. But I could have imagined it.

'Start,' said my friend, tapping his watch. 'I am keeping time.'

The boy hesitated for only a moment, straightened up, took a step closer to us, away from the comfort of the magnolia wall, and then his fingers began to fly over the cube, twisting and turning it with a dexterity that amazed me. I recognized some of the moves, and they were clever—*he* was clever.

'Done!' the boy said minutes later, the hint of a grin on his face. He clearly wasn't used to smiling.

'My turn,' said my friend in his clipped British accent, picking up the cube. 'And I start now,' he continued as he began to twist and turn the cube. When he finished a few minutes later, neither the boy nor the man needed to look at the watch.

'I lost, mate,' my friend said, putting a friendly arm around the boy's shoulders. The boy drew back immediately, his eyes darkening with fear.

He doesn't like to be touched, I realized, and my heart winced in pain.

'Now that you've won, I must give you a reward, right?' my friend was saying to the boy.

The twelve-year-old looked at the suited man standing in front of him with some confusion. He looked at Mark, who nodded encouragingly.

'Do you like cars?' asked my friend. 'I am a self-confessed petrolhead, you know.'

The boy nodded, his eyes shining.

'Do you want to see mine? It's quite ... I don't know how you Americans put it ... cool, I suppose?'

The boy's head bobbed with barely restrained excitement. *He's probably never been rewarded for anything*, I thought.

'Come on then!' my friend said and motioned for the boy to follow.

I moved to follow, and, in the process, I stepped on the boy's toe. He winced and looked at me properly for the first time, his eyes hard, boring into mine. I felt a little shiver run down the length of me. 'I am sorry,' I said, staring at the boy, my heart hurting.

I am sorry.
I am sorry for what's coming your way. The love and the lies.
Love you deserve and lies you don't.
I am sorry.

1

Heisenberg Enterprises Headquarters, Knightsbridge, London

May 2016

It all began, Ika would later conclude, with Francesca Harris.

'Hi, I am Ikadashi,' Ikadashi said to her reflection in the mirror in a thick Indian accent.

'Hi,' she said again, tossing her black, recently cut hair. She stood straighter, taller. 'I am Ika,' she said, effortlessly slipping into a clipped British accent.

'There are two of you,' she whispered to her image, 'which one is the real one?'

Ika drew back and squinted her eyes at the mirror. A blush-pink fitted dress from Warehouse, size 10—one size bigger still eight months on from the birth. LK Bennett heels, because if they were good enough for Kate Middleton then they were good enough for Ikadashi Kumar. And a Gucci scarf, because fashion influencers on Instagram said that an expensive scarf could elevate any outfit.

Ika did her makeup in peace. The metallic clock in her white-and-grey bedroom comfortingly hovered around the 7 a.m. mark. The room was messy: a few Massimo Dutti bags—remnants from the shopping spree from the day before—were still lying around. Good, then, that Vivaan was not home.

Her phone beeped.

The new nanny. She'd be in at 9 a.m. sharp. Gross rate of £15 per hour. Ika rolled her eyes and tried to not do the maths. Because if she did, she would feel tempted to leave her job as Head of Strategy at HE and find a role as a nanny somewhere. New mums back home in India followed a simple rule.

House help = Number of full-time or live-in nannies (which equals to number of kids) + cook + chauffer + gardener + cleaner, who all come in twice daily.

All of this in less than what Ika will pay her nanny for five hours every day, four days a week. The injustice of it stung. It really did. Why, could someone tell her again, was she not going back to India to raise her child?

Her phone beeped again.

Francesca Harris. Once neighbour and now best friend. Blonde-haired, green-eyed, life-of-the-party, very hot, Uber-fashionable lawyer: *Don't forget the Spanx.*

Ika typed back: *I don't need Spanx.*

Francesca: *Trust me, you do. Also, Fredrick Heisenberg.*

Ika: *Stop obsessing over him.*

Francesca: *Can't. TRTH.*

Ika: *TRTH?*

Francesca: *Too rich too handsome. Click a sneaky picture of him, ideally one with his bottom in it. I hear it's quite cute.*

Ika: *Heisenberg or his bottom?*

Francesca: *Heisenberg's bottom.* •*peach emoji*•

Ika rolled her eyes but could not help a grin. She typed: *Going with the pink dress.*

Francesca: *Will look fab against your beautiful 'olive complexion'.*

Ika snorted. The colour of her skin had horrified Dadi, her grandmother, back in Almora in India, so much that Ikadashi had been dunked in a mixture of water and coconut milk every week till she turned six and threatened to bite anyone who tried it again.

Ika? Came another text from Francesca.

Ika: *Mmm hmm?*

Francesca: *They are lucky to have you. You are the Carrie Bradshaw + Indira Nooyi of M&A. Bat your ultra-black eyelashes, flash your dimple and smile your dazzling smile that many have written poems about.*

Ika: *No one has ever written any poem about my smile.*

Francesca: *And don't get bogged down by petty details.* •*eye roll emoji*•

Ika chuckled and tossed her phone back on the crumpled, unmade bed.

Ika walked out of her bedroom, towards the room that Veer shared with his granny, Ika's mum, Himani and opened the door. The room was dark and comfortingly quiet. Ika closed the door as silently as she could and padded into her kitchen. She sat at the dining table, a chunky thing in dark wood, and poured herself a glass of warm water. She squeezed a slice of lemon into it and sipped it slowly—a habit from her growing-up years in India.

Imposter.

That was the word that came to her mind very often these days. Both as a mother and as a working professional.

To get through the ridiculous seven rounds of interviews at HE, Ika had had to sell herself brazenly.

'To the table I bring thought leadership, can creatively solve commercial roadblocks and am able to form coalitions in complex situations,' Ika had said to Jacob Carmen, her future boss, not quite sure what she meant by the jumble of words that she was sprouting. Jacob, sixty-two, who frequently featured in style magazines coming in and out of the hottest parties in town, had nodded his head so vigorously and beamed so brightly that, encouraged, Ika had carried on. Sat across from him in his office—overcrowded table, a bright yellow wall with a hundred post-it notes and bright blue cushions on a red sofa—Ika felt her body relax. Despite his Uber-posh Hugh Grant-ish accent, with his white hair and round Harry Potter spectacles, Jacob gave off comforting I-am-rich-and-powerful-but-also-kind-and-avuncular vibes. Very Joe Biden-ly, thought Ika, approvingly.

And then, last evening, at Kew Gardens, all the NCT mums were fawning over their spit-covered bubbas. As they picked on organic black-bean brownies (£3.45 each) from Whole Foods, they spoke about how incredibly special these months were and how wonderful they felt taking care of their little bubs and how they could not even think of going back to work just yet. Ika, the only one nibbling on a Jaffa cake, was sat on the grass with Veer a few feet away, trying to eat ants. She was hoping that she looked suitably maternal, smiling and nodding at their words. Those nights when she had to rock Veer for forty-five minutes so that he could then sleep for thirty? The mealtimes when he would grab the pasta and hurl it across the white walls of their three-bedroom Putney apartment? The poo explosions that would reach all the way up his back? *Ugh. Ugh. Ugh.* Like, really, was she missing a point?

A little wail broke her line of thought and Ika looked up to see a baby crawling over to her, his curly hair falling over his eyes and his pink lips, shiny with drool, open in a wide grin. Her heart melted. This, this right there, was her reason to live, she thought. The poo explosions did not matter, did they? They kind of did, a voice in her head said, but we could park them aside sometimes, couldn't we?

'Should I even be going to work, Mummy?' Ika asked Himani, who trailed in behind the little crawler. 'Isn't Veer too little?'

Himani, dressed in a polka-dotted M&S night suit, sixty, was eerily like her daughter in appearance: an older, fairer, dimple-free version cast from the same mould. She smiled.

'*Puttar*,' said Himani shaking her head and trying to remain patient, 'why did I take early retirement and travel all the way here from Almora if not to make this transition easier for you?'

'I feel nervous. I don't think I deserve this salary, designation or company.'

Just for kicks, Veer let out a blood-curdling wail that Ika was certain must have made neighbours all around spill their morning coffees.

Himani smiled at her daughter and her grandson.

'Nar ho, na nirash karo man ko,
Kutch kaam karo, kutch kaam karo!
Jag mein reh kar kutch naam karo
Ye jamn hua kutch arth aho.
Samjho jismein kutch vwayrth na ho,'

Himani recited her favourite Hindi poem in a silky, sing-song voice that wrapped Ika in warmth that only comes from a language you have grown up speaking.

'Please explain.'

'As a human being you are the most evolved of the Almighty's creations. No matter what comes your way, what challenges, doubts, problems you face, do not allow these to stop you from growing, learning, from getting closer to the purpose you have been put on this planet for. Keep moving. Keep getting inspired. You have one life. Do not waste a second of it!' Himani smiled, 'Written by Maithili Sharan Gupt. Give it a read.'

Ika looked thoughtfully at her mother, and then she grinned. 'Aye Aye, Mummy!' she said smacking out a salute that made Himani smile. 'I cannot be late on my first day. I cannot waste a second of it,' she barked with a straight face. 'I don't want to upset Mr Gupta.'

Himani glared good-naturedly at her daughter and turned her attention towards Veer who was now inching dangerously close to a stray pair of scissors.

Ika eyed the clock in the living room and, when she knew Himani was not looking, she dashed to the kitchen and opened the leftmost cabinet. An array of idols, the pantheon of Indian Gods and Goddesses, clad in bright brocades and adorned with flowers, stared benevolently back at her.

'*Bhagwan jee*,' gushed Ika, brow furrowed, hands folded, and eyes closed, 'please take care of everything. Veer and Mummy too. I feel anxious about this new big job. Please help me! Please. Please.' With that, she closed the door to the gods and goddesses and rushed out of the kitchen at lightning speed, lest Himani spot her little numinous sojourn.

At the door, ready to leave, Ika took Veer off Himani for one last cuddle. From the corner of her eye, she could see the clock. Twenty-five past seven; she really should leave now—the District Line sometimes felt like a little old lady trudging up a hill, and her first meeting was at half-eight with Jacob Carmen. There was no way she was going to be late, she thought as she threw Veer a little distance in the air. Veer gurgled with delight, and Ika thought to herself that she had just enjoyed one of those 'perfect motherhood moments' they all talked about. The mum impeccably dressed and ready for her first day at the big job. The baby, suitably cute, giggling happily. Her heart felt warm. This was wonderful. This—Veer and Ika like this—could be a scene from an ad on the telly about baby yoghurt. Or nappies. Or nappy rash cream. Or baby formula.

As these various products danced in Ika's head, Veer came back into the safety of his part-excited, part-nervous mother's arms, and obliged the world by projectile vomiting all over Ika's face, hair and clothes. The gong made a single gentle thud to remind everyone that it was exactly half past seven. Ika's eyes burned, and Himani gasped. Veer, always the one to bounce back from little misadventures like these with admirable speed, squealed with delight. Because, why not?

∼

'I'm Ikadashi Kumar,' said Ika to the stunning girl at reception, her heart sinking at the receptionist's perfect hair and makeup. Self-consciously Ika patted her damp hair and hoped fervently that it was vomit-free. Maybe she could carry off this fresh-out-of-the-shower look, Ika thought dismally staring down at her ancient, boring black trousers and pink frilly top that she had last worn about five years ago.

'Aah, I am Ella, Mr Carmen has been expecting you, Ms Kumar. He will be here in five minutes, please take a seat,' Stunning Receptionist said in a lilting voice.

Ika breathed deep to steady herself. She had reached the office in time, and she was clothed formally. Things could be a lot worse. A volcano could erupt. Aliens could attack. Walkers could stop making Sensations Thai Sweet Chilli.

Ika walked towards the plush, tan leather sofa set against the exposed brick wall. The wall, outlined in black iron, Ika noted distractedly, was adorned with framed newspaper clippings and pictures. She squinted at one picture in the far-left corner.

A tall, handsome man in a white shirt was smiling at her from the framed picture, presumably taken at an awards night. 'Fredrick Heisenberg, too good-looking for anyone's good,' she mumbled, recognizing the blue-grey eyes of the heir to HE, thinking of Francesca. She peered closer, pleasantly surprised that there was just that one picture of him on the wall.

And then she sensed eyes on herself and turned. And went still. She was now looking at the same blue-grey eyes across the room.

Ika stared at them, transfixed, unable to peel her own away, like there was a powerful, celestial rope that pulled her to them. The eyes were coming towards her she thought panicking.

'Just first-day nerves,' Ika mumbled to herself, perplexed. The eyes burned with fire, but the face that housed them was busy, stressed, a bit angry, a little bit scary. The face of a stranger, but goodness, thought Ika, familiar. So familiar?

Look away, a voice inside her head said, but Ika disobeyed until she heard a jubilant 'Ika!' which startled her out of her reverie.

'Why, Jacob, hello!' Ika said weakly, turning to look at the elderly British man standing next to Fredrick who had both by now walked up to her.

'I have not seen you in yonks! Welcome to Heisenberg! I am most pleased to see you,' Jacob said exuberantly and clasped Ika's arm in a firm grasp. 'Was the journey this morning okay? Where do you come from? Hammersmith isn't it? The trains okay?' he asked and then continued without waiting for an answer. 'Allow me to introduce you to Fredrick Heisenberg. You are lucky—this one is a tricky bean to catch hold of. Freddie, Ikadashi Kumar, we were speaking of her just this morning. She will be handling our strategy department and will be working closely with me and, I hope, you as well.'

'Ms Kumar,' came a sophisticated voice. Ika shook his extended hand. His fingers felt warm, and long. 'Delighted to make your acquaintance. We look forward to having you here at HE,' Fredrick was saying, and Ika nodded.

Say something smart.

'The weather is…ummm,' Ika fumbled, looking around helplessly.

Damn.

'Yes, it's appall—' Fredrick was now staring at her.

'Rather windy?' Jacob tried helpfully, looking first at Ika and then at Fredrick, a bit puzzled, 'The WeatherinLondon app is a bit rubbish, I dare say. I happened to check another app this morning, and they said cloudy, but at the moment it is decidedly awfully windy, though you could argue—'

'I'll get going. Flight to catch,' Fredrick said abruptly to Jacob who stared vacantly at Fredrick, his mouth open. Ika could only watch the air around Fredrick bristle angrily as he jammed his hands in his pockets and briskly walked out of the office like he carried the weight of the world on his broad, handsome shoulders.

∽

With one elegant step, Fredrick got into his Range Rover, but his mind was still with the new girl from work and that kind of annoyed him. He had allowed himself the amusement of watching her for a bit from behind the safety of the glass door that separated the offices from reception. He had seen her run into reception in the most dramatic fashion, her wet hair flying around her. She had looked around in utter panic, checked her watch and then breathed out heavily, slumping against a wall, visibly relieved. She had clearly made it in time against all odds. Fredrick wondered what they were, those odds. Had she woken up late? Had she missed the train? Had she walked the wrong way?

Fredrick had watched her stand at reception, consciously patting her wet hair, taking in her surroundings. He saw her eyes widen when she saw Ella and that almost made him smile. When the girl smiled at Ella, though, he watched transfixed, as the dimple appeared, lighting up her face. He saw her walk slowly towards the feature wall and wondered if it was just his imagination or did she actually single out his picture? And then she had about-turned.

His phone buzzed.

Ava.

American actress and his girlfriend of five years. With Dad gone, she was all he had. Fredrick stared intently at his phone for a bit and then accepted the call.

'Hi, poppet,' he said softly into the phone.

∼

After a flurry of meetings, Ika finally sat down at her desk at 2 p.m. with a suitably deep sigh, taking in her new surroundings. The furnishings were plush, the office layout open plan and people milling about seemed like they belonged in *The Crown*. Ceiling-to-floor windows looked down upon Brompton Road in contempt, and Ika sighed at the delicious prospect of shopping, *window* shopping, regularly at Harrods just down the road as she opened her laptop. Gmail. Office email.

Ika allowed her mind to go back to Fredrick Heisenberg. His eyes, blue-grey and piercing, seemed to be everywhere. Ika imagined them bouncing off the insides of her skull, and it made her giggle. Francesca would love to know more, Ika decided, and with that, she opened a new email. Her first from the HE account. Only right that it was for Francesca and detailed Ika's opinion of Fredrick in the looks department.

> Subject: Fredrick Heisenberg: Alas, a mere 6/10 in the looks department
>
> Fran,
>
> This is my new work email ID. Keep it please, quickest to find me here. Added bonus—I can pretend to work while talking to you. Yay!
>
> In news you have been waiting for—most unexpectedly, I met Fredrick Heisenberg almost as soon as I stepped inside the hallowed, and should I add, magnificent portals of Heisenberg Enterprises. HE HQ looks like the Queenie's lounge—or should I say, •posh accent• drawing room—they just need to add gold-framed paintings of the Heisenberg ancestors in the hallway. And maybe a few stern-faced butlers—imagine Jeeves.
>
> Anyway, Fredrick Heisenberg is tall—a foot more than me easily—broad-ish, if you know what I mean, the kinds

that fill the space they occupy. Looks a little bit angry, like someone has upset him and he will soon bark an 'Off with their head' at one of his many minions.

Oh, and also, he looks infinitely prettier in pictures. I'm sure he has a team of ten sat hunched over laptops busily editing his pictures before sending them off to the tabloids. Sad to report that the great FH is at best, a 6/10 IRL.

Speak soon.
Ika x

Her phone buzzed. A text from Vivaan, her husband of eight years.

Ika distractedly opened the message. Maybe he has messaged to ask how her first day was coming along?

Vivaan: *Have you paid the council tax? Or are you incapable of doing this as well and I will have to do it?'*

Ika felt a weird but familiar kind of hollowness appear in the pit of her stomach.

Her fingers felt cold, and listlessly she pressed send on her email.

Immeasurably delighted that she had found herself a seat in District Line at peak rush hour of 6 p.m., Ika found herself happily munching on a three-bean Mexican wrap hurriedly bought from Waitrose as others packed around her like sardines in a tin. The day had, in the end, not been that bad. Jacob's yellow glasses matched with the yellow of his Gucci pocket square and he used 'Golly gosh!' with alarming regularity, but apart from that he was really lovely. Fredrick... hmm... him Ika could not quite place. He was respected, even revered (though Jacob called him 'old bean Grumps' but Ika figured Jacob was some kind of a father figure to Fredrick). And then there was the bit where they had stared at each other like their lives depended on it. A blush threatened to rise up Ika's cheeks, but Ika shook it away. And then she went still.

Her eyes grew wider. She thrust the half-eaten wrap in her fake LV bag and with dirty fingers pulled out her iPhone, went to Outlook and then to the 'send' folders. A distinct sensation best described as 'sinking' began to consume her as she registered what she was seeing.

The email titled 'Fredrick Heisenberg is at best 6/10' meant for Francesca Harris had been sent to Fredrick Heisenberg six hours ago.

Argh.

ARGH.

ARGH!!!

2

Mumbai, India

June, 2016

Fredrick sensed eyes on himself and looked sideways. Ika, bathed in the yellow from the streetlamp, looked away hurriedly, walking faster. The ochre of her saree glittered when it caught the light in an oddly harmonious contrast to the black of her little bindi, her kohl-rimmed eyes and the night around them.

She looked around and breathed deep, hating every second of being around Fredrick. It was like waiting, with eyes closed, for the doctor to rip off the bandage, she thought, trying to not look at him again. Will he ever mention the email? Did he get it? Did he read it? Is he upset? So upset that he won't even talk about it? Waiting for one small mistake to fire her? Will he project her email in a leadership meeting and ask her to explain herself? Will he forward the email to friends at *DailyMail*, who will then write a 1200-word article about women who objectify men at the workplace? With her picture in it? Images of a grown-up Veer reading the comments section appeared in front of Ika, and a shudder ran through the length of her body. With Fredrick's contacts and power, Ika realized, a hollowness appearing in the very pit of her stomach, the possibilities were limitless.

She had observed him from a (safe) distance in her first month at HE HQ. His face was usually difficult to read and his eyes, despite their blue-grey colour, held a murky darkness to them. She'd imagined him sitting alone in his office at night when everyone was gone, the eerie yellow lamp on, thinking of ways to murder Pendy from finance—guilty of using the incorrect currency exchange rate.

'Isn't Fredrick umm … a bit ruthless?' Ika had dared while working late one night with Jacob. Ika was staring at Fredrick's plans for a little consulting company they had bought for pennies, literally, from a depressed, stressed owner.

Jacob had guffawed and then startled at his own laughter he had cleared his throat.

'All noise, my dear,' he'd said dismissively. 'He is a fluffy little teddy bear. All heart.'

Fluffy little teddy bear.

Ika thought of the toned, muscle-ly, twenty-foot billionaire who plotted murder of unsuspecting employees in his spare time and shook her head. No. Fluffy little teddy bear was one thing Fredrick Heisenberg was not. Sorry.

'You've known him for a long time?' she asked again, chewing her pen, mind racing back to last week when on seeing him approach, she had instinctively ducked under a table. *Is he likely to fire me for an obnoxious email?*

Jacob looked up from his laptop, peering at her from above his Harry Potter glasses.

'I taught him how to drive, wrote his college essay for him and chose his shirt for his first date,' he said with a faraway smile.

Ika could not imagine anyone teaching Fredrick anything. For all practical purposes Fredrick was born rattling the times tables.

'Amazing,' she had replied, hoping her voice carried more enthusiasm than she felt.

Ika and Fredrick walked past an ice cream vendor. Torn used white vest and faded shorts notwithstanding, the man smiled at her. Distractedly, Ika returned the uninhibited smile, then stumbled over a little pile of stones, many of which seemed to dot the roads, but steadied herself before Fredrick could reach out.

'Damn the stupid kitten heels,' Ika mumbled to herself, glaring at them, and Fredrick bit the insides of his cheeks to stop himself from smiling. She had been looking away the last few minutes, determined not to catch his eye, he could tell, he thought, wiping his brow with an already very damp handkerchief. It did not say on the tin how humid Mumbai was, he thought. Ika was comically fanning herself with her hands. It made him want to smile. A lot of things Ika did, Fredrick was beginning to realize, made him want to smile.

Awkward silence descended upon them yet again.

Fredrick jammed his hands in his pockets and craned his neck to find their car, feeling familiar listlessness creep up on him. Everything felt heavy and burdensome, and he knew why. It'd been tormenting him again. The darkness that surrounded it. How do you move on from a place like that even after all these years? How? How do you find your peace if you only have questions and no answers?

'Where's the car?' came Ika's voice and he turned to look at her. She was nervously twiddling her fingers, looking around distractedly.

'The driver said he will find us,' Fredrick replied, sneaking in another glance at Ika. There was the matter of the email, he thought allowing himself a smile. In the last month, Ika had provided him great amusement because of, he assumed, the email.

The day after the email, Jacob had asked Ika to sit closer to Fredrick in a meeting, she had stared at her boss, face getting paler by the second, mumbled something incoherent, got up and left. Fredrick had watched with a straight face.

On more than one occasion, on seeing him approach, Ika had executed military-style about-turns at lightning speed—once even colliding headfirst with Ella, the receptionist. There was also a time, or maybe Fredrick imagined the flash of yellow of her shirt, when she ducked under a table as he approached. Fredrick had half a mind to crouch under the table himself to confront her, but he had decided against it, unsure how that would ever come across as remotely professional.

At the moment, they were both returning from a party thrown in honour of HE by their Mumbai-based clients whom Ika and team had helped secure a win. Ika had been in Mumbai for the whole of last week, and Fredrick had flown in for the last day of negotiations. At 10 p.m., Fredrick was just about to leave the party when Jacob Carmen had asked him if he could drop Ika to her hotel.

Fredrick looked around the land of *Slumdog Millionaire*—this was his first trip to India—everything fascinated him. Even at the late hour, the shops on either side of the street were open, and people—some in shorts and chappals and others dressed up like they were headed to a royal wedding—milled around laughing, talking and eating. The cars on the roads seemed to follow no rules and honked with abandon.

'I hate when people think India is *Slumdog Millionaire*,' came Ika's voice and Fredrick reddened.

'Why?'

'There is so much more to my country,' Ika said extending her arms out as if embracing the city.

'And?'

'What "and"?'

'What other things do people say?'

'They wonder how I speak such good English. And they ask me if there are elephants in India—'

'Which there aren't?'

'No. There are.'

'In zoos?'

'In zoos and also on the roads, sometimes,' Ika said, matter-of-factly. Fredrick raised an eyebrow.

'But it annoys me that people assume that they are…' Ika said.

'Of course,' said Fredrick not quite understanding. A stray dog walked past him, and Fredrick looked at it, startled.

The sound of Ika giggling reached him, and he turned towards her.

'It's just a dog,' she said, now laughing.

'In the middle of the road? At ten in the night?'

She laughed harder.

'What?'

'Nothing,' she said. 'Naughty dog. Should have been home at this hour.' And with that, she broke into peals of laughter. For a moment the awkwardness between them dipped. 'You know,' she said nodding towards a lady dressed in a dazzling pink saree, laden with jewels, stepping out of the car that had stopped in front of what seemed like a huge palatial building, 'it's wedding season here.'

'Wedding *season*?'

The dimple appeared, and Fredrick tried to peel his eyes away.

'Long story but, yes, wedding season. Lots of weddings happening in the entire country this month and especially today. It's apparently a very auspicious day. The gods approve,' she said, mock-solemnly.

'So, this lady is getting married?'

'Gosh, no. She is just attending a wedding.'

Fredrick's jaw dropped. 'Whatever do the brides wear then?'

'Have you ever attended an Indian wedding?'

'No.'

Ika stopped in her tracks, stilling, her eyes growing bigger in size. She brought her hands to her face. 'What?' he asked.

'So … okay. Don't just say no. Hear me out first.'

Fredrick looked questioningly at Ika.

'Would you like to see what happens at an Indian wedding?'

And not have to go back to an empty room in an unfamiliar hotel to spend the entire night working only to keep the monsters that torment him at bay?

'Yeah, sure,' Fredrick shrugged his shoulders casually, careful to not appear too eager, 'but we need to be invited to one, right?'

'Wrong.'

'Eh?'

'You can crash one.'

Fredrick stared at Ika, horrified.

'So, see, I have done it before. I know the drill. I promise I won't let us get thrown out. And it will be a *lot* of fun.'

Stunned silence.

'Come on!' Ika pleaded.

'I'm suitably horrified that I'm in, but as it stands, I'm firmly in,' Fredrick said with a shrug and watched Ika's demeanour change.

'Sorry,' Ika's eyes darted everywhere, Fredrick noted, and she shuffled uncomfortably, 'no, I should not have proposed it. I don't know why I suggested this. It's not professional, it's not…I…'

When Fredrick said nothing, Ika looked up. He was staring intently at her.

'Ms Kumar,' he asked, smiling kindly and pointing towards the big building, 'are we crashing this one or do you have another place in mind?'

Maybe, thought Ika, looking at the handsome face of Fredrick Heisenberg, quite aghast both at the fact that she had actually suggested such a thing as crashing a wedding and that the great Fredrick Heisenberg was actually game? Maybe he was not *that* bad? Maybe he was not always just poring over his laptop or giving fancy speeches, one hand jammed in his pocket? Maybe he did not always glare at people presenting, looking like he was ready to have them for a light afternoon snack? Maybe sometimes he was a *bit* fun?

There must be things he liked to do? People he loved? Like truly, *truly* loved? How did he love? Was he fickle with his love? No, said a voice in Ika's head as she waited for the onslaught of cars to ebb so that she could cross the road; this is not the man who could ever be fickle with his love. Ika looked at Fredrick, his eyes intense and blazing even as he mopped his brow. He instinctively had his hand out towards Ika, protecting her from the cars, as they jumped into the traffic. In the glare of the streetlights and against the background of the oncoming cars, he looked devastatingly handsome. Angry, brow furrowed, annoyed at the world in general and Mumbai traffic in particular, but gosh, so handsome.

And then Ika felt a twang of jealousy run through her. Ika shook her head with some degree of surprise. She was, she realized, feeling jealous of the woman the great Fredrick Heisenberg loved.

3

Bharati Wedding Reception Hall, Mumbai, India.

June, 2016.

'And what exactly am I supposed to do?' Fredrick asked, aware of the film of sweat on his brow.

'For starters, relax?' said Ika, wringing her hands nervously, inspiring very little confidence.

'Relax? When I am about to lie my way into the most important day of a stranger's life?' Fredrick asked incredulously, rubbing his sweaty palms against one another.

'We're being a little bit dramatic, no?' Ika squinted her eyes at Fredrick. She crinkled her little button nose. The dimple appeared. A bunch of hair fell across her forehead.

'I don't think so.'

'Then we shall agree to disagree,' said Ika resolutely, and Fredrick looked at her amazed and amused. They had crossed the shiny lobby laden with chandeliers and were walking into a reception hall outside where a beautiful formation of red and pink roses spelt 'Asmi weds Arjun'.

A steady stream of handsomely dressed people were entering by the door, which was being minded by two men in suits, barcode scanner in their hands.

Dad must be turning in his grave. 'Bad idea. Abort. Let's get out of here,' tried Fredrick again, gulping with some difficulty, but Ika grabbed him by the elbow. He stared at her hand holding his elbow and then his eyes flew to her face. She now stared at her arm grabbing his and then let go like she had touched a hot pan. 'Too late to abort,' she hissed instead, 'just follow my lead. We will stick to the plan.'

'And what exactly is "the plan"?' Fredrick hissed back, leaning over so that they could whisper.

Ika seemed to ponder on this very important question for but a moment and then she shook her head dismissively. 'We will figure it out,' said Ika not looking at him.

'Are you kidding me?' Fredrick mouthed.

'Sorry Sir, Ma'am, invitations please?' said one of the burly men at the door.

Ika flashed a very wide smile, presenting to Burly Man the side of her face that held the dimple, Fredrick noted.

'I think we misplaced it,' Ika was saying sweetly to Burly Man who was visibly melting in the face of Ika's charm offensive, 'my memory is so bad these days, you know,' Ika added with a silvery laugh. And then she shrugged her shoulders and clasped her hands to her chest.

Fredrick shook his head.

'I cannot let you in without an invitation, Ma'am. I'm really sorry. I need the barcode.' Burly Man looked like he was going to start crying.

Ika's face fell, and Fredrick had to smile.

'Let's go,' he said softly to Ika. 'Another day, perhaps?'

Ika looked undecidedly first at Fredrick and then at Burly Man. Was their adventure going to end before it even started, she thought dismally.

'The Sweeeeeetttyyyyyyy?' came a shrill voice and a plump arm laden with a million shimmering bangles landed on Ika's shoulders. Ika turned around to see a lady in a bright blue saree, her hair done up like a bejewelled high-rise building holding her at arm's length. Thick makeup hid her real face. The lady looked at Ika and then Fredrick.

'The Sweety and the Sammie? From the London? The Preeti ji's daughter and her boyfrand? First time in the India?' the lady asked in a shrill voice, her chest heaving with excitement.

'Yes,' Ika heard herself say, 'I am Sweety and this,' she looked at the mighty Fredrick James Heisenberg, 'is indeed the Sammie.'

Fredrick glared at Ika, who shrugged. *Just trying to be authentic.*

'I am the Pushpa Aunty. The Preeti ji's cousin sister from the Ludhiana. Your Aunty,' said Pushpa fondly placing her palm against Ika's cheeks. 'I recognized you in a second. One minute.'

'Wowzers, Aunty. AMAZING,' Ika said, shaking her head like she could not quite believe how good Pushpa Aunty was at recognizing people. 'Sammie, Pushpa Aunty. Pushpa Aunty, Sammie.' Ika helpfully did the introductions.

'Pushpapa?' Fredrick tried. Why were all Indian names such tongue twisters?

'Why,' said Pushpa Aunty to the world in general, checking Fredrick out from top to bottom as he squirmed under the older lady's gaze, 'look at this Chikna munda! What a handsome man!'

Fredrick watched bewildered as Ika threw her head back and belly-laughed, mouthing *'Chikna munda'* on loop.

'The Sammie,' Pushpa Aunty purred, 'take the papa and push him off. But not full papa. Just push half the papa,' she said, and when Fredrick continued to look dazed, she explained, 'My name. Just pa. Push-pa. Don't push full papa, just half the papa,' she said, wiggling her index finger, 'Push-pa. Will you remember now?'

'I scarce think I will ever forget, Ma'am,' Fredrick said weakly.

Fredrick's eyes fell on Ika, whose shoulders were shaking with silent laughter.

'We misplaced the invitations, Pushpa Aunty,' said Ika looking pointedly at Burly Man.

Pushpa Aunty nodded her head, rapidly grasping the situation at hand. She drew herself to her full height of five-foot-two and a half (in heels).

'These poor peoples have travelled in a plane for forty hours,' Ika tried to interject that the flight was eight hours, but Pushpa Aunty brushed her aside; trivial details did not matter, 'to attend this wedding of cousin and you will stop them because they don't have a wedding invitation? BECAUSE THEY DON'T HAVE AN INVITATION? Who says that's a problem? WHO?!' she asked in her shrill voice, staring at Burly Man with the proverbial daggers, knives and swords in her eyes.

'No one,' replied the Burly Man meekly and allowed the trio in. Pushpa Aunty and Ika high-fived like they were best friends. Fredrick had to shake his head in disbelief. There was a lesson in leadership right there, a slightly murky one, but one that should be studied and imbibed.

'First Indian wedding, is it? Let me show you our magnificent Indian culture,' said Pushpa Aunty, gesticulating with her hands as they entered the wedding hall. Fredrick looked around and let out a breath. The sight that met his eyes was really nothing short of spectacular. Delicate white-and-pink flowers, creeper-like, fell from the ceiling, interspersed at regular intervals with heavy crystal chandeliers that added a sense of extreme opulence. People, lots of them, dressed in heavy, expensive-looking Indian clothes, milled around hugging and talking. Traditional musicians clad in what Ika told him were 'dhoti-kurta' played the flute and the tabla. At the far end of the room, under the glare of about a hundred ornate lamps, was a raised platform, stage-like, decorated in brocades of pink and red, on which stood the bride and the groom. Asmi in a heavy lehenga-chola that seemed to weigh more than her. And Arjun in a red and cream sherwani.

'Take note.' Pushpa Aunty winked at Fredrick and Ika who looked lost. 'The next one will be yours, you sillies,' trilled Pushpa Aunty.

Fredrick steadily avoided any eye contact with Ika, who was, he could only imagine, doing the same.

'I will introduce you both to everyone,' said Pushpa Aunty and Ika paled.

'No, no, Aunty. Sammie,' Ika looked indulgently at Fredrick, 'is one of those British men, you know, so delicate,' and Pushpa Aunty looked maternally at Fredrick, shaking her head understandingly, 'best to not tire him too much. We will just hang around, talk to you, eat and then leave.'

'In that case, come sit,' said Pushpa Aunty as she made her way through a throng of rich-looking people.

They had just settled into their seats when a few girls dressed in ornate skirts came up to them laughing and Pushpa Aunty introduced the Sweety didi and the Sammie bhaiya from London.

'Didi means elder sister and bhaiya is elder brother,' Ika whispered to Fredrick, who nodded his head, slowly absorbing now not just the colour and vibrance of the wedding but also the warmth of the people around him.

'So,' said Pushpa Aunty, chattily, 'tell me the whole story?'

Ika looked quizzically at Pushpa Aunty.

'So, I know that you are the lawyer in the London,' Pushpa Aunty said, patting Ika's shoulders.

'Am I?' Ika replied and Fredrick nudged her. 'Oh yes, yes, corporate law. In London. Sometimes in Paris too, one week in London and one in Paris actually. In *Zone Two*. In both London and Paris,' Ika added jubilantly—what a great response with the details—and Fredrick rolled his eyes.

'Why him? Against your beloved parent's wishes?' Pushpa Aunty craned her neck to admire, once again, the beauty of Fredrick Heisenberg. 'But seeing the Sammie, I think the hanky-panky must be great,' said Pushpa Aunty winking.

'Hanky-panky?' Ika looked confused. Fredrick had a massive coughing bout, and Pushpa Aunty jumped at the opportunity of gently stroking Fredrick's back.

'I am very modern. I go to the abroad at least twice every year. Hanky-panky before marriage is fine,' she said dismissively. 'Everyone is doing it in India also. But the Sammie,' she now looked intently at Fredrick, 'you do intend to marry the Sweety, don't you?'

Fredrick cleared his throat. 'I do,' he said. Very solemnly, *too* solemnly, thought Ika feeling heat rise up everywhere.

'And when you have the little kids, *nikke nikke bachche* in *chaddis*, you will not forget they are half Hindu.'

'Nikkay nik...eh?' Fredrick looked at Ika in bewilderment.

'Little, little babies in underpants,' she explained with an embarrassed shrug.

'You will let them go to the temple?' asked Pushpa Aunty.

'I'll go with them,' Fredrick said simply. Ika sat still, glaring at her hands folded neatly in her lap.

'Aww…' purred Pushpa Aunty as she leaned forward, 'and because the Sweety is this tip-top lawyer, you won't mind cooking and keeping the house?'

'I hope to be equal partners with my wife in all we do.'

'You will treat her like the stunning Indian princess?'

Fredrick paused, leaned in and said, 'I will treat her like the woman of dignity and substance that she is, Pushpa Aunty.'

Pushpa Aunty gasped, clutched her hands to her heart and breathed out a long, quivering breath. She grabbed Ika's hands and placed them in Fredrick's. She wrapped her own pudgy fingers around theirs and held on. Ika stared at the floor, deeply uncomfortable, not just because it was the first time in decades that she was holding another man's hand (and that, too, Fredrick Heisenberg's!) but also because, in the last few minutes, her impression of Fredrick Heisenberg as the rich, spoilt man with far too much money for his own good had shifted—just a little bit—but shifted for certain.

'Sometimes, I can see things—the future,' Pushpa Aunty said, staring ahead, a faraway look in her beady eyes. 'You are the Raj and the Simran. You are. You are.'

Fredrick looked bewildered again. 'Raj? Simran?' he asked.

'Characters from a Bollywood movie,' Ika said breathing out, shaking her head.

'From the most romantic movie that defined what the love really means for the India, the Sammie,' Pushpa Aunty explained. And then she continued, 'Such a shame then that the Sammie works at the Waitrose,' concluded Pushpa Aunty gently slapping Fredrick's knee.

'No, no,' said Fredrick waving a hand and thinking about the time he had thought of investing heavily into one of the grocery store chains, 'I don't own Waitrose, of course I don't.'

'Own Waitrose?' Pushpa Aunty laughed as if Fredrick had cracked the funniest joke of the century. 'I know you manage the till at the Waitrose. I do all my shopping from the Waitrose only when I go to the London. Just like the Charles?'

'Charles?'

'The prince?'

'Ah,' replied Fredrick, weakly looking around, unsure of how to respond to this.

A slow grin of understanding spread across Ika's face.

'No, no, Sammie does not manage the till at Waitrose,' Ika said after a pause, and Fredrick looked at Ika with gratitude. Ika leaned into Pushpa Aunty, looked around surreptitiously and whispered, 'Can I tell you something?'

Pushpa Aunty leaned in and whispered, 'Yes, of course.'

Fredrick leaned in, too, the glint in Ika's eyes making him deeply uncomfortable.

'Sammie manages the till at Aldi actually.'

Fredrick drew back indignantly.

'NO!' exclaimed Pushpa Aunty, bringing her hands dramatically to cover her ears, 'No! No! No! Maybe the Preeti ji lied to us! Aldi!' Pushpa Aunty brought a hand to her heart. Then she spread it across her forehead. 'We never go to the Aldi, the Sammie, and neither should you,' said Pushpa Aunty. 'Try getting a job at the Waitrose. Even when doing menial jobs, you should keep your dignity.'

'Please listen to the Pushpa Aunty,' Ika said to Fredrick, who could only glare back.

In the next hours, in the midst of great fanfare and lots of screaming and shouting, Asmi and Arjun put a garland around each other's necks as part of the wedding ceremonies. About five photographers clicked furiously.

'The Badi didi is coming to meet you both. She met you in London last year?' Pushpa Aunty said to them, once the excitement had come down a notch. Alarm bells ringing in his head, Fredrick turned to look at Ika, expecting her to take charge of the situation, but she had just paled.

'Just wait, here she is, the Badi didi,' said Pushpa Aunty, craning to look for Badi didi in the crowd around the stage. Nothing still from Ika.

'Push-pa Aunty,' Fredrick leapt into action, 'as you can no doubt imagine, the crowd is making me quite anxious.'

'What?'

'Yes, you know. British men, not very strong mentally?'

Pushpa Aunty's face cleared. Of course. 'Yes. NHS. Council estates. If you provide food, housing and medical care for every person, where do they go to face the challenges? Tell me?' Pushpa Aunty said, her eyes growing large. 'Look at us. We get the entire nation to face challenges. That's how we are so strong and have such high immunity.'

'Yes, exactly,' said Fredrick brightly. 'I am not meant for it—you know, this excitement—I just need my council estate flat and NHS. I also need fresh air or I will have a panic attack.'

Fredrick looked at Ika. She was still looking a bit dazed. He grabbed her hand.

'Bye, Pushpa Aunty,' Ika said to the older lady, wondering why she felt like she was bidding farewell to a real family member.

'You are coming back, aren't you? You are in Mumbai for a few more days, aren't you?' Pushpa Aunty looked from Fredrick to Ika. 'The Preeti ji told the Badi didi that you may be shifting to India. My husband has a masala factory in the Gujarat. I don't know if the Sammie can speak to customers properly,' Pushpa Aunty paused, went on her tippy toes and comically put a fond hand around Fredrick's shoulders, 'but if we can train him and he can manage one of the smaller shops for us. We sell a lot of garam masala there, you know.'

Ika giggled. 'So kind. Sounds a bit challenging for Sammie, but I am sure Sammie will try his best.'

'Of course I will,' said Fredrick, glaring at Ika.

'We need to go now, or Sammie will faint,' Ika said to Pushpa Aunty with a sympathetic nod.

'These British men. They all need to spend some time with Pushpa Aunty to build up stamina. At least the handsome ones.' Pushpa Aunty winked at a mortified Fredrick, and while there was still a chance, placed a firm hand on Fredrick's back one last time.

~

From the storm of the wedding, Ika and Fredrick walked into the raging gale outside. The trees swayed violently, dancing in the winds that howled.

'Let me try calling the driver again,' Fredrick said, standing at the steps outside reception and hurried with his phone. When he looked up a few minutes later, his brow furrowed, he saw that Ika had walked outside into the open. Fredrick strained his eyes in the darkness. The winds seemed to be calming a bit, and it had begun to rain.

'What a terrible nuisance,' thought Fredrick, feeling a bit irritated.

'The monsoons are here!' a boy, obviously poor, clad only in shorts, his parents nowhere to be seen, ran past him, across the streets, yelling happily. The rains began to hit the sun-parched earth and a heavy, beautiful smell much like that of coffee, but earthy and not coffee, began to take control of Fredrick's senses.

'It's raining! It's raining!' the security guard in a blue uniform shouted happily. Another guard joined him, and the two men grinned at each other. Fredrick had never seen people get so excited at the prospect of rain. That certainly did not happen in London, he thought ruefully, a tad amused.

The rains picked up strength, and Fredrick looked for Ika. She was a little distance ahead, on the side of the road, her hands stretched out, letting the first drops of the monsoon hit her palm. Her hair danced in the wind. Ika's saree and the raindrops caught the light from the street lamps and glittered like jewels. A million jewels.

Ika turned slowly. She was staring at her palm, mesmerized. She was smiling. Her eyes shone. She looked ethereal. Fredrick stared at her unblinking.

Fredrick did not know this then, but this, this right here, the image of Ika in the first rain of the monsoons in Mumbai, twirling as she breathed in the magic, oblivious of both the world and her own simple beauty, raindrops shimmering on her saree like a million jewels, would be an image that would never ever leave him.

He would come back to this moment countless times and wonder if this was when he began to fall in love with her.

4

The Tenth Floor, Burj Khalifa, Dubai

August 2016

'So, we should not bid?' Jacob asked slowly, peering at Ika from above his glasses. Jacob's turquoise glass frames matched perfectly with both his silk pocket square and his socks, Ika noted with grudging admiration. She thought she was doing well in a wine-coloured shift dress, pink lipstick and white peep toes, but clearly there was a lot left to be worked upon, she thought with a deep sigh.

Ten people, including Fredrick and Jacob, representing the core management team for the acquisition of Agex, a Dubai-based tech start-up, were staring at her in the plush meeting room on the tenth floor of Burj Khalifa.

'Ika?' Jacob prodded, cutting her line of thought, 'so we should not bid?'

'No,' said Ika resolutely, 'Agex is valued at sixty-five million pounds, and every extra penny is money down the drain. Harry Stiller, for *no* apparent reason, wants this company too, but in a bidding war, none of the bidders benefit,' she said decisively. From the corner of her eye, she saw Fredrick turn to look at her.

The Stillers and the Heisenbergs had been feuding for generations, Ika had been told, much to her amusement. Ika had grown up on a healthy dose of Bollywood films, and she was more than familiar with the *khandani dushmani* (family feud) plot line. The girl, innocent in blue and pink striped skirts meets cute boy in white Tee and joggers while on holiday in Ooty in India. They fall in love only to find out that their dads are both very powerful, AK-47-wielding sworn enemies. Drama unfolds (hammy acting done with utter incompetence and complete sincerity which makes it almost endearing), climaxing into a massive and unrealistic action scene where true love prevails. This feuding between Harry Stiller and Fredrick Heisenberg felt a bit like that to Ika.

'We need to pull out from the bid,' Ika said.

Jacob sat up straighter, raised his eyebrows and breathed out. And then he smiled. *Finally*, he thought, *someone who will confront Fredrick*. He tilted his head at the delicate-looking girl standing determinedly in front of him. She was not fire—oh no, *that* would be doused by Fredrick in no time. No, she reminded him of red-hot embers—seemingly harmless, beautiful to look at, but quietly powerful. Jacob looked at Fredrick and then at Ika. *Where's the popcorn when you need it?* He thought ruefully.

'You think Stiller is after Agex for "no apparent reason"?' Fredrick asked in a low voice.

Ika finally looked at Fredrick and felt her breath catch. *Good god, he's gorgeous*. And then she thought about the email. Argh, she groaned silently.

Think about tomatoes. Electric guitar. Rajesh Khanna. Pelvic thrusts. No. No pelvic thrusts. Electric guitar. Tomatoes. Aubergine.

'No apparent reason?' Fredrick asked again.

'That's correct,' Ika replied.

'Allow me to give you one. Stiller desires this company above all others because I want it,' he continued.

Ika was about to speak when Fredrick said, 'You give good advice, Ms Kumar, but only for someone who is looking at this acquisition as a transaction.'

He is clearly getting angry, and he is the boss. Do some simple maths and shut up, Ika, a voice in Ika's head warned her—a voice she promptly ignored.

'Mr Heisenberg, I'm sure I don't need to say it, but it's never a good idea to mix business and emotions.'

Ooh, Jacob thought, sitting up straighter. *Ika's giving it back.* The group, as a whole, expectantly turned their heads towards Fredrick.

'*Emotions,* Ms Kumar? Sometimes, business is everything but business,' Fredrick replied silkily.

'Numbers don't care about emotions.'

'But strategists should … no?'

'Not if they're good at their jobs,' Ika said pointedly.

'Or perhaps *only* if they are good at their job.'

'Are you suggesting I am not good at my job?' Ika asked, feeling the heat rising in her cheeks.

'We were speaking generally,' Fredrick said, and Ika wondered if she imagined his expression shift, a fleeting look of remorse crossing his face. Like he knew his words may have hurt her, and he wished he had not said them.

Jacob's phone beeped, breaking the tension. 'Stiller is going in at seventy million,' Jacob announced, the exasperation clear in his voice.

'We'll go in at ninety-five,' Fredrick replied, still holding Ika's gaze.

Ika shook her head helplessly. He was behaving like a dictator. A three-year-old dictator who wanted his toy NOW. Veer usually behaved in a more grown-up manner than this, she thought exasperatedly. 'There are times, Mr Heisenberg, when you have to walk away from a deal, no matter who the opponent is,' Ika said, amazed at her own bravado.

'Exactly, Ms Kumar. I know when to walk away from a deal. And it is not now.'

'It *is* now, Fredrick! No matter what you bid, Stiller will go in higher,' Ika said, throwing up her hands in her frustration.

'I can outbid him, Ms Kumar.'

Oh my lord, don't be a child, Fredrick! Ika groaned mentally. 'Just because you can doesn't mean you should,' she said out loud.

'Sometimes,' said Fredrick slowly, his eyes boring into Ika's as he got up and jammed a hand in his pocket, 'I do things simply because I can.' And with that, discussion thus concluded, Fredrick turned and left the room. Ika was left staring in his wake.

Thirty minutes later, Heisenberg Enterprise went in at ninety-five million pounds, and Stiller came in at a hundred million. Two hours later, HE raised the stakes to one hundred and five million, only to have Stiller win at one hundred and ten million pounds.

∽

Francesca: *Is it just me or was that to-ing and fro-ing between you and TRTH almost hot? Not as hot as my night with new nerdy boyfriend but hot nevertheless.*

Ika: *My first big project at HE was •pants emoji•*

Ika slumped into a plush chair that was, for all she knew, Ika thought sarcastically, feeling angry at the world in general, made of gold, too, because wasn't everything in Dubai made of gold? Ika's stomach growled, and she breathed out deeply, annoyed that her body needed three meals a day.

Francesca: *Anyway, coming back to Vivaan, you should stand up against that bastard you are married to.*

Ika: *Maybe.*

Francesca: *My blood boils. "It takes three times of me speaking nicely to you for you to listen to me. Just once if I shout at you. Do the maths." What kind of an idiot says things like that? TO HIS FUCKING WIFE?*

Ika sighed and glanced at her watch. 8 p.m. She was at the At.mosphere bar on floor number 122 of the Burj Khalifa, the restaurant in the clouds, as Jacob had dramatically labelled it with a flourish of his Louis Vuitton-clad arms earlier that day. Her phone beeped.

Francesca: *Remember what you compromise with, you are choosing.*

Ika sighed at the wisdom of her friend and listlessly looked around.

Ika's dress felt too tight now, her hair was in a very non-glam messy bun, her skin had eaten up all her makeup. Not that she cared, to be honest. All that could go wrong already had, she thought sulkily, her chin on her chest. Her one chance to impress Fredrick Heisenberg had gone up in smoke. The disaster today, plus the email, probably meant that her job was in real danger.

Ika breathed out, splaying her hands on her thighs and stared at the empty seat in front of her. Jacob had texted to say that he would be late to the dinner he had suggested they eat together, and Ika wondered if she looked as pathetic as she felt.

Her phone beeped again. Francesca is very bored, thought Ika with a grin and picked it up again.

Francesca: *Am googling pictures of hot, angry, petulant Fredrick now.*

Ika scoffed, taking a sip of her drink. Her phone beeped again.

Francesca: *Highly recommend googling pictures of hot, angry, petulant Fredrick. Also try "Sexy Fredrick Heisenberg in bathtub" in the search box and thank me later.*

Ika, smiling now: *Shut up! He is my boss.*

Francesca: *Fine, be a prude. Coming to your meeting today: a wise person we both know •wink, wink• once said—things that begin badly usually end well.*

Ika: *My dream job has begun badly, and it could end very soon. And who knows, that could be a good thing!*

Francesca: *If they threaten to fire you, forget women's lib and just flash the fucking dimple.*

Ika grinned and sent her best friend an eye roll emoji. It was just like Francesca to make her feel better no matter how far apart they were. She put her phone down and thoughtfully touched the rim of her glass, going through the argument with Fredrick in her head for the hundredth time. She closed her eyes and shook her head. *I should have handled it better.*

'Mind if I join you?' a familiar voice asked.

Startled, Ika looked up at Fredrick Heisenberg standing next to her table and felt heat rise up her cheeks. 'H—hi,' she stuttered, half getting up and then sitting back down again. 'Sure … of course.'

'I come in peace,' he said, smiling, which, oddly enough, seemed to make Ika redden further, Fredrick noticed.

He studied Ika with a half-amused expression and sat down opposite her. She looked exhausted, like she needed to curl up in bed.

'I am sorry…' Fredrick began.

'I am sorry…' she said at the same time.

They looked at each other, surprised.

'What for?' he asked.

'What for?' she asked as well.

They were both grinning now. He looked different now. More handsome. Kind.

What is wrong with me?

Fredrick put his hands up and said, 'Allow me to go first—I'm sorry for being stroppy at the presentation.'

'N—no, it's okay,' Ika said hurriedly, her heart feeling warm and woozy already at his apology.

'I didn't, *at all*, mean to suggest that you're not good at your job,' he said, distractedly touching his glasses.

Ika shifted uneasily in her chair.

'I think you're very capable. I … I think you are one of the smartest people I know. I am sorry—the words came out wrong.'

Her eyes flashed at him, and then she smiled. 'It's okay,' she said softly. 'Well, I was going to apologize as well,' Ika added, 'you lost business I was supposed to help you win.'

'But which you didn't *want* me to win,' Fredrick teased, straightening up.

It must be exhausting, thought Ika, staring at his well-tailored black suit, grey shirt and matching grey silk tie, to look this handsome all the time.

'That, sadly, is very true,' said Ika, shaking her head and smiling, for she could not deny her relief at Stiller's win. 'Sometimes, you can want and not want something at the same time. I am glad you didn't win at 110 million, but I am still sorry that you didn't get the company you wanted.'

'And, therein, Ms Kumar, lies the answer,' said Fredrick, a slow smile appearing on his face.

Ika frowned. Something didn't add up. She tilted her head and looked at him, her brain working fast. 'You know, you look remarkably happy for someone who just lost a valuable business.'

'The company was valued at sixty-five million,' he said, shrugging and picking his drink.

'And yet your last offer was 105?' she asked, looking confused. And the very next moment, she banged her fist on the table excitedly. 'You,' Ika said, '*never* wanted to acquire at all!'

Fredrick smiled. 'Not true. I did—but *only* until it was a sensible deal, and Stiller didn't want the business just because I wanted it.'

'You inflated the price for Stiller!'

'Again, *not* true. Stiller came in prepared to inflate the price till he got the business. I just gave him a taste of his own medicine,' he smiled. 'Someone said today that there are times when you have to walk away from a deal. You just have to know when. I think I knew when,' he finished with a grin.

'After offering forty-five million over the right price!' Ikadashi pointed out. 'Has Stiller figured out what you did to him?'

'I hear he is raging through the streets of Dubai, breathing fire,' Fredrick grinned.

'And that's making you so happy!'

'Christmas has come early,' Fredrick smiled, but the next moment his face became serious. 'We go back a long way, Ika, and at this point, I'm not even sure what the score is. And that is why I am sorry. I gave you a hard time, but you presented a strong, sensible strategy that I would have been happy to follow under different circumstances.' Ika smiled.

'Though, have to add, I didn't expect you to fight me at the meeting with the ferocity you displayed,' Fredrick added with an easy grin.

'I didn't fight you!' Ika said hotly.

'You one hundred per cent did.'

'I didn't!'

'You're doing it again.'

Ika opened her mouth and then closed it.

Fredrick laughed. 'Don't stop. Not many do—it's refreshing.'

'While we are at it with the apologies…' Ika said gulping and self-consciously scratching her shoulder.

Fredrick leaned in, curious.

'I have another one due…' Ika mumbled.

Fredrick watched as Ika fidgeted. 'Go on?' he said.

'That…errr…' She tucked a loose string of hair behind her ears, 'you know?'

Fredrick shook his head, not understanding.

'Err … the email…' she looked up at him helplessly.

Aah, that.

'Six out of ten? Off with their head? Team sat brushing up pictures? That one?' Fredrick offered and watched in mirth as Ika gulped with difficulty.

'Of course,' she said shaking her head, 'that's not true … I mean…'

'So, am I less than six?'

'No!' Ika exclaimed, and then she stilled, blushing.

'So more than six?' Fredrick asked, trying hard to keep his face straight.

Ika hung her head between her shoulders. This was terrible. Horrible. Then she heard a laugh. Startled, she looked up and watched Fredrick throw his head back and laugh. A proper belly laugh.

'You sent that email, and I put you through a rubbish meeting in there. I think we are even,' he said, shrugging. A huge wave of relief washed over Ika and she let out a big, deep breath.

Ika stared at Fredrick and realized that she was smiling.

Fredrick felt like an old friend, he had during their adventure in Mumbai too. But here was the thing: he was *not* an old friend. For most, Fredrick was serious, tacit and, like she had just seen, positively ruthless at work. The ease she felt around him, the effortlessness their conversation came blanketed in, the safe space that he had created for her to share her thoughts in—were they all misleading? Of all things Fredrick was in possession of—looks, money, power—it was this easy comradery that both pulled her to him and terrified her away from him.

The things, Ika thought with a deep sigh, confused at the complexity of her own thoughts, *the things we fear*.

'In other news,' Fredrick said leaning in, taking off his glasses, surprised at how relaxed he felt around Ika, 'thanks to Pushpa Aunty, I am fascinated by Bollywood now. What was that song playing when the Aunty in the pink glittery tent was trying to molest me, and you had to come to the rescue?'

Ika giggled at the memory of a very energetic, rotund, older lady splaying her hands across Fredrick's chest in the most disturbing manner, jigging her bottom to the beats of music.

'"London Thumkada" from the movie *Queen*. Compulsory to play it at every Indian wedding.' Ika said, raising her eyebrows. 'Give me your phone, I will find it for you,' she said extending her arm. Wordlessly, Fredrick handed his phone to her.

'And also, Raj and Simran—Pushpa Aunty spoke about them?' asked Fredrick.

Ika gasped dramatically. 'If you watch one Bollywood film in your lifetime, Fredrick, it has to be *Dil Wale Dulhaniya Le Jayenge*. DDLJ for short. Raj and Simran's story.'

Fredrick nodded his head.

'You know,' Ika said taking the phone off him, 'I watched a Hindi movie last night.' Ika knew she would never ever tell Vivaan about this, he hated the Indian-ness of Indian movies, but for Ika, Bollywood was oxygen.

'Mmm-hmm?'

'It's called *Disco Dancer*. So bad it is good, but you need to be a bit drunk to truly enjoy it.'

Fredrick was smiling already, and he wondered if he had smiled at all the entire day before meeting Ika. 'New movie?'

Ika shook her head, '1982.'

'Were you even born then?'

Ika shook her head again. 'My dad, Baba, he loved this movie. He said,' Ika sat up straighter and changed her voice to a mock baritone, which made Fredrick smile wider, '*DD* is not a movie, Ika, it's a state of mind.'

'Ha!'

'It sits between the trashy and the transcendental and very few movies can do that as successfully as *DD*.'

'Intrigued. What's it about?'

'A disco dancer.' Ika giggled, leaning in. 'So there is this kid called Jimmy played by this famous, hammy actor called Mithun. Jimmy lives on the street, has this plastic guitar and is really poor. And then he becomes this rock star who sings this super hit song called…well… "I am a Disco Dancer"—the song is epic by the way, let me find that for you on your phone as well. Anyway,

Jimmy is a *big* hit. Think Harry Styles in a golden, sparkly jumpsuit and headband, in the 1980s in India, pelvic thrusting like there is no tomorrow to a crowd that's going WILD. Jimmy is everywhere. Think Jimmy ice cream, Jimmy sweeties, Jimmy Jammies.'

Fredrick scoffed.

'This other guy David Brown—'

'David Brown?'

Ika nodded impatiently. 'David sabotages Jimmy's electric guitar with an intention to kill.'

'He does not!'

'But,' Ika paused dramatically, 'this girl calls up Jimmy's mummy, and Mummy runs and jumps right in.'

'Mummy saves Jimmy?'

Ika nodded. 'But Mummy gets electrocuted.'

Fredrick laughed. 'This is probably not supposed to be funny!'

'So, the scene where Mummy dies—you have to have to have to see it. On getting electrocuted, Mummy remains expressionless and turns different colours—red, blue, orange,' Ika was giggling uncontrollably now, 'and says "Aaah" and falls to the floor with her eyes open, still no expression on her face.'

Ika pretended to fall to the floor, and Fredrick burst out laughing again.

'Anyway,' she continued straightening up, and Fredrick leaned in further, enjoying every second of *Disco Dancer*, 'so the word "metrosexual" is many years away from being coined, but Jimmy is exactly that. When Mummy dies, Jimmy gets a bad case of guitar-o-phobia.'

'What?'

'He cannot sing anymore. Starts screaming every time he sees a guitar.'

'Aah, of course!'

'Enter Raju *Bhaiya*.'

'Raju Bhaiya? Bhaiya as in elder brother?' Fredrick asked, recalling what Pushpa Aunty had taught him at the wedding.

'Impressive,' said Ika nodding her head appreciatively, 'and yes. Raju Bhaiya. Played by Rajesh Khanna, top actor, in a "friendly appearance"—don't look at me like that, it says so in the credit roll—hamming like there is no tomorrow. He sings a very poignant song in the movie. Literally translating lyrics for your benefit now, "Not for the fair-skinned, not for those with a dark skin, this world belongs to people with compassion…"'

'Very inclusive even if not very politically correct. I am sure there is another meaning to the words?' Fredrick said laughing.

'You are being too optimistic, there isn't.' Ika laughed and added gleefully, 'Let me find this song for you as well.' And then she tapped on his phone again, and continued, 'Raju Bhaiyya begs Jimmy, "*Gaa*, Jimmy, gaa," he says.'

'GAA?'

'"Gaa" means, sing,' Ika said, 'so Raju Bhaiyya says "sing Jimmy, sing"' and guess what? Just like that, Jimmy finds his lost mojo and starts singing.'

Fredrick continued to laugh.

'But as we all know, Karma is a bitch. You know how David Brown gets killed?'

'How?'

'He gets electrocuted,' and with that, Ika dissolved into peals of laughter and Fredrick joined in.

'I—' Fredrick opened his mouth to speak, wiping tears with the back of his hands.

'Surprise!' came a loud squeal, disrupting their conversation, startling Ika. Fredrick turned around to face the commotion. A tall, skinny, stunning blonde was sashaying towards them, closely followed by an entourage of five or six women, reverently walking a few feet behind the goddess. The atmosphere in At.mosphere shifted perceptibly, thought Ika, allowing herself a smug mental pat for clever wordplay—Francesca would be proud of this one, she thought. A young girl who had so far been furiously clicking pictures of the Dubai skyline now shifted the focus of her camera to the lady. Some others followed suit. A murmur rose in the crowds.

'Ava?' Fredrick said, getting up, staring at his girlfriend in surprise.

Ava. The girlfriend. The Hollywood star.

Ava looked around like a mighty, glamorous dinosaur would at petty ants, gave her glossy hair one glorious toss and waved slowly at the lesser mortals gaping at her. And then she focussed her eyes on Fredrick. 'Hey there, handsome,' Ava drawled in a thick American accent. Even though she was wearing a simple white sleeveless top, blue denims frayed at her ankles and wedges, she oozed careless but overwhelming glamour. Green eyes, a sharp, tiny nose and very red pouty lips were framed by a golden, wavy bob so carefully arranged that it looked ever so slightly ruffled.

Ika watched, wide-eyed, as Ava placed her palms on either side of Fredrick's face and kissed him slowly, too slowly, on his lips.

'Weren't you supposed to be in LA?' Fredrick asked when she finally pulled away.

'One of the girls pushed stuff around in my calendar so that I could come see you, isn't it amazing?' Ava said, flinging a long, tanned arm carelessly over Fredrick's shoulder.

Ika had never met a Hollywood actor, so when Ava said, 'Oh, hello! I don't think we have met,' and extended a hand, Ika wondered for a moment if she should curtsy. 'H… hi,' Ika mumbled taking the extended hand, thankfully remembering just in time that celebrity was different from royalty.

Fredrick looked at the two women. They could not possibly have been more different. One was a fair, golden-haired, green-eyed actress, and the other an olive-skinned, black-eyed, dimpled M&A expert.

'Let's get going, poppet,' Ava said as she waved at Ika and tugged at Fredrick's arm. 'We only have a few hours, and I would *love* to make the most of them.' She winked at Fredrick, and Ika winced.

Fredrick and Ava together. In a posh hotel. Red satin bed sheets, flowers and wine—*shut up, shut up, shut up*! Ika shushed her brain. *Think about aubergines. No, don't, that's disgusting somehow. Think about teddy bears. Ladders. Triangles.*

'I'll see you in London,' Fredrick said, stealing another look at Ika, whose brow was furrowed as if she was having an argument with herself. He walked out, Ava by his side, chattering about things he felt very far removed from—something about something that was organic and gluten-free and cruelty-free and paraben-free—his mind was still with Ika. That smile. Oh goodness, that smile. Innocent, teasing, beautiful.

Stop thinking about her, Fredrick. And focus on the woman you love.

Back in the bar, Ika slumped into her chair and breathed deeply. The room around her that had stilled in the presence of Ava Smith now slowly came back to life.

That kiss, thought Ika, tugging at her scrunchie so that her hair fell around her shoulders, Ava's hands on Fredrick's face, her lips on his. A little voyeuristic shiver ran through her. How would it feel like to be physically that close to Fredrick, she wondered? And she shook her head.

What the hell are you thinking, she chided herself. *You're neither glamorous nor a world-famous actress. What you are is a married woman employed by someone who has spoken to you for a grand total of two hours. Use your brain, Ika, use your brain. He is not even thinking about you right now.*

Ika's phone beeped on cue.

Fredrick: *I will be watching* DDLJ *tonight.*

He *is* thinking about you, a little voice said inside Ika's brain. And with that, the dimple made its appearance.

5

Al Maktoum International Airport, Dubai

August 2016

*N*o. No. No. No.
 Ika squirmed in her seat. It had taken her a moment to recognize Fredrick, a moment during which she had been taken aback by just how gorgeous the man was. Fredrick was walking up the aisle, craning his neck to look for his seat, wearing his well-tailored light grey suit with an elegance that reminded Ika, perhaps because of the sharpness of his eye, of a leopard stalking his prey. His dark hair was a bit longer than usual, just beginning to curl where it met his collar. A slight stubble was the only indication of the long hours Ika knew he had been putting in at work. A few women turned to look at him as he passed them. Ika craned her neck looking for Ava Smith, and let out a deep breath when she realized he was alone.

I wonder what happened last night. No, actually I don't. Actually, I should not.

Ika fumbled with her phone and fired a few quick texts.

To Himani: *I will be back tomorrow morning at 7ish. Miss you. Miss Veer. Don't feed Veer any more lemons just to get funny videos. And DON'T PUT THEM ON TIKTOK. It's plain cruel. He is your grandson.*

To Vivaan: *Sorry I missed your call.*

To Francesca: *EMERGENCY: Fredrick is on my plane!!! Am wearing grey sweats and a hoodie that's two sizes too large for me. No makeup.*

Her phone beeped back instantly. Francesca. Obviously.

Francesca: *Hide. Or jump off the plane. Or lock yourself in the toilet and refuse to come out. Do not, I repeat, do not let Fredrick see you sans makeup. You look hideous.*

Before Ika could react with suitable indignation, 'Ms Kumar,' came a voice, a hint of surprise evident in it, and Ika looked up from her phone. 'It seems like we will be neighbours on the flight.'

What? How? No!

'Oh hi, Fredrick!' Ika said, nervously tucking a strand of hair behind her ears.

He reached up to stow his black leather bag in the overhead bin, his face disappearing for a moment.

Ika allowed herself the guilty pleasure of letting her eyes meander all over his well-toned body. The tip of her ears suddenly felt hot, and she fumbled with them.

'Are you okay?' Fredrick asked, leaning in, getting ready to take his seat.

'Eh?'

'Your ears?'

'No, no,' she said dismissively. 'It's hot. You know, aeroplane taking off and stuff.'

Fredrick looked like he hadn't a clue, but he didn't say anything. Instead, as she fastened her seat belt, he stole another look at her. The impeccably dressed, confident, straight-haired woman from work was now replaced by a curly-haired, innocent-looking girl who could, in her grey sweater and cropped jeans, pass for a college student.

Fredrick sat down, and as the plane readied for take-off, he felt familiar pangs of anxiety gripping his chest. He clutched the armrest and breathed deeply, readying himself for the flood of adrenaline that would soon be injected into his bloodstream. As usual, his face would give nothing away: he had learnt to hide his fears before most children had learnt to talk.

'It's okay, you know,' came a soft voice, and Fredrick turned to look at Ika. She was smiling gently at him. 'I hate flying too.'

'Flying is not a problem; it's the taking off,' Fredrick heard himself say. He paused, surprised at the words that he had just uttered. *Dad must be turning in his grave*, he thought with a mental chuckle. James had spent thousands of pounds on a battery of therapists to help with his fear of take-offs without Fredrick as much as opening his mouth.

'You know,' Ika said, turning towards him, chattily crossing her arms across her chest, 'when I was little, Baba, my dad, used to tell me that if I caused trouble on the aeroplane, it would distract the pilot and he would crash mid-air into Santa and that wouldn't be very nice.'

'You call your dad Baba?' he asked with a smile. He liked the sound of the word, there was a sweetness to it.

The aeroplane picked up speed on the runway.

Ika nodded and continued, 'This one time...' Ika said, giggling at the memory as Fredrick stared at her captivated, 'and I've NO idea how this happened: we were waiting for Dadi, my dad's mother, at Bombay airport, and an airline staffer brings a grandma in a wheelchair to us—all good except for one crucial detail. The grandma in the wheelchair isn't ours.' Ika began to laugh now, her shoulders heaving with mirth. 'Dadi ended up in Agra, a city far away, where, where…' Ika paused for breath, 'another attendant wheeled her out, and Dadi asked, "Why is Bombay so cold?" and the attendant made the mistake of saying, "*Arre*, madam! Age is catching up with you—this isn't Bombay, this is Agra." Rumour has it that at this point Dadi got up from the wheelchair, took a newspaper, rolled it up and thwacked him hard on the head. Twice.'

Ika's laughter was infectious, and Fredrick found himself grinning as the plane heaved into the sky.

'That boy …' Ika wiped tears off her face. 'That poor boy… stopped a security officer walking past them and proceeded to complain about Dadi. On cue, Dadi patted the attendant on his shoulder. He turned to face her expecting an apology, and she hit the top of his head with the newspaper again. The airport security guy was horrified and then called the police, like the actual police, and handed Dadi over to them. And Baba, panicking at Bombay airport, looking for his missing mother, gets a call from the Agra police saying that they have an elderly lady who has been hitting everyone at the Agra airport. And Baba says, "Stop, I don't need to know any more—that's my mother!"' Ika giggled, a hand on her stomach.

Clearly, it was a memory that had elicited many years of laughter, thought Fredrick, smiling as the plane steadied and straightened into the sky.

'And here we are, take-off all done,' said Ika, grinning. Fredrick craned his neck to see through Ika's window, surprised.

'Thank you,' Fredrick whispered. It also felt good, for a reason he didn't care to examine, to know she had had a happy childhood. Nothing kills your soul like a sad childhood, and no one knew that better than him.

'Today would have been my father's seventy-fifth birthday,' Fredrick said softly.

Ika turned to look at Fredrick. He was staring out of her window at the white tufts of clouds passing by. The sun shone on his eyes—they were, Ika realized, breathtakingly gorgeous.

'Our fathers share the same birthday,' Ika said, distractedly opening the food tray, crossing her legs, jamming her knees in between the tray and the rest of her body.

She is tiny enough to do that, Fredrick mused, looking doubtfully at his own long legs.

'Please wish your Baba a very happy birthday on our behalf,' Fredrick said, opening his own tray and placing his laptop on it.

She looked at him for a few moments. 'I lost him years ago,' she said finally.

Fredrick turned to look at Ika. 'I am so sorry. I just presumed ... I should not have... I...'

'It's okay,' she said with a small smile.

'How old were you when you lost your Baba?' The words were out before Fredrick could stop them.

'Twelve,' Ika replied.

The images of a happy childhood began to evaporate, and a coldness gripped his heart. 'That is too young to lose a parent,' he said.

'You're *always* too young to lose a parent.'

'Your father's passing must have changed your world...' Fredrick said.

'For weeks, I could not breathe…' said Ika, a faraway look on her face. 'But soon, life interceded. Baba was a doctor and the only earning member of our family. Suddenly, we didn't have any money. We live in a small city, Fredrick, called Almora. And like any small city in India, it is accepting of some things and not of others. One of the things it was not okay with was three women living on their own. The people we thought would help didn't. It felt like we were up against the world and its prejudices. People were waiting for us to fall. To fail. But thankfully, just when it all had begun to seem hopeless, Mummy found a job as a teacher, and her salary saw us through those years.'

Fredrick sat in rapt attention, listening to Ika's story.

'We had little money for luxuries, but I was safe and loved.' Ika smiled. 'I worked very hard to get into the top colleges in India—you see, they were a ticket out of a life where we needed to mind the money we spent on food,' she said, a quiet kind of a strength coming from her that Fredrick could not help but admire. Then she suddenly looked uncomfortable. 'I am sorry,' she said, pushing a strand of hair behind her ears. 'I don't usually speak about these things…'

'I am honoured you chose to share your story with me,' Fredrick said, resting his arms on the tray that he pulled out and turning to face her.

'Were you close to your dad?' she asked, looking at him.

Given her recent obsession with Fredrick's handsome face, Ika had spent many hours googling him. One of the images that she could not quite take off her mind was from James Heisenberg's funeral. Against the backdrop of famous men and women from across the world, stood Fredrick Heisenberg, his face expressionless save for the lone tear that had begun its journey down his face. The only window to his immense grief. Ika had stared at the picture for many minutes, her heart breaking at the vulnerability that emanated off Fredrick in the picture.

I've not had a full night's sleep since he passed away. I would give up everything I have for five minutes with him.

'He was my everything,' Fredrick said, still looking out of her window. He hesitated now, and Ika nodded encouragingly. 'May I ask you something personal? Please don't answer if you don't want to.'

'No, go on,' Ika said.

'How did you deal with it?'

'The loss?'

He nodded, his brow furrowed with painful memories.

'They told me that time would heal everything,' Ika said. 'However, when I was still crying myself to sleep three years later, I knew they had all lied. And with that, I understood something. Grief is like a hole in the street outside your house. Time does not fill that hole—it only teaches you its exact location so that you stop falling into the hole. That's what time does. Teaches you to sidestep the grief. Sometimes,' she said.

Sidestep the grief. How?

'You can't fill the void that losing a parent leaves, Fredrick,' said Ika, a thin film of water misting her eyes. 'You miss them for the rest of your life, but the grief becomes less raw. Less sharp around the edges. Sometimes, it disappears and then reappears in the weirdest ways, when you're least expecting it, rushing at you like a tidal wave, catching you off guard, leaving you breathless, hurting. But you understand that there is nothing you can do. You learn to live with it. You stop fighting it, and, in some weird way, you learn to embrace it.'

They stared at each other, shoulders touching in the limited space the economy seats offered. She looked away first, turning her gaze to her hands in her lap.

Fredrick heard her take a shaky breath.

'I am sorry—I upset you,' Fredrick said, gently peering at her face. 'It was very selfish of me.'

She looked at him, her eyes large and trusting. 'I am sorry you know this grief,' she said after a pause. 'Our grief is the last thing we have of the person that is gone, and so we cling to it. It's okay, though. You will let go when you're ready.' Ika bit her lower lip and shook her head.

'Thank you for sharing your story with me,' Fredrick said, looking at Ika. He wanted to wrap her in a hug. Would it be that inappropriate, he wondered? Would she—

'Ladies and gentlemen, this is your captain speaking,' a voice boomed across the aeroplane, breaking the spell. Ika and Fredrick hurriedly looked away, both red in the face.

Ika leaned forward to pick up her book from the bag at her feet and proceeded to bury her nose in words and pages she could barely focus on.

Fredrick opened his laptop, feeling a lot lighter than he had felt in the last seven months—seven months during which Ava must have sat him down a million times and begged him to tell her what was going through his mind. A million times when he had said that he was fine, not because he didn't want to share his feelings with Ava, but because the words would simply not come—unlike now, when they had tumbled out, tripping over one another.

He stole a look at Ika. Her face, sombre and pensive, told him she was not reading. She was thinking about their conversation. Just like he was.

Focus on the Excel sheet, Fredrick ordered himself, and focussed his attention on the laptop. A few minutes later, he felt a slight weight on his arm and turned to see that Ika's head was resting against him, her eyes closed, her book falling from her hands.

He allowed the book to fall. Her hair smelled of strawberries.

Fredrick shook his head and stared at the computer screen.

A bit later he felt Ika snake her arms around his arm, holding it close to her, snuggling in deeper, closer, gravitating towards the warmth of his body. Fredrick tried to concentrate on work but gave up a few moments later. He felt her shiver, so with one hand, he somehow managed to rip open the plastic bag containing his throw, leaned across Ika and wrapped it around her. And then he rested his head on hers and closed his eyes.

A few hours later, a very harried-looking Ika found herself hauling suitcases off the conveyor belt onto a rickety trolley. Twice she had picked up the wrong suitcase and the burly airport official in a yellow vest was now standing a few feet away from her, arms crossed across his chest, glaring at her obvious incompetence. Ika smiled timidly and shrugged. All bags collected, Ika threw her fake Gucci handbag on the trolley and began to push it towards arrivals. Her phone beeped again. With one hand she pulled it out of her pocket.

Francesca. *Obviously.*

Francesca: *So lemme get this straight. You pretended to fall asleep?*

Ika: *I am not a creep, for God's sake.*

Francesca: *Well...*

Ika: *Fine. Forget it. Not telling you anything else.*

Francesca: *Ok. Fine. You REALLY fell asleep.*

Ika: *I just kind of...you know...rested my head on his shoulder...*

Francesca: *ooooo...SCANDAL*

Ika: *Bye.*

Francesca: *Ok. Temme—why did you do it? It's unlike you...*

Ika: *He was telling me about his Dad, and I wanted to give him a hug which would have been inappropriate...so...*

Francesca: *The award for the single most pathetic thing I have heard in a long time goes to...why wouldn't you hug someone if you want to hug them? It's just a hug!*

At this point, Ika banged, trolley first into a pillar, looked around sheepishly, said sorry to no one in particular but the world in general and went back to her phone.

Ika: *I don't know. It just. I don't know.*

Francesca: *What happened when you woke up?*

Ika: *We both looked suitably embarrassed, what else, looked everywhere but at each other. Captain announced descent right then, so we were both glad for the distraction.*

Francesca: *So?*

Ika: *So what?*

Francesca: *What was it like?*

Ika: *What was what like?*

Francesca: *Sleeping with the Fredrick Heisenberg.*

Ika: *Shut up.*

In the brightly lit car park at Heathrow, Fredrick nodded at Red, his chauffeur of fifteen years. With one step he was inside the car. He placed his laptop bag beside him.

'Home, Mr Heisenberg?' Red asked, looking at Fredrick in the rear-view mirror.

Fredrick nodded. He took out his phone and opened WhatsApp. He searched for Ikadashi's number and opened her picture. It was a selfie. She was on the beach, probably West Wittering, thought Fredrick. She was smiling a wide happy smile. A little boy who looked remarkably like his mother peered into the picture from Ika's lap.

As the Range Rover picked up speed, Fredrick's mind went back to the flight. He had slept for four hours, head resting on Ika's, their arms intertwined. Four hours of deep, uninterrupted sleep. The longest he had slept in years without waking up anxious or restless.

Why did he so desperately want to be around her, he wondered, breathing out and slumping into the comfort of the car seat. He had never been unfaithful to Ava, despite the many women who regularly expressed interest in him—he was not the sort, whatever that meant. Why did he feel like he had little control over himself around Ika? What he had done was not cool, was it? He had asked Ellin, ex-investigator and now his executive assistant, to find out which flight Ika was on and had paid a lot of money to buy the seat next to her.

He shook his head. What was he thinking?

Wearily, he closed his eyes, but they flew open the next instant for all he could see was Ika.

6

Mumbai

2009

Twenty-five-year-old Ika was yet to figure out how to use a hair straightener. And so, her hair was perpetually in Medusa-like curls, spiralling out of control in every possible direction. But she liked it. Just like she liked the rest of herself.

That evening, the winds were picking up, and the trees lining the road leading up to her Colaba flat swayed gently. Ika got out of the cab that had brought her home from her office in Nariman Point and walked up the stairs, running her hands through her hair. It was a good life—the money was good, she liked consulting and didn't mind the long hours. Her family was well too. Dadi had recently discovered the wonders of YouTube and was too preoccupied with videos of old Bollywood movies to drive her mother crazy. And Vivaan—well, Vivaan was about to finish his MBA from Stanford.

Vivaan.

She slowed down and bit her lips thoughtfully. They had been seeing each other since they were eighteen. When she had first met him, he had an all-encompassing acceptance of her that had captivated her heart. She could be Ika with him. They had laughed themselves silly at corny Bollywood jokes, he had enjoyed *bhel puri* and *golgappa* on the streets as much as she did, and he loved her curly hair.

Then it had all changed.

Going to the US had done something to him, and Ika wanted to stop it, but she knew it was beyond her. All he spoke of when he called was his career, rarely about anything else. She agreed it was good to be ambitious, but Vivaan's ambition was beginning to define him. The gentleness in his eyes had vanished, replaced by a mean glint. He now made constant jibes at her clothes; and she could tell that her hair and mannerisms had begun to embarrass him—like the last time they'd gone to a very posh restaurant and Ika asked for a doggy bag. Or the time Ika had been getting dressed to meet some of his friends, and he'd asked her to change into something more grown-up. Or that time when she'd told him that she would take up a job that meant more to her over one that would pay her more, and he looked at her like she was an idiot.

Ika shook her head as if to clear it. He was killing the light and the lightness in her.

'In seven years from now,' a voice in her head asked, 'do you want to be in a posh office in London earning a bigger salary than you can imagine now, thinking about how you wasted the last fourteen years on a man who didn't deserve your spirit? I don't think so.'

Standing outside her door, just as the first drops of rain hit the ground outside, she made a decision. 'I will call him tonight,' she mumbled under her breath, 'and tell him we need some time apart.' With that thought, she turned the key in the lock, stepped into the darkness as she felt for and flipped on the light switch on the nearest wall.

'SURPRISE!' Vivaan yelled, and Ika screamed.

Vivaan was standing in her living room wearing jeans and a white Tee that screamed 'STANFORD'.

At six feet three, Vivaan was a foot taller than Ika, and she looked up at him, her eyes wide with surprise. Black eyes, sometimes sharp, sometimes shrewd, a wide smile and a mop of wavy, black hair grinned back at her.

Gosh, he is good-looking, thought Ika.

Ika looked around in shock, stuttering, 'Wha—what is going on?' As she took in the room, she stilled. There were more people in the room—his parents and sister and her mum. 'Why are you all—what is—'

'Ika, the last seven years have been the most wonderful of my life. I've accepted a job in London, but I don't want to leave without you. I don't want to live without you. I think the time is finally right,' Vivaan said without preamble. He was wearing a big, indulgent smile as if he was awarding Ika the biggest gift life would ever give her. Ika feebly noticed that the living room was decorated with streamers and a big cake lay on the coffee table in anticipation of a celebration.

Going down on one knee, Vivaan extended his arm, opening up his hand. There was a little jewellery box sitting open in the centre of his palm and in it was a huge diamond ring.

'Will you marry me?' he asked, pushing his spectacles up his nose.

Ika looked at her mother, who was staring at her, a message in her eyes. Ika felt her mouth go dry. *No, say no, Ika. Just say no. NO. SAY NO.*

'Will you marry me, Ikadashi Joshi?'

Say NO! the voice in her head shouted. *For god's sake, you wanted some time out of this relationship. That was not TWO MINUTES ago! Get a hold of yourself, Ika!*

'Yes,' she heard herself say.

7

Putney, London

October 2016

Fredrick pressed the doorbell of Flat 26 and glanced at his watch again. 8 p.m. Not too late, he reassured himself, tapping his foot restlessly. Fredrick looked around the bare hallway, walls painted in a dull marigold. Most of his formative years had been spent in rooms doused in marigold, and now even as an adult, Fredrick had not managed to rid himself of the hate he had for the colour.

The doors opened with a flourish, breaking his line of thought, and Fredrick did a double take. An older Ika in unfamiliar clothes had just filled the doorway against the backdrop of a child's angry wails.

'Hi,' older Ika looked surprised to see Fredrick, 'how can I help?'

'I am Fredrick. I need to drop something off for Ika, please,' Fredrick replied. 'Ikadashi, I mean. Ms Kumar, I mean.'

'Mummy, can you please hold Ve—' Ika came onto the scene, carrying a baby on her hip and froze when she saw Fredrick at the door. Ellin, Fredrick's Swedish executive assistant, had promised to send the memory card through 'someone', Ika groaned mentally, letting out a deep breath.

'Oh hi, Fredrick,' she said out loud, trying to yank her very, *very* short shorts a little lower. 'Sorry, I was not expecting you.' The baby, who had now forgotten to cry, took this opportunity to yank at his mother's hair, and Ika yelped in pain. 'I am okay, I am okay,' she mumbled looking at Fredrick's horrified expression. 'Come in, please?' she said, grabbing Veer's hands as they reached for her hair again.

Fredrick nodded, staring first at Ika, then at the baby boy version of Ika, and then at the elderly lady version of Ika. Genetics was fascinating, he thought to himself.

'STOP!' Ika yelled just as Fredrick had taken his first step inside. Shocked, Fredrick looked up.

'No, no,' said Ika, feebly catching his eye, 'Veer, stop. Not you. Veer is pulling my hair, please come in. Please.'

Fredrick smiled at the horrified expression on Ika's face and entered her house.

Ika followed Fredrick's eyes around the room, utterly dismayed. About a hundred plastic toys covered the floor of the living room. The remnants of Veer's dinner were still clinging to his £12 IKEA highchair (thank god Ika had cleaned the floor). Veer himself was in his bedtime onesie, so clean even if badly behaved, Ika realized with some degree of relief.

'Fredrick?' Himani repeated, leaning back to look at Fredrick again, her eyes wide with surprise, 'Heisenberg?'

'I see you have heard of me,' Fredrick said with a smile, standing awkwardly in the middle of the room. 'Apologies, I did not mean to barge in on your personal time…'

'Oh, yes,' Ika said, putting Veer down before he shot towards his toys with admirable speed, 'introductions. Mummy, Fredrick. Fredrick, Himani, my mum.' Ika was still carrying a box of baby wipes, Fredrick noted with a smile. She had the air of a busy, harried mum. A *beautiful*, busy, harried mum. A far cry from the put-together lady at work, but it suited her. Just as the comfortable, lived-in mess of the living room suited her, Fredrick thought. Lots of pictures on the walls. Little nooks and corners with stuff collected from travels abroad. The house smelled deliciously of lavender and baby. The house looked lived in. It looked like a *home*.

'And this is Veer,' Ika offered when she saw Fredrick staring at her son.

Hearing his name, Veer turned around and pointed towards Fredrick. He grinned the grin of the devil and then went on to babble a complete sentence in baby language, drool pouring down his chin.

'Ellin told me to give this to you,' Fredrick said, handing Ika the memory card, 'I was driving by anyway,' he lied. 'Nice to have met you, Mrs Joshi, Ika,' Fredrick said, nodding at Ika's mother and was about to leave when Himani spoke up, 'Fredrick, *puttar*, have you eaten?'

Ika glared at her mother.

Meanwhile, Fredrick had stilled. *Have you eaten?* So basic. So kind. So mother-like, he supposed?

'No, I have not, actually,' Fredrick replied, looking first at mother and then at daughter, 'but please don't trouble yourself.'

'Fredrick's staff probably plans his dinners a year in advance, Mummy,' Ika said.

'That may be true sometimes,' Fredrick grinned, 'but I happen to love last-minute ones too.'

'Mummy,' said Ika desperately, diving in to save the situation, 'Fredrick probably needs to be somewhere.'

'No, I don't.'

'You don't?'

'Nope.' Fredrick said. 'You don't want me to stay for dinner?'

'No!'

'No, you don't?'

'No, I do!'

Fredrick laughed at Ika's horrified expression, as did Himani.

'Your plan did not work, Iku,' Himani said, laughing too. Ika glared at her mother, and Fredrick mouthed, 'Iku?' at Ika.

'Come on in, Fredrick, the table is almost set, we just need to add another plate,' Himani said, taking Fredrick to their large wooden dining table, busy like the rest of the house with flowerpots, jars of pickles, candles.

A loud wail from Veer and Fredrick turned around to see Ika struggling to put Veer in the highchair.

'It's like he sprouts extra tentacles when I have to put him in the highchair,' Ika said, and Fredrick leaned in to restrain Veer, allowing Ika to buckle him in. Veer grabbed onto Fredrick's arm and held onto it with all his might.

Fredrick tried to tug himself away, but Veer, his displeasure at being put into the highchair forgotten and replaced with an obsession for Fredrick's arm, let out the biggest wail.

'Okay, fine,' Fredrick heard himself say, and he handed his arm back to the ten-month-old who grabbed it greedily.

'Veer probably thinks it's something he can eat,' Ika said shrugging.

'My arm?'

Ika nodded. 'They are not all or always very cute. Sorry! Let me get your arm back.'

'It's actually okay.'

Despite usually hating kids, I like Veer drooling all over my arm, thought Fredrick with amazement.

'Well, this one seems to have taken a shine to you,' Himani said, laughing as she came to the table. 'There is daal, and chapatti, and aloo gobhi with some pickle. Simple.'

Himani looked at the spread and beamed. Her positivity was infectious, thought Fredrick, staring at the older lady.

Fredrick turned towards Ika. 'Your husband won't join us for the meal?'

'No, no,' Ika fumbled, Fredrick noticed, 'he works most of the week in Lucerne. Here only on weekends,' Ika replied and poured a ladle full of steaming *daal* into a white china bowl for Fredrick.

'So, tell me everything, Fredrick,' asked Himani with a wink, sitting down at the table. She put some salad on Fredrick's plate, Fredrick noted before even touching her own plate. He watched, almost transfixed at Himani who bustled around Veer now, a longing searing his heart. There was a busy simplicity to Himani that was making his heart ache in a weird knotty way. Most of his friends had mums who were dolled up in designer clothes for tea at 6 a.m. Some of his friends at Eton had needed appointments to meet their mums. Himani, Fredrick could guess, was different. More real. More heart. More mother? The kind of mother he would have loved to have. Fredrick cleared his throat and picked up the embroidered dusky blue napkin that matched the table mats and runner. He would never even know the true enormity of what he had been denied, he thought ruefully.

'Exactly how terrible is Ika at work?' Himani asked with a cheeky smile, picking up a spoon.

'That's going to be a very long conversation,' said Fredrick, his face serious.

'Mummy!' Ika looked sternly at her mother who laughed and then she turned to glare at Fredrick.

'She is wonderful, Mrs Joshi, one of the best we have,' Fredrick said with a smile, and Ika reddened.

'Both of you, start eating,' said Himani with a kind of authority that can only come to a mother, and both Ika and Fredrick obliged.

And as they ate, Veer babbling away, mutilating a carrot stick that his mother had handed him with a stern 'do NOT throw it', steady, easy conversation flowed between the three adults. Himani was, Fredrick realized, articulate and funny, keeping him laughing with a steady dose of anecdotes from her days as a professor at a girls' college in Almora.

Himani reminded him of two people, thought Fredrick, oddly both men. Albus Dumbledore and Fredrick's own father, James. The same air of good-natured wisdom, as he knew James had, and had imagined Albus Dumbledore to possess when he had first read the Potter books sat crouched in a dark corner in the humongous library of the Swiss chalet James took him to soon after his adoption. With Professor Dumbledore and James for company, Fredrick had, for the first time in his life, felt safe…just as he did now in the company of the tiny Mrs Joshi.

8

HE HQ, London

November 2016

The Grape and the Dodger had often been called the 'biggest meeting room at HE HQ' and for good reason. The office trooped down to the local pub every Friday, and even though Fredrick didn't drink, if he was in HE HQ on a Friday, he made it a point to join in. Today, however, despite the general bonhomie that came with partly drunk colleagues—Jacob was debating if he could tap dance on the table—Fredrick felt restlessness consume him.

Ika had definitely been in the office, and Fredrick was sure he had seen her at the pub—a flash of her dark pink dress had caught his eye. For the past hour, though, she had seemingly vanished.

Fredrick glanced at his watch. Half seven. Maybe she left to put Veer to bed, he reasoned and sternly told himself to focus on what his CFO was saying. A few moments later, he found himself, yet again, distractedly craning his neck for Ika. They had been talking a lot more since the cozy dinner with Himani a month ago—mostly in hurriedly snatched snippets about Himani or Veer when they bumped into each other in corridors or meetings.

These were, more often than not, the highlight of his otherwise stressful days and Fredrick found himself looking forward to them more than he would have liked.

'As I was saying—' the CFO said but had to leave his sentence midway when he saw Fredrick abruptly get up, excuse himself and walk away.

Fredrick walked out of the building into the pretty, well-lit garden. No Ika, though, he noted, scanning the area quickly. Fredrick was about to go back in when his eyes caught a flash of pink. He walked closer and spotted a figure huddled over the blue light of a mobile phone in the far corner of the garden.

Closer, though, he stopped.

She was talking on the phone, in a hushed, pained voice.

'I was trying, I really was' ... 'please don't say that' ... 'no one deserves to hear such bad things, please, just please stop.' The winds carried snippets of Ika's pleading voice to Fredrick, and immediately a coldness snaked around his heart.

Fredrick watched unmoving as Ika cancelled the call, wrapped her arms around herself against the chill of the night and cried softly.

Stay here, leave her alone.

Slowly and in measured steps, Fredrick walked up and sat down on the big boulder next to her. Ika looked up, startled. Her eyes were red from the crying.

'Fred—' she tried. Her voice faltered, and the tears started. Hastily she wiped them away but more rushed out, persistent and rebellious. She shrugged helplessly, looking away.

'If it's okay,' Fredrick asked in a soft whisper, leaning in and looking at her intently, 'I'd like to stay here with you for a few minutes.'

Ika vehemently shook her head, a fresh bout of tears spilling forth. She wiped them with the back of her hands furiously, continuing to resolutely look away.

'Please?' Fredrick asked again, his voice softer, gentler. Ika shook her head, still staring ahead, but less vigorously than before.

Fredrick let out a deep breath and got up to leave, hating it but aware that Ika deserved her privacy. The next instant, ice-cold fingers grabbed his elbow. He turned to look at Ika—she was still staring ahead. She tugged at him to sit down. He felt her fingers tighten around his arm in a silent request.

Fredrick sat down. And they sat like that, shoulders touching, in silence, for a long time. When the tears did not stop, Fredrick put an arm around Ika's shoulders. They felt delicate. Fragile. She rested her head on his shoulder, and they shuffled in closer.

'Are you cold?' he asked. Ika shook her head, but a shiver ran through the length of her body. Fredrick took off his black turtleneck and carefully draped it around her shoulders. Ika protested but gave in.

'I am sorry,' she said in a watery voice when the tears finally subsided.

'Did someone at HE do something to upset you?' Fredrick asked, his eyes blazing.

Ika shook her head.

'Did someone at HE *say* anything to upset you?' he asked again, leaning in a bit more.

Ika shook her head again.

Fredrick breathed out loud and stared ahead of him into the darkness that engulfed the rear end of the garden, a million questions jostling for space in his head.

'It is tough to learn how to do this,' he began finally, choosing his words carefully, 'but it is important to not take personally how other people treat us. It is very counterintuitive but a powerful tool to learn. Almost a superpower.' He looked at her with a small smile, which Ika weakly returned. 'Because,' he continued now staring at her, cried-out she looked as pristine as a porcelain doll, 'how others treat us is rarely a measure of what we are, but almost always a mark of what *they* are. How people behave with us is a function of their own mental state, upbringing and experiences. It has very little, if anything, to do with us, our actions or our words.' Ika nodded slowly, allowing the wisdom of his words to sink in, and Fredrick continued, 'Do not let someone else's vitriol become the voice in your head.'

'Thank you,' Ika whispered, large, cried out eyes staring at Fredrick.

'I don't like seeing you upset,' Fredrick heard himself say, tightening his arms around her. Ika snuggled in.

'Why are we whispering?' Fredrick whispered with a smile after a moment.

'I don't know,' Ika whispered back, finally grinning. Fredrick stared at the dimple, feeling relief flood through him.

∽

Later that night, sat at the dining table, Ika watched Vivaan, who was at the sink. 'Forget about doing the dishes—that's expecting too much out of you, of course. It's difficult for you to put all the dishes in the effing sink,' he was saying. His back was turned towards Ika, but she could imagine his face—eyes wide with barely controlled anger, nostrils flared.

On the telly, someone scored a goal, and the crowd exploded.

'Vivaan,' Ika tried nervously, 'you have been belittling me for one thing or the other the entire day today.'

'Then stop being a continuous disappointment?'

Ika let the comment pass.

'I was about to put the dishes in the sink and wash them too, but Veer started to cry so ... so I got distracted ... I meant to do it, but you came early...' she said, trailing off helplessly, feeling small.

'The kid is the biggest excuse this woman has,' Ika heard Vivaan spit out.

'I have to look after him, don't I?' Ika tried in vain, hating yet again how weak her voice sounded. She was, she knew, about to start crying anytime now. The thought of more crying exhausted her.

At her words, Vivaan turned around slowly. He was still in formal clothes, his shirt a sparkling white even at the end of a long day. Sleeves rolled up, he carried the green Fairy Liquid bottle. He squished it in anger now, and a few small bubbles escaped from the bottle in mute protest.

'You look after him?' He raised an eyebrow, and said in a low growl, 'you are barely able to manage him even with your mum and the nanny. You are probably the most incompetent mother I know.'

And with that, he turned around and went back to doing the dishes.

No, she was not going to cry. Not again. Not after the hours she had spent crying in the pub garden. And with that, her mind went back to Fredrick. Had he really put his arms around her? Had she really sat that close to Fredrick, head resting on his shoulders? A longing cut through her chest—what would she not give to be back in the garden, in the cold night, huddled into the kindness that was Fredrick. His whispers came to her now, his smile, his gentle eyes. And his words.

How we treat others is rarely a measure of what they are, but almost always a mark of how and what we are.

The countless times Vivaan had handed Veer back to her saying that he could not manage such an unruly child. The innumerable occasions when Veer had started crying within minutes of being with his father. The multiple days that Veer had gone without even speaking to his father—they all came back to Ika. She sat up straighter. She cleared her throat.

'It's not me who cannot manage Veer. It's you. You cannot manage our child,' she said in a small voice that did not even reach Vivaan as he angrily clanked the dishes around.

The words were whispers, but they were brave. The bravest, Ika realized as she got up from the chair and walked to the safety of Veer's nursery, they had been in a long, long time.

By the time Ika opened the door to the nursery, she was smiling.

'Hello, my favourite people,' she said peeping in. Himani and Veer were ready for bed, cozy in their pyjamas, huddled over a 'Peppa Pig' book. Himani looked up and smiled at her daughter.

'Pee pee,' Veer babbled, grinning and standing up.

'He is saying Peppa Pig,' Himani said proudly.

'Of course he is.' Ika grinned.

'Someone is looking happy,' Himani teased as she beckoned Ika to sit with her on the bed.

'Fredrick helped me today, Mummy,' Ika said, climbing into the already overcrowded bed and stretching the duvet across her legs. Veer clambered over, settled comfortably into his mother's lap, grabbed her fingers and started to chew on them.

'Did he, *puttar*? Himani beamed. 'I like him. Tell me everything?' she asked leaning in, already smiling. If she had a son, Himani thought, clutching *Peppa Goes On Holiday* to her chest, she would have wanted him to be exactly like Fredrick. And then, just as Ika launched into her story, Himani stilled.

A baby.

A baby boy.

A lost baby boy.

Even after all these years, the secrets she carried weighed so heavy on her chest that, sometimes, Himani felt like she would crumble under the weight of the lies and the deceit.

Across London, in his Knightsbridge penthouse, Fredrick tapped on his phone to switch off the lights in the bedroom, sinking the room into darkness broken only by the moonlight seeping in through the closed window. Ava let out a content sigh and nuzzled into his chest. Fredrick fingered the little mole on her shoulder, his mind elsewhere.

'Pat my head, darling?' Ava mumbled, half asleep, and Fredrick did as he was told. Her hair was done in blonde curls today, and absent-mindedly, he played with them.

'I sleep my best in your arms,' Ava mumbled again into his chest. 'You are my home, honey.'

In the darkness of the night, Fredrick wondered why he had never felt the same kind of love for Ava, powerful and verdant, as he knew she did for him. He had hoped that her love for him would be enough for the two of them and now he wondered if that was wise. She had been upset earlier that evening— something about her mother marrying thrice and never really caring about her—but Fredrick had not felt any of her pain. He had tried to empathise, but his words, as he comforted her, sounded fake to him.

'We have both been betrayed by our parents, Freddie,' Ava was saying, 'but our experiences will make us better parents, not worse. I really need a family, Freddie, our family. I really want kids. I know you hate them. I know you don't want any, but please think about it. Please?'

Fredrick thought about Veer and his babbling. And he wondered what he was doing right now. Sleeping with his mummy?

And then he thought about Veer's mummy. And her tears. And even now, far away from the dark, cold garden of the pub, in the luxury of his flat, his heart fluttered. And a restlessness overcame him.

I hope she is smiling, Fredrick thought to himself, continuing to fiddle with Ava's hair. Ava was saying something about a baby, and Fredrick nodded in the darkness, not really hearing her words, his mind occupied elsewhere.

When Ava was fast asleep, head resting on his chest, snoring delicately and rhythmically, Fredrick leaned across to pick up his phone from the side table. He flicked open WhatsApp.

Fredrick: *You okay?*

One tick.

Two ticks.

Typing.

Ika: *Your words give me strength. Thank you.*

Fredrick stared at the phone screen for a few moments. *Did you see your husband again? Did he say anything? Did you cry? Are you happy?*

Fredrick: *No problem.*

9

Shaftesbury Avenue, London

December 2016

Ika stared at the nest like something planted right on top of the Harry Potter signage outside the Palace Theatre, transfixed. It was mind-boggling to even consider that in a few years' time, Veer would be big enough to accompany her to watch the *Cursed Child*. The things she would do with him, the places she would show him. A walk down South Bank on a sunny day, looking at the boats and the shops, eating slices of pizza (and buying cheap second-hand books because obviously Veer would love books)? Hours spent in that cool-looking aquarium close to the London Eye? Stare at dinosaurs in the Natural History Museum? Feed the ducks in the Serpentine at Hyde Park after a round of skating, which Veer would soon get better at than she was? Be giddy with excitement and give in to buying overpriced toys at Hamleys?

Lost in thought, Ika looked around. She loved this part of London. The sometimes dodgy tourist shops that sold keychains with the Queen on them, because well, what is more British than a key chain with the Queen on it. The tourists themselves walking around painfully slowly, looking around in wonder. The food shops that hung on to the aromas of long, boozy nights, high heels and short dresses.

She walked forward, still staring at the nest, lost, when long fingers wrapped themselves around hers and yanked her back. She tumbled into Fredrick's chest.

Startled, she looked up. A black cab honked at her.

'Come back to earth?' Fredrick said with a smile. Ika smiled weakly in return, still a bit bewildered. Fredrick held her hand tighter and tugged her away from the traffic on the road. 'We need to wait a few more seconds for the green man,' he said, nodding ahead.

'Sorry, I got lost in my thoughts…'

'I know,' Fredrick said, looking straight ahead.

They crossed the road a few minutes later and walked towards Fredrick's car and Red. Fredrick did not leave Ika's hand, and Ika did not tug hers away.

~

'Jacob?' Ika noted that his blue tweed jacket contrasted shockingly well with the pink satin pocket square. She leaned under the table to check out his socks. The same shade of pink as the pocket square. How? How does he do this, Ika wondered plonking a sea salt crisp into her mouth, *how*?

'Yes, my dear?' Jacob replied, looking up from his laptop. The duo had been working in companionable silence in Jacob's office for the last two hours.

'I was reading about Mr Heisenberg…you know, the older Mr Heisenberg…'

Jacob raised an eyebrow, clearly a bit surprised that Ika wanted to talk about this.

'Aah. James.'

'Yes.'

'What about him?'

'He only ever adopted Fredrick? Not again?'

What a silly question to ask, Ika chided herself mentally.

Jacob drew back into his chair.

'You know, Ika,' he said, taking off his spectacles and placing them on the table in front of him, fixing his eyes on her, 'when you find your person, you don't need anyone else. You never need anyone ever again.'

'And Fredrick was that person for James?'

'And James for Fredrick. The Fredrick and James' story is one of the most powerful 'love' stories I have ever had the honour of witnessing.'

Ika planted her elbow on the table and rested her chin against the heel of her palm, cupping her face in one palm.

'James was coming out of a very public divorce. Fredrick was twelve and ... they were both ... I think, at their lowest,' Jacob's voice trembled, and Ika looked at him surprised. 'I sometimes think Fredrick and James were like broken pieces of glass, sharp-edged, ready to hurt, maybe even dangerous, when they met...but they fit in together like two big pieces of a puzzle, eating up each other's sharp edges, becoming whole. And beautiful.'

Ika stared at Jacob. *Twelve.* Twelve is too old. What was Fredrick's life like before that? Who did he live with? Where? Was he safe? Did he ever get hurt? Ika bit her lower lip anxiously, surprised at how her heart was beating. The unknown, the truth, scared her.

'James' passing has been very hard on Fredrick.'

'I can imagine. He mentioned it to me.'

Jacob looked up, startled.

'Did he?'

'When?'

'Flight back from Dubai.'

Jacob nodded his head slowly. He drew back further and stared at Ika. 'He does not usually talk about James,' he said finally.

Ika nodded.

'He did not speak to anyone for a week after James passed,' Jacob said, staring unblinkingly at Ika. 'He talks more now, and smiles more now, not that he ever really smiled a lot.'

Ika met Jacob's eyes squarely. Was he trying to say something to her?

'What about Fredrick's birth parents?' she asked.

Jacob breathed out deeply.

'Ah. That. I don't know.'

'What do you mean?'

'We know very little about them. Almost nothing.'

'Fredrick does not know who his birth parents are?' Ika tried hard to keep the surprise out of her voice. With his resources, it was difficult to imagine that.

'No.'

'Really?'

Jacob shrugged. 'We've been trying for years. It's killing him,' he said shaking his head.

'That's very hard,' said Ika, rubbing her hands. Why did she feel everything in HD for Fredrick, she wondered, unable to shake away the annoyance?

'It's something Fredrick struggles with, my love. He is not a bad guy. I know he is reticent and sometimes comes across as aloof but all of that is part of his defence mechanism.'

His fingers around hers a week ago in Central London. The questions that came with that—what was happening? Where were they headed? What was right? What was wrong? What was she supposed to do?

'You know, Jacob,' Ika said breathing out, splaying her hands on the table, 'love, if you find it, in whatever shape or form, is double-edged.'

'Interesting you should say that. What do you mean?'

'If you love powerfully, you get to experience the huge-ness of love but when that person leaves, it's so much harder. If you do not experience a love very intense, you don't get to feel the beauty of love in the same way, but the pain is lesser. Because all things end, right? Love, friendship, life.'

'What would you much rather have, Ika? Love—intense and huge and all-encompassing that may come with heartbreak? Or an insipid and uninspiring life where your heart does not get broken.'

Ika smiled and shrugged.

'I will, any day now and from experience, take a broken heart over no love.'

'Would you now, Jacob?' Ika smiled wider.

'I would, most certainly, my dear.'

10

HE HQ, London

January 2017

Mothers of young kids will acquiesce that nights can sometimes be interesting. For Ika, too, it had been another such night. Veer had decided that he was not having any more of this preposterous sleeping at night business. Outdated and not for him. He woke up at 2 a.m. bright and chirpy, ready to take on the day, err, night. Ika obviously did what any mother does in a crisis situation—she googled. No matter what Ika tried—and God knew she tried everything from not catching his eye (yes, a crucial tactic as per Google), to not playing, to playing loads to tire him out, to lights off, to lights on, to singing, to not singing, to dancing, to well, not dancing—Veer refused to sleep. At half six, just around the time Ika's morning alarm went off, he quietly went to his bed, closed his eyes and fell asleep.

Understandably, a few hours later, groggy-eyed Ika found herself walking unsteadily into the office. The idea that she could head straight to the ladies, sit on the toilet, close her eyes and doze off for half an hour presented itself, and Ika allowed herself a smile. The smile vanished when she recalled that she was due to attend a high-profile meeting with Fredrick sometime that morning. Hastily, Ika pulled out her phone and checked first her calendar and then her watch. She was already three minutes late. Fredrick hated tardiness.

Damn.

Ika ran to the meeting room and stopped at the door. Gingerly, she opened it and peeked inside—as expected, the meeting was in full swing. Fredrick was at the head of the table, tall, broad and handsome, sharp in his light grey suit, tapping his ice blue tie as he brought home a point. Feeling smug about choosing a moment when his back was turned, Ika slid into the room, quiet as a mouse. She walked along the wall and sat down in the first chair she could find.

'Any questions? Anyone?' Fredrick asked, his eyes scanning the room. They flew past Ika and then came back to focus on her at record speed. Then they narrowed at her. Someone asked a question, but the eyes did not leave Ika's face.

Did she have food on her face?

Paint?

And then her heart lurched. Baby vomit? There had been another incident that morning just as Ika had handed Veer to Himani.

Fredrick began to walk towards the door, an air of urgency, a kind of restlessness clinging to him.

'I'll be back in a jiffy,' he said to the room in general and to no one in particular. 'Ms Kumar,' his eyes had still not left hers, 'may I borrow you for a moment, please?'

Ika got up and followed Fredrick out of the room. Once outside, Fredrick grabbed Ika's wrist and led her briskly into the corridor and then straight into the gents.

'Fredrick, this is the gents,' Ika mumbled looking around her eyes wide, scandalized beyond measure. A very expensively decorated and thankfully deserted, gents toilet stared back at her.

'What's this?' Fredrick said, his eyes boring into her face. Ika paled. So, this is how strict he was about someone being three minutes late? Really? You grab the latecomer and whisk them into the gents? Was this the HE way? However, common sense dictated that the situation be salvaged as best as it could be for the time being.

'See, Veer was up the whole night…' she said raising her arms defensively.

'Okay?' Fredrick stared intently at her, looking flustered.

'I literally got ten minutes to sleep before the wretched alarm went off and…' Ika fumbled and tried to look ashamed, 'I am sorry. It won't happen again. I promise.'

'What won't?'

'I won't be late to meetings,' Ika said in a small voice.

'Late?'

'Okay,' she said giving in and looking a little bit exasperated, 'very late?'

'Who is talking about that?'

'You are!'

'No, I'm not.'

'Yes, you are.'

'Ika.'

'Fredrick.'

Fredrick breathed out impatiently and dragged his hands down his face. 'This bruise on your forehead. Where did it come from?'

'Bruise?' Ika looked perplexed for a minute and reached to touch her forehead. 'Nothing.'

'The *other* side,' Fredrick said getting more impatient.

Ika moved her fingers to the other side of her forehead and winced when she touched a big-ish bump. 'Ouch!' she squeaked.

'Be careful!' Fredrick exclaimed, grabbing her arm away from her face.

'I don't know. I've been up with Veer the whole night. There was a lot of rough playing and bumping into things happening,' Ika shrugged, feeling sheepish.

Fredrick stared at her.

'Are you sure?'

'Yes.'

'No one has hurt you?'

'Maybe my year-old son, but no, no one apart from him,' Ika said smiling, and then it struck her. 'Who do you think did this?'

'The same person who made you cry in the pub?' Fredrick said blankly.

'Fredrick…' Ika breathed out.

'I know,' Fredrick said, shoulders slumping, looking uncomfortable, 'I am crossing a line here. But … but rude words are one thing, hurting someone physically is a completely different thing.'

Ika stared at Fredrick. He was breathing heavily; he looked so … so flustered, almost vulnerable, like he did not want to be here, holding her arm, asking these questions, but there was no way he could not ask them.

'Vivaan may be a lot of things, but he is not a wife beater,' she said finally. *Not yet, at least.*

'Okay, okay,' Fredrick breathed out and let go of her arm. 'I'm sorry, I didn't mean to…'

Ika grabbed the cuff of his jacket. 'Don't worry so much about me,' she whispered, heartbroken in a weird achy way.

'Okay,' he mumbled, running his fingers through his hair, listlessly.

They stood like that for a few moments staring at each other; Ika against the wall and Fredrick in front of her.

Close.

Fredrick reached out and gently pushed a strand of Ika's hair behind her ear. 'You need to put something on this,' he said softly, nodding at the bruise, 'and make sure playtime with Veer does not result in bodily harm to either party.'

'Bodily harm.' Ika smiled. Fredrick's hands dropped, but instead of dropping to his side, he let them rest at her waist. He gently lifted Ika's chin. And then he leaned in.

Ika stilled, wide-eyed and staring at him. His eyes—blazing, his nose—small and sharp, his lips—beautiful.

He came closer. Their eyes locked.

Don't think, a daring voice in Ika's head ventured, and with that, not quite believing what was happening, Ika took a step closer to Fredrick. Fredrick leaned in further. The air around them bristled.

The door to the gents burst open noisily, and a man entered, coughing and sputtering. He looked around and stilled, coughs forgotten when he saw Fredrick and Ika.

'I am so—' he began to mumble. Fredrick, eyes burning and face hard, slowly turned to face the unwelcome intruder.

'OUT!' he growled.

The man about turned and vanished at record speed.

Fredrick pulled away from Ika, and Ika stared at her feet, breathing out and rubbing her clammy hands against the rough fabric of her navy blue jumpsuit.

'You have a lot of people waiting for you in the meeting room,' she said finally, her voice steadier than she would have expected it to be.

'After you,' was all Fredrick said, using his hands to indicate towards the door.

11

HE HQ, Knightsbridge, London

February 2017

Ika grabbed the two empty and washed lunch boxes and stuffed them inside her bag. Jacob had been asking for a *tarka daal* forever and Ellin for a curry. Ika had, yet again, for one last time, tried to explain it to Ellin. The truth, as she had called it, about the omnipresent curry.

'No, Ellin, let me break it to you. Santa does not exist. And there is no Indian dish called a curry.'

'It is. There's even curry houses, all very Indian,' Ellin had insisted in her thick Swedish accent.

'Don't even get me started on curry houses. And a curry is as British as shepherd's pie.'

'It's not.'

It reminded Ika of another conversation she recently had with someone at work who had insisted that people from India were called Hindi and the language Hindu. Ika had tried to stress the fact that she had lived in India for the first twenty-five years of her life and was quite clear that the language was Hindi and people Hindu, but the gentleman had refused to take her word for it. You had to let a few pass, Ika had thought then. And that is what she thought now.

Ika had exhaled deeply.

'Okay, fine, Ellin, whatever you say.'

Over the last eight years, Ika had had to learn to live with this. Case in point: the chief executive that Jacob had introduced to her that morning. He had taken one look at Ika, and when she had said hello, he had replied with a, 'I love chicken tikka masala'.

'I work in the M&A team and look forward to closing this million-dollar deal for you,' Ika had responded. Jacob snorted, which he quickly converted into a cough.

Laptop firmly in a TUMI laptop case and heels replaced with trusty VEJA sneakers, bought online at a 60 per cent discount at the ungodly hour of 5 a.m. on 26 December last year, Ika was ready to trek her way home. She glanced around the office floor one last time and then craned her neck to look at Fredrick's office. The door was closed; there was no way to know if Fredrick was still in.

Innumerable times since their rendezvous in the gents, Ika had found her mind wandering to what had *almost* happened. Would they really have kissed, she wondered again and again. Maybe he would have stopped? Maybe she would have moved away? Ika's shoulders slumped, and she let out a deep breath. What storms, she wondered, did the future hold?

'Hiya,' came a familiar voice breaking her line of thought. Ika looked up startled and then blushed a deep red.

Fredrick had been watching Ika intently for the last few minutes. She was doing it again—shaking her head repeatedly as if having an argument with someone sat inside her head, and then when she saw him, she blushed like she had been caught red-handed. It made him smile. It was, he knew, his first smile of the day.

'Are you leaving?' Fredrick asked nodding at her bag.

'Do you need me for something?' Ika asked staring at Fredrick. There was a darkness on his face that reminded her of rain-laden clouds ready to burst. His brow was furrowed, and even though he was smiling, the smile did not quite reach his eyes.

'Umm ... okay if I walk you to the station?'

'Yes, of course, that would be lovely. Knightsbridge Station.'

The two walked out together from the spacious office floor into reception. Ella waved them an ultra-cheery 'have a great evening' to which Fredrick did not bother to reply, and they were out on the road, in the midst of the well-heeled of the Knightsbridge area.

Even the air in some areas of London smells posher than the rest, and Knightsbridge, Ika thought to herself, was definitely one of them. Crowds—not as much the tourists but definitely the locals—walking past were often both sartorially inspiring and intimidating. An elderly lady, about seven feet tall, most definitely an erstwhile model, dressed in a bright yellow woollen coat, matching sparkly shades and two feet heels, now walked past, four dogs on leash. Of course, thought Ika ruefully, that's exactly how you dress to walk the dogs.

'Your forehead looks fine now,' Fredrick mumbled after a few minutes of silence as the two walked towards Hyde Park, the station forgotten. Ika nodded.

'For some reason, Hyde Park always makes me think of Princess Diana,' Ika said as they entered. 'You know,' she said looking at Fredrick, 'I was working on an art project for school when the news of Princess Diana's car crash came in. Some of my friends were in tears that evening.'

'Was Princess Diana that popular back in India?'

'Back in a *small* city in India'—Ika smiled—'we all hoped to be Princess Diana's future daughters-in-law, you see.'

Fredrick smiled. A weak, watery smile, Ika thought, looking intently at him.

'No harm in dreaming, eh?' Ika grinned widely, determinedly. 'My friend, Anu, she was certain that one day Prince William would travel to India on a royal tour as a dashing man of twenty-five and see her walking down the road, in slow motion, her colourful *salwar kameez* flowing around her. She would toss her glorious hair, and Prince William would watch transfixed, taking but a moment to fall in love with her. He would be so gobsmacked by Anu's exotic Indian beauty that he would send MI5 agents to track her down, leading to the most epic romance in the British Royal Family.'

'And?' Fredrick was smiling widely now. His smile reached his eyes. *Almost.*

'Well, the Royal Tour never happened. Anu is now happily…? married to a potbellied accountant who recently had a hair transplant and is currently taking herbal treatment for pimples and snoring.'

Fredrick laughed.

'Not that these things matter, of course.' Ika grinned.

The Serpentine loomed statesman-like in front of them, dotted with ducks and swans. Fredrick smiled again—James had an inexplicable and rather disturbing fondness for these ducks, he thought ruefully. Ika and Fredrick sat on a bench a few feet away from the Serpentine.

'Something is bothering you, isn't it?' a small voice reached Fredrick a few minutes later, breaking the silence.

'Day after is the first anniversary of my father's passing away,' he said finally.

Beside him, Ika's shoulders sagged. Yes, of course.

You will get by. Somehow. I know how hard this is.

I am sorry.

I am very sorry.

Ika sat silently, uncomfortably crossing and uncrossing her legs.

'He transformed my life. I owe him everything.'

'You are lucky to have found him…'

'He found me, and then he saved me. Again and again and again for years,' Fredrick said staring straight ahead. It felt nice, he thought, to be actually speaking, even if indirectly, about the adoption. Also, good to know that she had done her research and knew he was adopted.

'From?'

'Myself.' Fredrick paused and thought. And then decided to say it. 'My mum…' he faltered, 'she kind of messed things up for me.'

'How?'

'I know three things about my biological mother,' he raised three fingers. 'One, her name was Valerie. Two, she was a prostitute. Three, she was a drug addict.'

He shook his head. He had never volunteered information to anyone, *anyone,* about his birth parents.

'A mum's a mum, whatever else she might have been,' Ika said after a pause.

'You really think so?'

'Yes.'

'You know why I don't even touch alcohol.'

'Why?'

'Who knows what I get from my mum? Maybe I am genetically predisposed to addiction?'

'You are the single most determined, disciplined and focussed man I have ever met in my life,' Ika said in a low voice, 'you need to give yourself more credit than that.'

'Sorry, Your Highness. Forgive me,' Fredrick half smiled.

Ika slumped into the wooden bench and inhaled deeply. The winds were picking up, and she wrapped her H&M scarf tighter.

'I don't belong, Ika,' Fredrick said, softly staring at the Serpentine, 'I've never belonged.'

You belong to me.

'You may not have belonged *before* you met Mr Heisenberg, Fredrick, but you do now,' Ika said, her brow furrowed. 'Life before may have been tough, but with your father...' Ika trailed off helplessly.

Fredrick stilled, staring ahead in the darkness that was with each passing moment deepening around them. After the adoption, James had whisked him away to a quiet chalet in Cologny in Switzerland so that they could get to know each other away from the madness of London. Thousands of hours with more therapists than he could count followed, all of them desperate for any detail the sulking twelve-year-old would offer about his past life. Fredrick had not opened his mouth *once*, not even to say 'hello' or 'thank you'.

'Before Dad, there were a lot of foster homes,' Fredrick said, looking straight ahead, eyes vacant.

The one where, when the foster mum had come to give him a cuddle and say hello, he had bit her neck. The other foster mum who was, now he could tell easily, mentally unstable, and had charged at him with a knife. The other one that only gave him food sometimes, forcing him to steal stale sandwiches from the local store. The foster dad who slapped him so hard that he saw shiny white stars dancing around his head.

'Were they all horrible?' came Ika's voice, soft around its edges. She was staring ahead, too, looking at the silhouette of the ducks, trying to not focus on the little grey-eyed boy, sad and alone, the images of whom her brain was conjuring up for her.

'Mostly,' he said, looking down at his hands, 'but often I was too.'

'Were you safe?' she asked. Fredrick cast a sideways glance at Ika. She was staring ahead, wringing her hands nervously.

'Yes, I was safe,' he said and watched her still and then breathe out in relief. 'I was a very difficult child,' Fredrick said, 'Dad changed it all for me. I understood in being with him what it meant to live in the midst of love. And that transformed my life.'

'It does that, doesn't it? Love? It transforms lives,' Ika said softly.

Silence descended upon them, and it stayed there, hovering around them, wrapping them like a warm blanket.

'You must have looked for your birth parents?' Ika asked breaking the silence.

Fredrick nodded, slowly, thoughtfully. 'Spent crazy amounts of money on it. Ellin and Jacob have been helping, too, but nothing,' he shrugged.

'Did you ever get to meet Valerie?'

'She passed away when I was fourteen. Jacob found out about her a few years after her death.'

Ika nodded slowly, wrapping her head around the facts.

'So...'

'Yes. For fourteen years Valerie lived a few hundred miles away from me but did not bother to find me. Of this sob-fest, this hurts the most,' Fredrick did not even try to keep the bitterness out of his voice.

'A mother always does her best, Fredrick. Her best may not be *your* best, but it is her absolute best.'

'You are defending my mother? The woman who abandoned a sick, one-day-old baby?'

'You were sick?'

Fredrick shook his head and breathed deeply. 'I was born with Neonatal Abstinence Syndrome. NAS. I was born addicted to drugs … because she could not stop taking them while pregnant. They had to wean me off it…'

Ika sank back into the bench. She bit her lips. Sick babies—there was nothing worse in the world. An image of a poorly little baby with beautiful blue-grey eyes came to her now, and Ika felt her eyes moisten.

'Sometimes I don't know what to do with my past. It just hurts.'

'Maybe that is why God sent Mr Heisenberg to you. To make up for all the love you missed out on.'

'Later today, I am due to speak at a private event to mark Dad's first death anniversary. It's his closest friends and business associates, those that mattered most to him.'

'And?'

'I…I…don't think I am up for it.'

'Why?' Ika asked softly.

'It's hard to speak about Dad without…umm…you know… umm…'

'Getting emotional?' Ika offered.

Fredrick shrugged, looking away.

'And what's wrong with that, Fredrick?'

'Maybe I should ask Jacob to speak for me,' Fredrick mumbled and was fishing his phone out of his pocket when Ika put a gentle hand on his arm.

'Don't you think Mr Heisenberg deserves his son to speak about him?'

'I don't want to be an emotional mess on stage, in front of fifty-odd people.'

'You won't be.'

'Will you come?'

'To the event?'

'Yes.'

Ika felt a rush of love for the man sat next to her who had only shown her kindness. She leaned in, took his face in her hands and kissed the top of his head. His forehead felt warm.

'Yes, I will,' she said drawing back, and suddenly shy, avoiding his eye.

Had she really just kissed *the* Fredrick Heisenberg like he was a little puppy, she wondered suitably horrified, a moment later as she sunk lower and lower into the bench.

'Is anyone else here carrying VEJA shoes and two lunch boxes in their bags?' Ika wondered two hours later, sat in a second-row seat at the majestic Orangery in the Hurlingham Club in Fulham. Ika's makeup had washed out and her legs still hurt from all the walking. Fifty-odd finely dressed men and women, intimidating to look at, the air around them sombre, sat in rapt attention. Fredrick, clad in a well-sharp black suit, stood in the centre of the room, one hand in his pocket, speaking about James Heisenberg, commanding the room with each word that came out of his mouth.

'Like many in this room, I too will,' he was saying, 'never forget.... the...the kindness...'

Ika's toes curled on themselves as Fredrick faltered. His eyes were red, and he now spared a hand over his forehead. He paused, stared at his shoes, trying to regain composure. And then he shook his head and shrugged helplessly, obviously in the throes of intense emotion that was poised to overtake any moment now.

Look at me.

Fredrick looked straight up at Ika the very next instant like he had heard her silent request.

I can't go on, his eyes said to her.

Yes, you can, she said silently to him.

The crowd murmured encouragingly. The lady sat next to Ika sniffed.

Fredrick breathed out and turned around to face away from the crowd. When he turned back around again, a few seconds later, his eyes were still wet, but when he began to speak, his voice was steady.

~

Jacob stopped a few feet away from James' grave in the Kensal Green Cemetery. James' father was also buried here, incidentally, only a few feet away from Charles Babbage, who invented the computer, and this had always made James laugh, Jacob thought now, a lump forming in his throat. This year had been hard, a lot harder than he had anticipated.

A couple of tourists walked past Jacob, giggling noisily. 'How the VIPs RIP,' said one to the other, and Jacob shook his head at the disrespect. Jacob then turned around to focus his attention on the two people he had spotted at James' grave when he had arrived a few minutes ago.

Fredrick was sat at his father's grave, a bouquet of lilies, James' favourite flowers, in his hands. He sat still, crouched in his oversized black woollen coat, stately against the backdrop of the grey and white mausoleums.

A few feet away from Fredrick was a lady in a well-fitted black woollen coat and heels. She had been standing there for a long time, Jacob could tell, and now, as Jacob watched, she started to walk towards Fredrick. The lady sat down next to Fredrick. Fredrick held his face in his hands; his shoulders heaved, and Jacob's heart lurched. The lady shuffled in so that their shoulders were touching. She put an arm around the mighty Fredrick Heisenberg, who crumpled into her embrace. She held him tight, gently rocking him from side to side, not saying anything.

The winds rustled; the clouds gathered. Jacob wiped away the tears that were streaming down his face. While it had been hard to live without his best friend, it had been harder to see Fredrick's pain. He was immeasurably glad, Jacob thought, that Fredrick had finally found someone in whose arms he could find some peace.

'You would have dearly loved Ikadashi Kumar, James,' Jacob mumbled to himself, about turned and, with one last look at Fredrick and Ika, began the long-ish walk to the gates of the cemetery.

His phone buzzed. Ava.

'Hello, my love,' Jacob said into the phone, trying hard to keep the exasperation out of his voice, readying for the avalanche of words he knew were headed his way.

'Hi Jacob, do you know where Freddie is? Imma sooo worried about him. He just won't say anything! It's James' death anniversary, and he still won't talk! Like what, man? Just keeps saying he is okay. Is he? Do we know? Do we ever know?' Ava exhaled deeply, throwing up her heavily manicured hands. 'Do ya know, he has never even mentioned his adoption to me? Like EVER. He won't talk about his birth parents. Or now James. Or the million other things he should be talking to me about. Everything I know about him is from the tabloids!'

'Take a breath, my girl,' said Jacob into the phone, his ears already hurting, 'relax. Fredrick does not speak to me either, you know. He speaks to no one. He bears the cross alone.'

'He does not need to!' Ava shouted, exasperated, and then added in a lower voice, 'Why can't I be the exception? Why can't I be the one person in the world he shares his pain with?'

'I wish I had an answer to that, Ava,' Jacob said quietly, turning around once again to glance at the emotional mess his favourite boy in the world was in at the moment, still being rocked gently from side to side by Ikadashi. 'Fredrick is in a meeting, honey. I am sure he will call you as soon as he is out.'

12

Putney, London

March 2017

'It's his first Holi, for God's sake!' Ika said, trying hard to keep her voice steady, fearful of crossing some kind of line. A red burning line that cropped up unexpected and unannounced in arguments with Vivaan and burned it all—her pride, dignity and self-respect—in its wake.

'Don't say things that trigger me,' Vivaan had warned her in an eerily calm voice the last time they'd argued, 'you know you'll regret it.'

'He won't remember a thing,' Vivaan retorted, bringing Ika back to the present, zipping up his handbag. He tucked his crisp white shirt into his trousers and put on his spotless black suit jacket. He glanced at himself in the full-length mirror and nodded in silent approval. Ika watched this with growing annoyance.

'Vivaan,' Ika tried again, scrambling out of bed, 'how are we going to make sure Veer remains in touch with his roots if we don't make an effort to introduce him to our culture?'

'One, he is not even one. And two, throwing colour at random people is hardly culture, Ika. It's hooliganism. And three, no one asked you to leave India. If you are so worried about your son missing out on all things Indian, go back.'

Ika took a moment to absorb the stings.

'I grew up playing Holi. And so did you. It's part of being Indian,' she tried again.

'Okay, listen,' Vivaan replied, turning around so that his eyes, dark and hard, bored into Ika, 'it could be *your* thing. It isn't mine. I can't prioritise throwing colour at Veer over my meetings in Lucerne. Please feel free to celebrate our culture with our son. I need to get on this flight now.'

'Why are you so angry all the time?' Ika hated the pleading tone in her voice.

'Try doing things then, Ika, that do not make me so angry?'

Tears began to sting her eyes, and Ika knew that this would be another battle she would lose. 'I wanted—'

'And also, consider cleaning the dishes today? Or is that too much to ask of the High Highness?'

And with one last acidic look, Vivaan about turned and walked out of the bedroom.

Ika slumped back into her bed and drew the bedsheet closer to her. She hugged her knees and then buried her face in them.

I'll break your face. I'll smash your face to the floor and drag you through the blood.

He'd said that to her in a fit of anger last week. And the words had not left her, no, not yet. Maybe these kinds of words never do?

The worst and the scariest was that she had not reacted at all when Vivaan had spoken those words. Like it was acceptable, almost? It wasn't right, right? What would another woman do in her place? Another modern, educated woman who earned six figures at one of the most coveted firms in Europe? Disregard them as words spoken in a moment of anger, like she had? Or ...

A little shiver ran through Ika's body.

Was she in an abusive marriage? Is this how they looked? Was she one of *them* now? It must be her fault, right, at some level, to have let things come to this?

Surely, it must be her fault.

All of this was her fault, she thought, sinking lower into the comfortable safety of the bedsheets.

∽

'Where are you running off to?' came the baritone and Ika stopped in her tracks just as she was about to open the main door and step onto the road.

'Hi Fredrick,' she said, turning back, smiling.

'Gosh!' Fredrick exclaimed, looking at the harried-looking girl in front of him. 'What's going on?'

'It's Holi today,' Ika replied.

Fredrick narrowed his eyes at Ika, and then his face cleared. 'The festival where everyone throws colour at everyone else?'

Ika laughed and nodded. 'Last minute decision to have a bit of a celebration, because why not? Jacob has, very kindly, dismissed me for the day.'

'Of course, will be great for Veer to be exposed to Indian festivals—it's his culture...'

Ika's smile vanished, and Fredrick wondered if he had said something inappropriate.

'Yes, I know,' Ika replied, smile back on a moment later, 'heading to Alperton for starters.'

'Alperton?'

'Yes. Lots of Indian shopping to be done. Food, colours, clothes. Then pick up Veer from nursery, get him home, play colours with Veer, scrub him top to toe and then a nice Indian meal with Mummy and Veer with some Indian music.'

'Sounds lovely. Your husband?' Fredrick jammed his hands in his pockets and tried to keep the edge out of his voice.

'He's in Lucerne,' Ika replied, and Fredrick wondered if he imagined a darkness clouding Ika's face. *That jerk.*

'Okay. How are you getting to Alperton?'

'Tube-ing it,' Ika said cheerfully.

'Fancy Range Rover-ing it?'

'Oh no. Red needs to be with you here.'

'Well, maybe I can come with you along with Red?' Fredrick offered.

'To Alperton?' Ika asked with a giggle, taken aback.

'To Alperton indeed.'

'To shop for colour and buy jalebi?'

'To buy jabeli.'

'Ja-le-bi'

'Ja-be-li.'

Ika giggled. 'Jabeli it is. Are you sure though? Mind you, Alperton is no Mayfair.'

'I'm quite bored of Mayfair, truth be told.'

'Meetings?'

'Can be rescheduled?'

'Gasp. Horror.'

'Gasp, horror indeed.'

'In that case—let the Alperton adventures begin!'

13

Putney, London

March 2017

When the bell rang at six, Himani, who had spent the last three hours getting the terrace ready for their last-minute Holi celebrations, gave it one final satisfied glance, threw the dupatta of her salwar across her shoulders and hurried towards the door, opened it and stilled.

Ika was at the entrance, holding about a million bags. Fredrick was standing next to her, looking handsome in his black suit, the open top button of his shirt giving him a relaxed air. On Fredrick's shoulders sat Veer, clutching onto his hair with all his little might, giggling as he readied to eat it. Fredrick was holding onto some shopping bags as well as Veer's Peppa Pig nursery backpack. Ika and Fredrick were both laughing.

When was the last time she'd seen Ika and Vivaan as a happy family, Himani asked herself. Her mind drew a blank.

'So, you convinced Fredrick to celebrate with us?' Himani asked with a grin, beaming at Fredrick. Veer squealed with delight on spotting his Nani.

'I did not take much convincing to be fair,' said Fredrick putting Veer down and surprising Himani with a quick hug.

'Fredrick tried jalebi, Mummy,' Ika squealed. Himani looked expectantly at Fredrick.

'Exquisite! Jabeli … err … I mean Ja-le-bi … is exquisite!' Fredrick said with a laugh, slowing down to pronounce the name of the Indian dessert.

'Too sickly sweet!' Ika retorted.

'Crunchy. Sweet. Warm. What is there to not like!' Fredrick responded. Veer now bounced back into Fredrick's arms.

'And Fredrick went to the samosa shop with me, the little shop with the awning, you know, down the main street,' said Ika laughing. 'The mighty Mr Heisenberg lined up to buy ten samosas. The shop lady blushed red for no reason and gave us an extra samosa,' Ika looked pointedly at Fredrick who mouthed a happy-to-help. 'And we bought clothes for everyone. Indian clothes.'

'And there was no changing room in that shop,' Fredrick laughed.

'No, there wasn't. And Fredrick was so scandalized when the shopkeeper asked him to just try on his kurta right there on the shop floor.'

'Mortified is the word,' chimed in Fredrick.

'Did Fredrick buy an Indian dress?' asked Himani, surprised.

'Yes!' replied Ika and Fredrick together, looking at each other in surprise and laughing.

'And then we went to this store with all the Indian groceries...' Fredrick added.

'And Fredrick just loved it. We got the bhaang powder and gujhiya and the colours. The ladies there, too, could not take their eyes off the great Mr Heisenberg, needless to add.' Ika giggled. 'I think the whole of Alperton thoroughly enjoyed Fredrick's visit. We may get a letter from their council requesting a repeat visit for the general amusement of the female residents and shoppers.'

'Come on!' Fredrick chided Ika good-naturedly and then turned to Himani, 'Ika took me to this tiny shop that sells chaat. You know, Indian street food?'

Himani nodded indulgently. Yes, she knew chaat—Indian street food, she thought with a smile. Ika and Fredrick looked like little schoolchildren, back from their day out, excitedly telling the parents all that had happened.

'And Fredrick tried golgappas, Mummy. I had to teach him how to eat them in one go.'

'Eating them is an exercise that requires military precision, I must say, but once in, they are delicious!' said Fredrick. 'Where has all this food been my entire life?'

'I think Fredrick is closet Indian,' said Ika.

'"Closet Indian"? Ha! I'm very proud of my newfound love for all things Indian.'

At his words, Ika turned red. She looked everywhere except at Fredrick. Fredrick coughed delicately. Himani watched the two, her arms folded across her chest, trying hard to not smile.

'And then,' Ika continued, 'we picked Veer up from nursery. Paula, the nursery teacher, she gave the day's update to Fredrick only, completely ignoring me.' Ika was giggling now. 'Gosh, it must be so hard to be Fredrick Heisenberg!'

Fredrick rolled his eyes, and Himani smiled, looking first at her daughter, looking so different from the sad girl who had left for the office that morning and then at Fredrick.

'Anyway, we thought we would call more people. Jacob is joining us,' Ika hurried inside, 'as is Francesca.'

'Your boss Jacob?' Himani asked, taken aback.

'Yes, boss Jacob,' Ika smiled. She looked around her spotless home. 'Thanks, Mummy!' she squealed hugging her mother. And then she craned her neck and saw how Himani had decorated their terrace with multicoloured streamers—all in less than four hours when Ika had called Himani to tell her of her last-minute plans to celebrate the festival. If Vivaan did not want to celebrate, that was fine, wasn't it? Veer deserved a happy day; all of them deserved a happy day.

On cue, the bell rang, and Jacob and Francesca trooped in together. Another round of welcomes and introductions and hugs and hellos. Jacob looked around in wonder, folded his hands, handed Himani an elaborately wrapped gift and said, 'Namaste Himani ji' and won about a million brownie points in that one instant and with those words.

'I told you to wear old clothes. These will get dirty, you silly girl,' Ika pulled Francesca in to a corner and hissed at her puff-sleeved, blue Ted Baker dress.

'Look at him,' Francesca nodded helplessly in Fredrick's direction, 'just *look* at him. I don't care if I destroy this dress, but I am not wearing old clothes in front of that God on Earth.'

And with that ensued an hour of Holi. The group, led by a very excited Veer, trooped to the terrace. Himani put on some music.

'Rang barse bheege chunar wali'

'Holi khele Raghuveera'

Bollywood songs that had been the backdrop of every single Holi celebration Ika had been part of growing up in India took Ika back into time. The sun would shine bright, people—multicoloured and happy high—would sing along and dance, throwing fistfuls of dry colour into the air or at each other in parks and on the roads, both of which would be unrecognisable by the time the festivities concluded. Bucketfuls of coloured water would come out. Water pistols. Water balloons. And battles of a different kind would rage on the roads, leaving happy, tired kids and laughing parents. Old disputes would be forgotten over mithai and bhaang and music and dance. And even sworn enemies would let go of prejudices on this one day to celebrate.

As memories gathered force, Ika looked around wistfully, her eyes a bit moist. It was hard, even after all these years, to be away from her own country. How long, she wondered, did you have to stay in a place for it to become home? Would London *ever* become home?

'Help, missy!' Francesca poked Ika in the ribs, bringing her back to Putney. 'Take the food around?'

'Oh, yes, sorry. I got lost.' Ika smiled.

Francesca paused to stare at Ika and then smiled.

Himani put the gujhiya, laddos, samosa, jalebi on colourful plates and passed them around.

'Jacob ji,' Himani said shyly to Jacob, 'please have some gujhiya?'

'And what is this gujhiya? I did some reading up on Holi when Ika invited me this afternoon, but I don't think I came across gujhiya,' Jacob asked, picked up one and took a large bite. His eyes widened. 'What is it, Mrs Joshi? This heavenly, crumbly, sweet food of the Gods?'

Himani laughed. 'It is delicious indeed. Special Holi delicacy. A firm favourite in our house.'

'Is it okay if I take some more?' Jacob asked, aghast that he was speaking with his mouth full. And again, without waiting for an answer, he picked up three, making Himani laugh out loud. Himani could see why Ika liked Jacob so much. She could easily see that.

On another set of plates were little mountains of dry colour. Pink. Red. Green. Yellow. Blue. Happy little perfect mountains awaiting their destiny to amuse and entertain.

'Oh my god, these look so pretty,' Francesca squealed walking into the terrace, staring at the mounds of colour and fingering the streamers billowing in the slight breeze.

'Do they?' Ika asked with a wicked smile, grabbed a handful of blue colour and mercilessly smeared Francesca's face with it. 'To go with your Ted Baker dress.'

'You. You…' Francesca fumbled for the right words and then grabbed colour and smeared Ika with it.

Jacob—clad humbly in his plainest Gucci tee, Ika noted with a roll of her eyes—looked alarmed for a moment. 'Is that how you play Holi?' he asked, his eyes wide with both surprise and excitement.

'No, no,' Ika said innocently, turning her now yellow face towards the man who had so quickly become a dear friend, '*this* is how you play Holi,' and with that, she grabbed a generous amount of blue and rubbed it on Jacob's cheeks. 'The blue looks lovely on you too, Jacob,' she laughed.

'You messed with the wrong gent, my lady,' said Jacob, getting into the spirit, lunging towards the plate of colour, grabbing two fistfuls and then dashing after Ika who had taken off the moment Jacob had looked like he meant to have revenge.

And with that, they were off. Colour flew everywhere. The blue and the red and the pink and the green—the world around them was soon in multicolour. Veer squealed in delight and threw microscopic amounts of colour at Fredrick, who crouched low to humour his littlest friend. Himani joined in with gusto that surprised her. Sounds of laughter and squeals and 'don't you dare' carried through the evening to the neighbours. The food vanished at alarming speed. And jugs of bhaang were tipped empty. The clean faces from an hour ago were all multicoloured now, the terrace was a mess, Veer was sitting in a corner, exhausted from his long day, but everyone was smiling.

Himani observed the scene with a smile on her face. She watched Ika and Fredrick walk towards one another. Fredrick took a bit of colour and gently rubbed it against Ika's cheeks.

'Happy Holi,' he said.

She took some pink, and he bent low so that they were at eye level. She smiled and slowly smeared some of it across his already multicoloured face.

'Happy Holi,' she said, almost shyly, 'thank you for making this day special.'

They stood like this for a moment, awkward and shy, like teenagers, grinning stupidly. And Himani realized she was smiling widely.

'They look good together, don't they? Even in shades of blue and pink?' came a voice, and startled out of her reverie, Himani looked up to see a blue, pink and green Jacob standing next to her.

Himani nodded, and in wordless camaraderie, Himani offered Jacob another gujhiya which, again wordlessly, he accepted with a wide grin. And with that, a friendship was born.

∼

Later that night, after having dropped her ruined Ted Baker dress that had cost Francesca all of £148 in the bin, she plonked herself on her black leather sofa.

She stared at her open diary and chewed her pen for a bit. There was a lot that was going on in her head.

Francesca began to write.

'What do you fucking do when you find love is the all-important question. You should embrace it, right? YOLO and all that? But what do you do when you find it while fighting for the survival of a shitty marriage you do not have the guts to leave? Also, fuck, how handsome can a man be!'

She stopped writing and chewed her pen some more and then got up and made herself a big drink.

It was all too much to think about, she thought to herself taking a sip of her Pincer Vodka.

∼

Ika buried her face in Veer's curls. She could still feel the heat of Fredrick's palm across her cheeks from when he had put colour on her. In the darkness of the nursery, as she found Veer's pudgy little hand to hold on to, flashes from the day came back to her. Fredrick's face—comically impressed—when he had tried the now famous jalebi (or jabeli as he continued to call them). Fredrick walking out of the bathroom after the madness of Holi, dressed in a simple white kurta, looking like an Indian prince. Veer sitting in Fredrick's lap as he ate his dinner. Fredrick and Jacob laughing over something Veer had just said. Fredrick rushing to help a very shocked Himani with the dishes. The two of them, her mother and Fredrick, hanging out in the kitchen by the dishwasher, surrounded by soap suds and a pile of dirty dishes, talking and laughing like they'd known each other forever. Fredrick's hug before he left. His arms, strong and powerful around her. She had wanted him to stay. How she had wanted him to stay.

Ika sighed, shaking her head in the darkness, allowing, hoping almost that the black around her would hide her thoughts from herself and the world.

Her phone beeped.

Fredrick.

Her heart skipped a beat.

I've never really known what family feels like. But standing on that balcony, celebrating Holi with you came very close to the real thing, I'd imagine ... I won't forget today for a long time. Thank you for letting me be a part of it. F X

∼

Himani cried softly into her pillow. There was something about Fredrick that always got to the core of her and stirred up memories that she knew were best locked up in the darkest, deepest dungeon of her heart.

Every time she did something for Ika, like the time she was helping her wash her face, or putting food on her plate or randomly patting her head, she knew Fredrick was watching. Watching and yearning.

As the evening had progressed, she had found herself doing little things for him too. Insisting he wear a jumper once he had changed into the Indian kurta, patting his hair down when it became ruffled after play with Veer, making sure that the duvet covered his legs when they had all sat down post dinner—on the floor—for a game of cards.

He had bid her farewell first and then said bye to Ika. He was about to get into his car when he had caught her eye. He had walked up to her and wrapped her into a quick, wordless hug. But the hug had meant something. It spoke, like hugs always do. It said thank you.

Some mother had lost so much time with such a beautiful son.

Himani cried for Fredrick and his mother.

She cried for herself and the baby she never got to meet.

~

In the darkness of their bedroom, Jacob propped himself on his elbow and looked at his wife of almost four decades. Her sleep mask—which read BADASS GRANDMOM in red—always made him smile, but not today.

Jacob's heart felt all kinds of heavy. It had been a beautiful, beautiful day. Ika's home was simple, but there was so much love between mother and daughter and they had welcomed them all with such warmth that there were few social gatherings he could think of having attended recently that had meant more.

No, all that was good. It was Fredrick who haunted him.

Jacob had seen Fredrick in the biggest of events, in the midst of the rich and the famous, standing tall and erect, one hand in his pocket, unaffected, unfazed.

But at Ika's, he had looked around with such … such…

Pain seared through Jacob's heart and he felt his eyes sting.

And then there was that unsaid, unspoken 'whatever' going on between Ika and Fredrick. Would Fredrick have the strength, Jacob wondered, or would he be like his father? How far, he mused, had the apple fallen from the tree?

The restlessness inside him gathered force. Casting one final glance at Florence to make sure she was asleep, Jacob made his way out of the bedroom. Once in the dimly lit plush den, he sat at his table.

Hurriedly, he brought out a pen and paper.

He needed to write. Now. That was the only thing he knew from decades of pain that would bring him any kind of peace.

Brow furrowed, he began to write, urgency dictating his movements.

'Dear Isla,' he wrote, letting out a deep, shaky breath. Then he drew back and scratched the words. 'Dearest Isla,' he tried and then scratched the words again. He thought for a moment, and then a slow smile appeared on his face.

'My Love,' he wrote in a neat cursive...

14

Putney, London

April 2017

The animal-like growl coming from Ika's bedroom reverberated in the nursery, and a shudder ran through Himani's body. Himani scrunched, her eyes shut and pressed her palms against her ears. More screaming. Himani's hands trembled as she picked up her phone from near Veer's cot and upped the volume of the white noise. The sound of something crashing now and Veer woke up with a loud wail.

Himani groaned, but secretly she felt glad of the distraction. Maybe she should tell Ika how much her fights with Vivaan distressed her. Maybe she should go and fight alongside Ika? Try and sort it out?

Himani hurriedly picked up Veer, who continued to wail loudly, his little face turning red at a rapid rate.

Himani shut off the white noise and plonked a dummy in Veer's mouth. There never used to be throwing of things before, Himani thought, putting Veer back in his cot.

What if Vivaan hit Ika? A shiver ran through Himani, and she hurriedly walked out of the nursery. She saw Vivaan in the hallway, coming out of his bedroom, his eyes wide with anger and his hair dishevelled. His hand, Himani noticed with alarm, was bloodied.

'Vivaa—' Himani tried, but Vivaan rushed past her, slamming the main door behind him.

Gingerly, Himani opened the door to Ika's room. The first thing she noticed was the blood on the wall. And Ika, sat on the floor, hugging her knees, tears streaming down her face.

'How did he get hurt, *puttar*?' Himani asked rushing to her daughter's side, 'and are you hurt?'

'He banged his wrist against the wall,' Ika said in between her sobs. Seeing his mother cry, Veer let out a blood-curdling wail.

Despite the crying, a wave of relief washed through Himani. So, they had not hit each other. Not that Ika would ever have, but Vivaan, with his increasingly angry demeanour, had started scaring Himani.

Himani sat down on the floor next to Ika and took her hands in hers.

'I just said to him that I wished he spent some time with Veer,' said Ika helplessly shrugging, tears pooling in her eyes, 'and it snowballed into this,' Ika gesticulated with her hands.

Himani stayed quiet for some time, looking at her daughter, at her dishevelled hair, at her broken spirit.

'Call Fredrick,' she said finally.

Ika looked at her mother, startled. 'What?'

'Talk to him. He is a sensible man who will give you good advice.'

He will tell you what I should tell you but don't have the guts to.

'No, I don't need anyone to—'

'If you won't call him, I will, puttar,' said Himani, pulling out her phone. 'This has gone on for far too long, Ika. You need to speak with someone you trust.'

'Mummy, I will call Francesca,' Ika tried.

'Francesca is dating three guys at the moment, Ika, including the building plumber,' Himani said ruefully. 'I love her, but I am not going to let you take her advice right now.'

~

The cuckoo clock that Ika had bought from Switzerland on her honeymoon struck one.

'Should I take him off you?' Himani tried again, getting up from the chair but Veer clung to Fredrick like his life depended on it. Veer opened his mouth to wail, and Himani cowered. These days, fewer things scared her as much as Veer's wails did.

'It really is okay, Mrs Joshi. He looks very sleepy. I think he will doze off soon anyway,' Fredrick replied, patting Veer's head. Veer, his fascination with Fredrick growing by the second, snuggled into Fredrick's shoulder with an authoritative grunt. Fredrick rested his face against the little boy's dark curls.

Despite the tears, Ika smiled.

'I'll clear the table,' Himani said and picked up the seven cups of coffee that lay on the dining table where the trio had been sat for over two hours.

'Your home needs to feel safe to you as well, Ika,' Fredrick said when Himani was gone.

'He has never hit me,' Ika tried.

'Well…are you waiting for him to?' Fredrick shot back and then his shoulders sagged. 'Look—I'm sorry, I don't mean to be rude. The kind of anger issues Vivaan has that you and Himani have told me about, I don't see why you or for that matter Veer should be putting up with them. Your home needs to feel safe as well, Ika, and from how you were looking when I walked in, this,' Fredrick made a circle in the air with his index finger, 'does not feel safe to you.'

'Baba died when I was twelve,' Ika said staring at the floor.

'So?'

'I want Veer to have a father…'

'Even if it's one that goes around smashing his own wrist at the drop of a hat?'

Ika spared a hand across her face. There is such shame in admitting that your marriage is not what it should be. She'd experienced it first-hand when, upon his arrival, Himani had asked Ika to tell Fredrick everything that had happened. Ika had remained quiet, and it had finally fallen upon Himani to give Fredrick the details, which he had heard with growing horror.

'Your husband should love, respect and honour you, Ika.'

Ika stared at the table.

'You have to stand up for yourself. Because if you don't, no one will,' Fredrick said solemnly. 'Vivaan was not like this initially, right? How did it all change?'

Ika shrugged. Did she know the answer to this? Had she allowed this to happen to herself?

'I have grown up with the narrative of women's liberation, supported it and been vocal about it. Heck, even been part of protests back in the day, but when it has come to my own life, I have…' Ika's voice faltered, 'I am a lie, Fredrick. A weak woman who is waiting for someone to rescue her.'

'It's immensely hard, Ika, I know. I get it,' Fredrick placed a hand on hers. 'But hear this—you, and no one but you, have to be your own hero, Ika,' Fredrick said leaning in, his eyes sincere, 'you have to save yourself.'

Ika stared at him. He was close, distractingly close. She could feel his breath on her face. His eyes, the flecks of brown in them shining, looked worried. Her eyes wandered to his lips.

A gentle snore from Veer broke the spell of the moment. Ika looked around and then cleared her throat.

'I ... I'll take him to bed...' she mumbled and took Veer from Fredrick. Ika scuttled away, letting out a deep, shaky breath.

Sat alone at the table, Fredrick blew out a long breath going through the events from the last two hours in his head. Getting the hesitant, 'Any chance you are awake' message from Ika at close to midnight, followed by him frantically calling her up knowing that something had happened, to her quivering voice on the phone that soon turned into sobs, to him racing his car to Ika's apartment to finding her sitting on the floor, in pyjamas and tears. Fredrick had somehow known even before Himani appeared on the scene, lips pursed, and told him that this was about Vivaan.

As the story had poured in, Fredrick had had to clench his fists many times to stop himself from an angry reaction. How had Ika allowed this to happen? Was she not smart and funny and clever and would not any man be lucky to have a woman like her by his side? Why could Vivaan not see this, and more importantly, why could Ika not see it, he wondered, staring at the helpless-looking girl who now walked back into the room.

'You knew much before I told you today that something was wrong, didn't you?' she asked sitting down again. She looked tired. Beautiful but tired.

Fredrick sighed.

'I'd hoped I was wrong, Ika,' he said softly.

Himani came into the room now and sat down at the table.

'I shared all this with you, Fredrick, for some advice. What do you think Ika should do?' Himani said, cupping her chin with her long fingers. Ika's eyes flashed towards Fredrick.

'I think she should leave,' Fredrick said in a low voice.

'Why?' Himani asked.

'Because she does not deserve this. No one deserves to be in a relationship with someone who constantly puts them down, finds faults with everything they do. These things,' he looked at Himani now, 'these things kill a person from inside. I think Ika should save herself and leave.'

Himani nodded.

'Ika deserves someone who will love her, respect her and cherish her, Himani. Not some idiot with anger issues. I cannot even understand why she has been putting up with this for so long,' Fredrick said, his brow furrowed, his face pained. He had suspected this for some time but to have Ika and Himani tell him the details had been more painful than he had imagined.

He looked at Ika now, sitting cross-legged on the wooden chair, hugging herself. Frail. Scared. Fragile.

Something dropped, yet again, in the pit of his stomach.

Fredrick had to fight the urge, yet again, to take Ika in his arms; she would be safe with him, away from the world that contained Vivaan. He spared a hand over his forehead. This was killing him from the inside. He could get that idiot beat up, he thought angrily to himself, or better still, beat him up himself. Or get him fired. Make him unemployable. That would be very satisfactory, he thought. How dare Vivaan, Fredrick thought biting his lips, how dare he treat Ika like this.

'There is blood on your wall. Who knows what that man is going to do next?' Fredrick asked.

'I don't have the courage,' Ika said.

'Then find it, Ika. How long can we go on like this?' Himani said shaking her head, her brow furrowed with worry.

Ika stared at the table and then at the two people sat at it. Her mother and Fredrick. And in that moment it hit her. She felt an electric energy run through her body. She picked up her phone. She had to do it now, right now, before her fears raised their heads again and stopped her.

'I need you to move out,' she typed hastily lest she stopped, 'and I want a divorce.' She pressed send and then waited for the avalanche of tears to come, but it did not.

~

'You must think I am pathetic,' Ika said. She opened the door to the stairs and the lights flickered on automatically.

'It takes courage to stay in a marriage like this, and it takes courage to get out. Either way, to me, you are brave,' Fredrick said, and Ika looked at him surprised.

They walked down a few steps in silence.

'After he smashed his wrist on the wall, I thought he was going to come for me,' Ika said staring at her feet, her voice small. Saying this felt like a confession. Like *she* had done something wrong.

'It doesn't need to be like this,' Fredrick said softly, 'it *shouldn't* be like this.'

Ika turned to face Fredrick. The yellow of the bulb casting weird shadows that danced around them.

'I don't know what will happen tonight when he comes back,' she whispered, her eyes fearful.

'I can stay?'

Please let me stay.

Ika shook her head. That would never work.

'Just call the police if you feel scared. Don't let him hurt you in any way. Keep Veer away,' Fredrick spoke fast, as he knew he did when he felt anxious.

Ika nodded, biting her lower lip. Fredrick took her hand in his. The air around them—it already felt heavy. Heavy with unspoken words, promises and desires.

Fredrick and Ika stood still, staring into each other's eyes, on the lower steps of the back stairs, bathed in yellow, in the midst of shadows, at crossroads.

'I'm sorry, I pulled you into this…'

'I'm glad you did,' he whispered back. Fredrick took a step closer to Ika, so that their faces were but a few inches apart. 'Leave him, Ika,' he whispered, 'he does not deserve you.' He paused, his brain whirring. There was one particular thing he wanted to say. He knew he should not say it. But he also knew it was what he desperately wanted.

'Leave him,' he repeated himself, his eyes boring into Ika's, 'and come with me.'

Ika's eyes flashed at him in surprise.

'Fredrick…' She shook her head helplessly.

Fredrick took her face in his hands. 'I can't let anyone hurt the person I love,' he said, shocked that he was giving the thoughts that had been whirling in his head for months, eating him from the inside, a voice. Finally, a voice.

'I've tried very hard not to, but I've fallen in love with you, Ika. Everything about you, what you say, what you think, what you do—matters to me. I have never felt this way about anyone.'

Ika could only stare at Fredrick. From this close he was stunning. Transfixed, she reached out to place a palm on his cheek.

'Leave Vivaan and let's give us a chance?'

Ava? Veer? Vivaan? A thousand questions raised their heads.

I am not a model or an actress.

I am not half as pretty as the rest of them.

I am not a bazillionaire.

I don't come from a family that is friends with the Prime Minister.

How will this ever work?

Fredrick came in closer, his blue-grey eyes—green in the yellow of the lamp—blazing with emotion. He pulled Ika in, and when their lips met, Ika found herself shushing the noise in her head. She allowed herself to give in to the moment and the powerful pull that Fredrick had been since they had first set eyes on each other.

'I love you too, Fredrick, I love you,' Ika mumbled just as their lips met, even in the heat of the moment, shocked that she was saying this out loud.

15

Putney, London

May, 2017

Ika was sat at the dining table, exactly where she had been sat not an hour ago with Fredrick. Vivaan was at her feet, tears streaming down his face, wrist wrapped in a bloodied handkerchief. He had never looked more pathetic, thought Ika, disgust of an unfamiliar kind rising in her chest.

'Ikadashi,' Vivaan grovelled, 'don't leave me. I won't be able to live without you.'

Do you know, truly know, anyone, yourself included? Ika wondered, feeling far removed from Vivaan's theatrics. Ika tilted her head and stared at the man she had been married to for eight years. He had run inside not five minutes ago, reeking of alcohol, phone in hand, open to Ika's text.

'How do you think I'll live without our son? Without you? What have I done to make you want to leave?' he asked in a screechy voice, grabbing her feet.

You have been disrespectful. There have been days without an end where I have only heard cruel heartless jibes from you. You have left me entirely alone in this parenting gig. I am too scared to ask you for help. You have called me a fucking bitch. You have continuously disparaged me, chided me, treated me like I am inferior to you. Your vitriol is the voice in my head that refuses to leave me. Your poison lingers in me.

'Tell me,' he beseeched her, 'tell me what I did wrong, and I promise, I will change.'

Ika, her happy pink night suit oddly out of place, sat silent. Unmoving. In another world. Would Fredrick ever really leave an actress for her? A world-famous actress?

'You can't do this to us,' Vivaan begged Ika.

You did this to us, she thought, but no word came out of her.

One text from her about a divorce had him at her feet, she thought, tilting her head to one side, genuinely surprised.

'Say something, Ikadashi. I promise, I'll love you. I'll be the best father in the world. The best husband. I'll change my job so that I have more time for us. I—'

The kiss at the bottom of the dark stairs, she thought, a shiver running down the length of her body. His lips on hers. His arms around her...

A loud wail from Veer from his nursery reached Ika now and something inside her woke up.

'I'll be to Veer what Baba was, is to you,' Vivaan was saying, his head hanging low like he was suddenly very tired. 'I've been so mean to you, Ikadashi. I've tried to be a good husband, but I've not been one. I don't want to lose you or Veer. I'll do what I need to.'

Ika sat up straighter, suddenly more aware of the situation she was in. Veer's wail had popped the bubble she had been in since the kiss. The reality, Veer, taking its place. She gasped. She had for a bit forgotten that at the centre of all this was Veer.

For her, Fredrick was a hundred times better than Vivaan. But for Veer?

Her heart stood still, and she looked at the father of her child sat at her feet.

Ika's heart sank. It sank because in that one moment of clarity she knew what she was going to do.

Sometimes leaving is selfish. And when it came to Veer, gosh, God knew she could not be selfish. No, not with Veer.

She was going to stay. Whatever it did to her, whatever it did to Fredrick.

And with that, she began to cry. For herself. For Fredrick. For the love they shared that would never, she knew now with scary clarity, come to anything.

'Let it all out, my darling,' crooned Vivaan, looking hopefully at the mess his wife now suddenly seemed to be. This was promising, Vivaan thought, very promising.

∼

When Fredrick's phone finally buzzed at six, he had been pacing his room for three hours.

A message from Ika. His heart thudded.

Hurriedly he opened the message, anxiety ripping through him and then he stilled. He read the message again, and then again. And then one more time.

And then in a rare display of anger, Fredrick threw his phone across the bed. Shoulders slumped, he then sat on his bed and hung his head low.

Ika: *I can't leave Vivaan, Fredrick. No matter what I feel for you, I don't think I can find that courage.*

Fredrick let out a deep breath. He wondered if he would ever forget these words. He blew out another big breath. Once, twice, thrice. He shook his head because he felt his eyes get wet. He clenched his teeth. No, there were not going to be any tears because he had been foolish enough to bare his heart to some random girl from work.

Gosh, that woman, he thought, restlessly lunging to pick up his phone. Maybe he could call her? Talk to her? Maybe Vivaan had been violent? Scared her into staying?

He opened her contact on the phone but stopped just before he hit 'call'.

Pathetic. So pathetic. Like one of those morons in love.

He sat on the edge of the bed. And then got up. And then sat down again. He wondered what he could do with his hands and legs.

Maybe smash a window?

And then I would be exactly like the man I asked Ika to leave.

His phone rang shrill, startling Fredrick, who stared at it like he did not know what to do with it. Ava's name was flashing on the screen.

∽

Francesca: *You had two fucking options. Vivaan and Fredrick. And you chose Vivaan? Do I have that right? DO I FUCKING HAVE THAT RIGHT?'*

Ika sobbed harder. She leaned over and pulled some more tissue off the toilet roll, dabbing her eyes with it. The floor of the toilet was cold and a shiver ran through her. She could hear Veer crying in his room and Vivaan trying to pacify him. Cry, Veer, cry. Your mother has just ruined her own life.

Ika: *Everything feels heavy, Fran*

Francesca: *Ika, this is not right. That man is golden. You are lucky he loves you. How can you throw it away?*

Ika: *What if he does not love me?*

Francesca: *Ika...*

Ika: *How does it even make sense, Fran? Why would he love me? What if I leave Vivaan and then Fredrick does not want me?*

Francesca: *Whether Fredrick wants you or not, you need to leave that jerk.*

Ika: *He apologized. He said he will change.*

Francesca: *Fredrick says he loves you and you don't believe him. That idiot—Vivaan—who has been the worst husband in the world for a decade tells you that he will change, and you believe him? Get a fucking brain.*

Ika stared at Francesca's message and tossing the phone aside, cried more. *What was she doing?*

A gentle knock on the door, followed by an 'Ika beta?' reached her a moment later. Ika crawled on her fours and opened the door.

'Oh, my poor baby,' mumbled Himani and got on her knees to take Ika into her arms.

'I said no to Fredrick,' Ika said to Himani in a whisper broken by sobs.

'Oh no, oh no,' mumbled Himani, 'he asked you to come with him?'

'Leave Vivaan and come to me—that's what he said, Mummy...' Ika said taking unsteady breaths. 'What if Fredrick did not mean what he said? What if he changed his mind? What kind of a life would Veer have? Shuttling between two homes? How would Vivaan treat him? He does not deserve this, does he?'

Every word that came out of Ika seared through Himani's chest like a poisoned spear. It was all painfully familiar. No, no, no! Himani wanted to scream out loud. No.

'I understand,' she said instead in a gentle voice, 'I understand, puttar. You are just trying to protect your home, your family, your marriage. I know. I understand.'

'Why is it so hard, Mummy,' said Ika burying her face into her mother's shoulders, 'I'm behaving like a teenager.'

You are behaving like someone in love.

'It's hard because your heart is saying one thing and your mind another,' said Himani, staring straight ahead and gently patting Ika's hand.

'Am I doing the right thing?'

'By whom?'

'Veer?'

'Probably?'

'By myself?'

'Probably?'

'Mummy...' Ika looked pleadingly at her mother, 'please don't do this.'

'Ika. Only time will tell. You are doing what feels right in this moment. Leave the rest to time.'

Time will heal, thought Himani listlessly; it's supposed to heal. Hadn't it in her case?

No, her heart replied obstinately; she was still crying at night, wasn't she?

Himani stared at her daughter and crumbled inwards. Poor Ika, poor, poor, poor Ika, she thought to herself, her eyes brimming with tears.

~

Ika craned her neck to look for Fredrick. It was 10 a.m. The last eleven hours had been exhausting. She needed Fredrick. She needed to talk to him. To explain everything to him. To—

She shot up when she saw Jacob walk past.

'Jacob!' she waved frantically. Jacob nodded and walked over to Ika. He pushed his glasses, rimmed pink today, up his nose and stared intently at his colleague. There was no makeup, her eyes looked cried out, and she clearly had not slept a wink. Fredrick had looked a lot like this as well when Jacob had met him a few hours ago.

'Do you know where I can find Fredrick, please?'

Jacob's expression shifted.

'I need his signatures,' Ika mumbled, looking everywhere but at her boss.

'You can find him mid-air,' said Jacob with a forced smile. He shook his head sadly.

'Mid-air?'

'He is on his way to LA.'

'LA? When will he be back?'

Jacob shrugged.

'You don't know?'

Ika's eyes now had a sheen to them, and her voice carried a desperation that struck Jacob as very painful. He did not know the details; he would probably never get to know them, but he knew he could hazard a guess.

Oh, you two, Jacob said silently to himself. What have you done?

'He does not know,' Jacob said gently, for, by now, it was clear to him that the last thing Ika needed were signatures, 'he said something about … err… shifting our headquarters to LA. So that you know…' He faltered now. 'He … he could be with Ava, and also, you know about his birth parents, right? So he can spend more time there so … You know…' he trailed off realizing there was no way he could be kind to Ika while telling her this.

He fiddled with his neon pink tie and touched the rim of his matching neon pink glasses.

For Ika, the world had stilled.

Fredrick had not bothered to even reply to her text. The last she had from him was the kiss and him telling her that he loved her and now he had shifted base to LA? To be with his girlfriend? This was the man she was seriously thinking of leaving the father of her kid for?

'Ika darling?' Jacob placed a hand on Ika's arm. The girl's face had lost its colour.

Ika stood up straighter. Her eyes, focussed far ahead, became hard.

'Jacob,' Ika said, a decision made in a matter of seconds.

'Yes, my love,' Jacob replied, wondering why Ika looked so different suddenly.

'I am sorry this comes as a surprise to you. Actually,' she faltered here, and listlessly, she picked up her trusty black BIC, 'I wanted to speak to Fredrick to submit my resignation.'

'Your what?'

'I am leaving HE.'

'Ika, honey, let's talk.' Jacob looked first at Fredrick's empty office and then at the harried-looking girl in front of him desperately trying to hold on to her dignity, and he felt his heart break.

'Later, please, Jacob,' Ika mumbled, and before the avalanche of tears could hit her, Ika picked up her bag and ran out of the office floor, to reception and then outside.

An hour later, Himani pressed the red button on her iPhone and breathed deep, her daughter's sobs reverberating through her ears.

It was my fault, Mummy, for even thinking for a moment that Fredrick meant anything he said. I don't want to see his face ever again, Mummy, he left me all alone in this when I really needed him.

King George's Park was lovely at this time of the year, but all its beauty was lost on Himani at the moment. She walked past the little lake, not noticing the ducks, into the Southside shopping centre, her legs taking her to Waitrose on autopilot. The guard at the door nodded at her, recognizing the lady who usually came in with a cheeky little boy. She picked up a basket and headed towards the vegetables, a shiver running through her.

She picked up a bag of organic Waitrose carrots and put it in the basket, biting the insides of her cheeks, but the tears won and soon they started flowing shamelessly down her face. This, this mess that her daughter was in, if you looked closely enough, was all her fault.

Kids do what they see their parents do. And Himani had done exactly what Ika was doing, Himani thought, and she wondered if her heart would break from the pain and guilt that was searing through it now.

At that very moment, just as Ika got into the tube to come home, her face awash with tears, and Himani bent to listlessly pick up a strikingly purple cabbage that no one would eat, her own face wet with tears, Fredrick rested his head against the plush seat of the plane he had borrowed from a friend for the hurried trip to LA and let out a shaky breath.

It had been a mistake, a terrible, terrible mistake. Those moments with Ika had meant nothing to her. He closed his eyes, exhausted. His heart hurt. It hurt so much. To be betrayed, relentlessly and by those he loved seemed to be in his destiny.

Their story had ended even before it had started, Fredrick thought. Ended for good.

Part Two

16

Amritsar, India

August 1965

Five-year-old Himani slept on a charpoy under the stars, hands clasped around her mother Paramjeet's comfortingly thick waist.

The charpoy, placed in one corner of the courtyard, or the aangan, looked tired, perpetually sagging in the middle, worn from years of carrying weight. The rooms in the house, most of them barren, much like those in the other fifteen hundred houses in their tiny village in Punjab, had never been painted and were spread across two floors.

The red of the exposed bricks, the beige of the mud floor, the green of the fields that surrounded them and the smell of the cows in the shed—even many years later, every time Himani thought of the first years of her life, these sounds and sights would come back to her, adding colour to the otherwise dusty, unclear images her brain held for her to revisit.

'Why do you waste your energy on a girl, Paramjeet *puttar*?' Biji, Himani's paternal grandmother, would often say to her daughter-in-law. 'Focus on giving birth to a son who will carry our name forward instead. This kudi will be married off to bear sons for another family—she is of no use to us.'

Himani would listen to Biji say such things and wonder what she could do to become a boy. She often thought how wonderful it must be to be a man as she walked, stick in hand, across the yellow expanses of the mustard farms that dotted her village, a wistfulness on her face. To come home from the fields and eat fresh food served on a plate by a dutiful wife? To angrily hurl it across the courtyard if the salt in the daal was not to your liking? To hit the women whenever you wanted? To come and go as you pleased? To live a life of freedom?

But despite its inequalities, Himani loved the home she shared with her grandmother Biji, grandfather Darjee, parents and a host of aunts, uncles and cousins.

Darjee had a small business producing jaggery from sugar cane juice. Himani would sit for hours on the terrace of her house and stare, transfixed, as workers in blue turbans boiled the juice in what were surely the biggest iron kadhais in the world. The men sang in Punjab: *Pagri sambhal Jatta, pagri sambhal oye*—as they cooled the mixture. And Himani, tucked behind the large hibiscus plants on the terrace, hummed with them.

Sometimes Darjee would spot Himani lurking behind the huge pots, and he would beckon her closer with his wrinkled finger, his face distorted in mock anger. 'Himani, puttar, girls of the house should never be seen around the workers—whatever will our neighbours say!' Himani would hang her head and try to look ashamed, but then he would smile, his eyes crinkling behind his thick glasses, and the world would be wonderful again.

Apart from her own mother, the only other person Himani loved was Darjee. He always wore the same clothes—a salwar, a light kurta that reached his knees, white pyjamas and a white turban, the pride of a Sikh man.

That August morning, Himani called out for her mother when she woke up, vaguely aware of the dreams she'd had of her sixth birthday just around the corner. Surprised to see dozens of people from the neighbourhood swarming into the *aangan*, Himani propped herself up on one elbow and craned her neck. When Biji's scream, dripping with horror, reached her a few moments later, Himani knew that something terrible had happened.

The sun was just beginning to rise, but the sky was still smeared with shades of the night gone by, unwilling almost to take on the day and the horrors that awaited them all. Smoke from where Biji had been lighting the *chulha* with dried wood and dung cakes made the air hazy. These were the sights and smells of an early morning in an Indian village—only this was the day that everything changed.

The men seemed to be pulling something out of the well. Himani heard a faint thud followed by a woman's wails.

'Mataji!' Himani called out, desperate to be in the safety of her mother's arms, fear rising in her belly. 'Mataji!' she shouted again. But there was no answer. Perhaps Mataji was inside the house. Himani looked around, confused and scared.

A moment later, her mother's sister came running to her and clasped the girl to her chest. 'Your mother has left us, Himani *puttar*,' she said, tears streaming down her face. 'She jumped into the well this morning.'

Himani stared at her aunt and turned to look at the limp figure lying on the floor of the courtyard, a puddle of water spreading out around it. Even from a distance, she could make out her mother's form, her long hair tied back in a plait like always. She was wearing the pink salwar and blue kurta she had on the previous night. Himani had never seen her mother without a dupatta, and now, as she lay dead, it was missing.

Himani turned and looked at her charpoy, and the dupatta, pink with small blue flowers printed on it, lay across it. Slowly, she bent to pick it up and then walked to her mother's dead body. She bent and spread the cloth across her mother's chest.

And then she howled.

When the tears stopped, she stared at the sky and counted the kites that dotted it. She sat there, alone in her grief, fully aware even then that she would grieve forever. That her life would forever be incomplete no matter. That she would forever live in pain.

The muffled cries of turbaned boys playing games under the fierce afternoon sun gave way to the shouts of the sabziwala announcing his wares as he cycled across the village in the evening. No one came looking for Himani. No one stole ghee for her milk. No one, Himani knew, ever would.

Paramjeet's ashes were collected the next day and immersed in a river nearby. Darjee conducted a sahaj path bhog at the gurudwara a day after that to conclude the antim sanskar, the last rites. And thus, with a reading from the Sri Guru Granth Sahib, the life that had been the centre of Himani's universe came to an end.

The family had just come back from the gurudwara, and Himani was still crying, her hands wrapped around her knees, her mother's dupatta wrapped around her shoulders, huddled in a corner of the *aangan* when an impatient knocking at the wooden door made her get up to open it. Her father, Keerat, was standing at the door, a young girl by his side. The girl was overdressed in a bright red salwar kurta, the red dupatta with golden tassels covering her head. She was smiling, and Himani wondered how anyone could smile.

'*Sat sri akal,*' Keerat greeted everyone and then looked at Himani. 'Say "*sat sri akal*" to your new mother, Himani puttar.'

Himani felt like she would throw up.

∼

Biji sat on the charpoy and looked at Himani. At thirteen, Himani's peaches-and-cream complexion, doe eyes and easy smile had begun to attract the attention of the boys and the envy and appreciation of girls in the neighbourhood. She sighed as Himani played hopscotch with some girls, her pigtails flying around her as she laughed.

'Thank god she's a good-looking girl,' Biji remarked as she took a big gulp of lassi from her brass tumbler.

'She's been happy since she started school,' Darjee said, coming and sitting next to Biji. 'She has nothing,' Darjee's voice was heavy with worry, 'except for a father who wants nothing to do with her.'

If only Keerat would take her to Delhi and enrol her in a school where Himani could make something of her life. How she would love that! But would she, he wondered, be happy away from him and Biji? 'We are Himani's home; we are her parents. We are everything to her. As long as she is with us, she'll be fine,' Darjee mumbled.

'You are blabbering now,' Biji said resignedly.

'Let's eat?' Darjee asked.

'That is all that you men want. Food, food and more food. I've spent my entire life in front of that godforsaken chulha making chapattis for this ungrateful family.' Biji got up, a deep sigh escaping her. Her knees were killing her and years of smoke from the chulha had given her a cough that refused to be cured. 'Himani *puttar, dasso,* help me make rotis,' Biji shouted over the din the girls were creating.

Dinner was simple and wholesome—roti and dal served with a dollop of homemade ghee. Given how much Biji had grown to dislike cooking, it was a good last meal that she cooked. She went to bed at 8 p.m. that night never to wake up again.

Amidst all the commotion that accompanied Biji's death the next morning, almost forgotten, stood scared little Himani. She was not really fond of Biji, she thought, so why was she crying? 'You're crying not for Biji,' a voice in her head explained wisely, 'you are crying because of how Biji's death will now change your life.'

Later that day her father arrived to take Himani to Delhi with him.

When she left, wordlessly touching Darjee's feet as a mark of respect, Darjee found himself a quiet corner in the aangan away from everyone. Hiding in the shadows of the night, Darjee rested his head against the cool of the mud wall encircling his home. He put his hand on the banana tree, seeking warmth from its cool trunk.

'It's all right, it's all right,' he mumbled to himself, taking off his glasses, the world blurring. 'It's all right, it's all right,' he mumbled again, but now his voice shook.

'She'll be all right,' he whispered to no one as tears racked his body and the words sounded incoherent even to him. He covered his mouth to muffle his sobs and told himself to stop crying, but the truant tears refused to listen.

'My poor Himani puttar, my poor, poor Himani puttar,' he chanted in between his sobs.

17

Vauxhall, London

February 2019 (2 years later)

Bus number 87 stopped at Vauxhall Bus Station and Ikadashi Kumar stepped out, pulled her ponytail tighter, her lips pursed determinedly. Her legs, sore from leg day at the gym (ugh), protested and Ika winced.

Ignoring the pain—she was quite the expert at that, Ika thought ruefully to herself—she hauled her laptop bag and began the eleven-minute walk to the office, lost in thought. It was her 36th birthday, a good pitstop to assess her life a bit.

Life that had become the eye of a catastrophic whirlpool when Fredrick left was beginning to calm down, she could finally, if a bit cautiously, say. Case in point, she had slept full nights that entire week (also largely thanks to Veer no longer waking up to play at crazy o'clock). Veer was almost three—gosh, when had that happened? Any day now, he could bring home his bride and announce that Ika was soon to be a grandmother. Anyway, the nice GP with salt and pepper hair who had, two years ago, looked intently at her and prescribed antidepressants—which she threw in the bin as soon as she got out of the surgery—had told her that week that he was 'delighted' at her progress. 'Clearly, the meds are working,' he had said with the trademark intense gaze, and Ika had smiled innocently. Francesca, currently six months pregnant and miserable, identifying more with grumpy, medium-sized whales than with *Homo sapiens*, had said to her that the anger inside Ika was no longer like an Australian bushfire that destroyed everything it touched but more like a half-hearted little campfire Year Two kids had tried to make while on summer camp. That was, Francesca had insisted, a clear sign that Ika was finally 'moving on'. Yoga, weight lifting (she was still wobbling at forty kilos though), changing her diet to include extraordinary amounts of sprouted mung beans, burning pieces of paper that had Fredrick's name written on them, crying non-stop, forbidding herself from crying non-stop, learning to kick-box, imagining that she was kicking Fredrick and then missing him terribly, not allowing her mind to wander to what could have been, constantly telling herself that Fredrick was not just her soulmate but also, and more importantly, a world-class jerk who had simply disappeared—all of this had helped. Or not. Or whatever.

No one tells you, sighed Ika, running her fingers up and down the straps of her backpack, how tough this moving on business really is.

A grey building about as interesting as a public washroom now loomed up, and Ika opened the glass doors without the proverbial spring in her step.

Aqua Limited: *Where dreams begin.*

So here was the thing about AL, thought Ika, climbing up the stairs; the only dreams that began in this advertising agency were those that employees dreamt of as they dozed off in meetings.

Becca at reception looked up from filing her nails and nodded at Ika as she walked in. Ika took a moment to absorb Becca's newest avatar. Becca Fringe's fringed bob, which had been blue till last Friday, was jet black and rod straight today. A thick lining of black eyeliner, black nail polish, black lipstick and an all-black ensemble completed her look.

'Goth, are we this week?' Ika grinned.

Becca nodded. 'Dimple, Pimple is losing his shit man, he's gone all Scottish again, go save him.'

Dimple and Pimple. Ika groaned. Pimple, aka Preston MacLeod, Ika's boss, the life and soul of AL, its beloved CEO.

Ika pushed open another set of glass doors and squinted. They should hand sunglasses at reception, Ika thought, entering the tiny, brightly coloured office and finding her way to her desk. The walls, chairs and tables were all a mish-mash of neon rainbow colours, which, frankly speaking, hurt the eye.

Someone someday is going to end up in epileptic shock thanks to these walls, thought Ika angrily putting down her H&M backpack.

Was there ever a time, not so long ago, that she only used fake branded handbags, Ika wondered with some surprise. How pathetic was that? And ate only dainty sandwiches from Pret with a side of disgusting veggie crisps—yuck! And wore only sophisticated-looking dresses from boutique stores, the names of which she could barely pronounce—absolute waste of money. H&M, New Look, Zara, Mango were all absolutely grand.

'Hoo's it gaun? How ye daein?' came a thick Scottish accent, and a ginger-haired, pimpled man in his early thirties materialized at Ika's side a moment later.

Preston MacLeod. The boss. Harry Styles gone wrong as Becca Fringe had very aptly once quipped. The life and soul of AL (or not), also as Becca Fringe had aptly once quipped.

'Hey, Pim—Preston, what's up?' Ika replied with a nod. She took off her down coat and slung it on a chair next to her table.

The table was parrot green and the chair neon pink—as far as was possible from the decadent elegance of the HE HQ, Ika thought with a content sigh.

Ika's mind went to how it all started at AL. She could never quite recall applying for AL, but then she could not quite recall much from those dark days after Fredrick had legged it across the pond and effectively vanished from her life. After a remarkably inane conversation with someone who sounded and behaved like a freshly minted, thoroughly bored intern, Ika had said she would be happy to meet the AL Chief Executive to see how they get on. When the man on the other end replied that he was indeed the CEO, Ika felt like she had found both her dream manager and dream job.

Preston was comfortably unattractive, and as Ika said to Francesca later that day, out for the first time in almost three months after Fredrick's departure, a slab of cement possessed more personality than the AL Chief Exec. Preston had treated Ika with an aloofness that convinced Ika that there was never going to be any danger of any kind of romance either way. That had kind of sealed the deal for Ika, despite the significantly lower salary.

'Aye, a wee problem…' Preston drawled, and Ika tried to not groan.

'Which account and what's happened?' Ika asked, taking out a little sachet of her Earl Grey from the jade blue drawer and beginning to walk towards the canary yellow-coloured kitchen. Preston followed her, making Ika think of a little puppy. 'Also, normal English, please?'

'Aye … I mean, yes,' Preston said, grinning sheepishly, his yellow teeth on display. 'You did M&A, in another life, right?' asked Preston, walking in long strides, fingering the collar of his yellow and black shirt which the fashion genius had paired with black shorts.

Another life. That's exactly what it felt like.

'Yes,' Ika said. Preston raised a ginger-haired eyebrow at Ika but she offered nothing more.

Preston watched Ika make her tea. It was no joke to have HE on your CV—in fact, it was the main reason he had offered her a job—yet Ika avoided all conversation about her time there. And for the hundredth time, he wondered why. Had something happened? If yes, what? With that, yet again, the first strings of the *Casino Royale* soundtrack began to play in Preston's head.

The girl, he thought, shaking his head, fascinated him on so many levels. There was, Preston was convinced, a lot going on in her life.

'T'was nice to meet Vivaan on Friday for drinks,' Preston said trying to keep the edge out of his voice.

'Great,' Ika nodded. The Uber ride back home came to her now, and as was often the case, she could not even recall why the argument had started.

'I can't stand to even look at you,' Vivaan had said loud enough for the Uber driver to hear. 'Makes me sick.' And then he had paused, his eyes hard and narrowing at her in the darkness of the cab. 'Go on, go on, threaten me with divorce. Try the antics again?' he had chided her.

Ika had taken a big breath. A couple of years ago, before Fredrick actually, Ika would have listened to this quietly, tearing up, willing Vivaan's tirade to stop.

Now she leaned in towards the driver and asked him to pull over, which he did with visible relief. And then with poised calm, she stepped out of the cab. Vivaan stared at her. He'd had too much to drink, she could tell.

'I don't need to listen to your drivel, Vivaan. I will find my way home. See you there,' she had said, waved a cheery farewell and walked off before Vivaan could open his mouth.

And then, somewhere near Battersea Park, she had sat on a bench by an unfamiliar road, and as cars had whizzed past, in the midst of the winter darkness, she had cried.

'So, you were saying,' Ika said, unwilling to dwell on the Friday evening any more than was necessary, 'something important has come up?'

'Huh?'

Preston was pouring hot water in to Ika's cup, staring at the water. What if, he wondered, Ika was actually an Indian Princess in exile, hiding from cruel rebels out to get her kingdom and—

'Preston?' Ika tried again.

The rebels rush into the AL offices, their long hair and beards flying, wielding whatever weapons it is that they use in India these days. Preston pushes Ika aside so that he stands brave and tall in between the princess and the rebels. The air around them is charged with danger. In one swift movement, and with elegance that can only come to a seasoned warrior, Preston pulls out his sword and the rebels are slain in one grand strike. Slowly, Preston turns around to face the Indian Princess. Ika's hands are clasped to her chest, and her face furrowed in consternation. She opens her mouth to speak, 'Wow, Preston—'

'You are annoying me,' Ika growled. Preston looked up startled and then reddened. 'You were telling me something?' Ika asked, rolling her eyes.

'Aye,' Preston cleared his throat, coming back to the Vauxhall office of AL, 'so a company is keen to buy us out.'

'What?'

'Good offer.'

The door opens yet again and another set of rebels storm inside. Preston readies himself for war. He leans in—

'Preston, if I lose you to your dreams one more time, I swear I'll take this half orange half pink table,' Ika pointed to the table by them that held the sugar and the coffee pods, 'and smash my own head in it.'

'Errr…' Preston blushed and looked, Ika thought, with his orange hair and now bright pink face, remarkably like the table Ika had not a minute ago threatened to smash her head in.

'So, there is a catch though, with this buy-out…' Preston threw up his hands defensively and then put them on his slim waist. 'Just before you started work with us, a company called Benny Limited bought a majority stake in AL. That gave us a lot of cash, which is how we,' Preston gestured around, 'were able to update the office. But now Benny don't want this new acquisition to go through…'

'What?'

'Aye, makes no sense because they stand to make a lot of money if it does. I was wondering if you could please have a look at the paperwork before I start involving legal…'

'Yes, sure,' Ika said, frowning. She picked up her mug and walked back to her desk, leaving Pimple behind.

A few hours later Ika found herself sat in the meeting room, an ocean of empty coffee mugs surrounding her, neck deep in documents. Forget the new acquisition; many things about the Benny Limited majority stake in AL did not make sense.

Ika googled Benny Limited and just as Google spat out results, the door of the room burst open and Becca, Jamie from finance, Mike and Judy from Design, and Preston barged in singing 'Happy Birthday to you' loudly and tunelessly. Becca carried a rainbow-coloured cake decorated with multi-coloured sprinkles. Ika wondered weakly if she could take any more colour anywhere.

'Oh, guys!' Ika squeaked nevertheless, pretending to be surprised and getting up from her chair. The usual AL gift—a £100 Amazon voucher—would soon be handed to her, she knew.

Much singing, back-slapping and enthusiastic cheering ensued. Preston stared at Ika, his arms crossed, the same annoying smile plastered on his face like she was his favourite niece going up on stage to collect her third prize in the school flute-making competition.

'Open your gift!' Judy yelled, and Ika unwrapped the little package that contained the voucher.

'A voucher for £100?' Ika exclaimed with mock surprise.

'There is more!' Judy yelled again, and Ika opened the other packet that Preston handed to her with a knowing smile.

Me Before You bumblebee tights in black and yellow stripes fell into her hands.

'Because you said once,' said Preston leaning in closer, making Ika draw back, scared that he might give her a hug, 'that you loved the book.'

Ika spared a hand over her head feeling a bit weak.

'Is Preston dressed to match the bumblebee tights?' Becca howled, pointing a finger at Preston's yellow and black shirt and Ika shook her head vehemently. However, one look at Preston's pink face and Ika wondered where she could hide.

'You said you'd forward details about the company trying to acquire us. You still have not done that,' Ika said hurriedly lest Preston said anything that would make matters worse.

'Huh?' Preston was lost in his other world again, eyes narrowed and face hard.

'Stiller Group,' Becca offered.

Ika froze. Someone was playing a song on YouTube to mark her birthday. Mike was dancing.

'Stiller? The American company?'

Becca shrugged.

The chaos that surrounded Ika melted into nothing and Ika sharply turned towards her computer. Information about Benny Limited sat there waiting to be read. Benny Limited, Ika read hurriedly, was part of the Rubiks Group. Rubiks. There was always a Rubik's cube on Fredrick's desk; her mind raced, goosebumps all over her body. Her fingers quivered as she typed in 'Rubiks Group + Fredrick' into the Google search engine.

Nothing.

Silly, her brain chided her, and then familiar anger and helplessness came over Ika.

'Can you stop looking for Fredrick everywhere? It's been two years,' Ika said to herself, tears welling up in her eyes. 'Stop it. Stop it. STOP...FUCKING...IT. He is not the man walking towards you in the crowds at Regent Street. He is not the man coming out of the car at Veer's nursery in Wandsworth. He is not the voice that calls after you. He is not—'

My father loved the Rubik's cube.

Fredrick's words from two years ago came back to Ika, and she stilled again.

Ika leaned into her computer at record speed.

'Rubiks Group + James Heisenberg,' she typed.

0.18 seconds later, Ika drew back.

Rubiks Group was one of the many companies owned by James Heisenberg.

Rubiks Group owned Benny Limited. Benny Limited had bought a majority stake in AL a week after she had accepted the job offer.

'Happy birthday, happy birthday,' sang Mike, and, in a rare display of joy, Becca joined in with a helpful and creative— 'Pimple and Dimple. Hope they don't get shingles. Only get the wrinkles. If you don't like this jingle, Pimple and Dimple.'

Becca wrapped her arms around Ika, and Preston glared. He hated the Pimple-Dimple thing.

But then he noted how Ika had suddenly paled. Like she'd seen a ghost.

Curious, very curious, thought Preston, walking towards Ika, his mind racing.

'So, Aye, apparently, we are part of, in some weird way, the Heisenberg Group, Ika. They've let us be for the longest time but seem to have woken up because of the Stillers,' he said, narrowing his eyes at Ika, intently watching her expression. 'I dunno, I just got a call from someone called Ellin from HE. I was wondering if you could liaise this for us, Ika? Jacob Carmen wants a meeting with us, and I think,' and he crossed his fingers, 'Fredrick Heisenberg might be calling me up too,' he said with a wide grin displaying his yellow teeth, the awe in his voice unmistakable. 'That actress girlfriend of his is so hot. If I get a chance to meet him,' Preston said gesticulating, his eyes wide, 'you can tag along too,' he finished generously.

Ika mumbled incoherently, getting paler by the second, displaying a remarkable lack of enthusiasm, thought Preston, rubbing his chin. He caught a ripe pimple and wondered if he should head to the gents to pop it.

18

Karol Bagh, Delhi

March 1979

Darjee got into the rickety bus that would take him from the New Delhi Railway Station to Gaffar Market. He wiped his forehead with a handkerchief, and to ignore the oppressive heat, he focussed his mind on the sights and sounds of the city he had heard so much about. Ambassadors and Fiats—the only two brands of cars available in the country—whizzed past the bus, and Darjee gazed at them in wonder. Keerat had told him that the waiting time to get a scooter was thirty months at the very least, and he had counted at least eleven on the roads. Delhi was wonderful and amazing, he thought to himself, wide-eyed.

The young man sitting next to him slurped a fizzy drink from a glass bottle and paused when he saw Darjee looking curiously at it. 'Since they banned Coca-Cola, I only drink Limca. It's not the same though,' offered the man, clad in tight trousers and a polka-dotted shirt, without preamble. Darjee nodded, not understanding a word, his mind already wandering to Himani.

He had not seen her in three years. She would be almost twenty—an adult.

'Your stop is the next one, Dadajee,' said the young man a little while later. Darjee nodded and went back to peering outside his dust-stained window.

So many banners, he thought. Some still shouted patriotic slogans about India's 1971 war with Pakistan. Others were about the Asian Games due to be held in 1982. And still others were about the *Garibi Hatao Andolan*, aimed at reducing poverty. India was a nation of seventy crore people living across twenty-four states and with less than 50 per cent literacy, but while Indians were poor, they were resilient—hopeful but angered by rising prices and lack of food grains, and the banners reflected these issues.

The bus ground to a halt.

Darjee made his way out, carrying his tin suitcase. He squinted in the sun and smiled when he saw Keerat.

Keerat, tall and broad, wearing fancy trousers and a white shirt, a younger version of Darjee, smiled warmly and bent to touch his father's feet.

'*Jeete raho, puttar,*' Darjee said by way of blessing, putting his hand on his son's head. 'Take me to Himani. Quickly now.'

Darjee walked as fast as he could through the lanes of Gaffar Market and breathed deeply when Keerat finally stopped outside a black wooden door and knocked.

A tall, slim, salwar-kurta-clad girl opened the door. There was a daintiness about her that struck Darjee. Her eyes, large and expressive, stared at Darjee for the moment that it took Darjee to recognize her. 'Himani *puttar! Tussi kiwen ho?*'

'Darjee!' she said softly and bent to touch his feet. Darjee pulled her into a hug and when they pulled apart, both Darjee and Himani had tears in their eyes.

'It's been too long, *puttar*,' said Darjee, feeling emotions well inside him. Himani welcomed him inside the house, and the entire family including Harpreet, and Keerat's three boy sat in the living room. The maroon sofas, with their fabric covers intact, contrasted harshly with the marigold walls. A tray with homemade besan laddus and samosas lay on the table in the centre of the room. Harpreet covered her head respectfully, and the boys sat awkwardly, unsure of how to behave in front of the ancient Darjee. Conversation—a bit forced—came from Keerat, who spoke to fill the silences. Darjee contributed in monosyllables, finding it hard to focus on anything apart from Himani.

'Show me your room, puttar,' Darjee asked Himani when the group had broken up, the boys leaving to play cricket and Harpreet heading into the kitchen to cook dinner. Darjee noted that Himani got up to follow her stepmother, but Harpreet looked back sharply and shook her head. 'Sit,' she hissed.

Himani looked quizzically at her grandfather.

'Your room?' Darjee prodded again.

Himani pointed to the floor of the living room. 'I sleep here. I just push the sofas back and spread out a thick *razai*.'

This was what Darjee had long feared. 'I see. You go to school—like your brothers?' Darjee tried again. He had, in every letter he'd written to his son, pleaded with Keerat to continue Himani's education.

'Sometimes,' she said, innocently.

Darjee's heart gave way. 'What do you mean?'

'Actually,' she said chattily, unaware of how every word was piercing Darjee's heart, 'there is so much work at home, and I can only go if I finish it all. But even if I get up at 4 or 5 a.m., I am never able to. Sometimes, Harpreetji lets me go ... maybe once or twice a month.' She brightened up as she continued, 'I love it when I go, though.'

'Harpreetji?' Darjee asked, as Himani lowered her gaze, uncomfortably adjusting her dupatta.

'What kind of work do you have to do?'

'Cooking, cleaning, clothes,' she shrugged. 'All of it.'

So, you're a maid, thought Darjee, *in your own house*. 'And Harpreet?'

'Harpreetji has a bad back...' Himani hesitated.

Darjee scoffed as images of his daughter-in-law carrying four shopping bags came to him.

'But forget about that! Look at this, Darjee,' Himani said, her eyes brightening as she pulled out her secret collection of well-thumbed books, most of them in Hindi but a few in English, from behind the settee.

'I've taught myself to read English, Darjee!' Himani whispered conspiratorially. 'Bhaiya,' she said, referring to the oldest of the boys, 'has an English and maths tutor, and they study here,' she pointed towards the wooden table in the corner of the room. It was covered in blue plastic and in the centre was a tray with three of four bottles of pickles. 'I make sure I am in the kitchen at that time. I keep a notebook hidden while I pretend to cook and make notes from what I hear Masterji teach Bhaiya. I can also do multiplication and division and can sometimes solve sums that even Bhaiya can't!'

Himani had expected praise from her grandfather, and she felt very confused when she saw tears in his eyes.

Darjee put a hand on Himani's head. 'Are you happy, puttar?' he asked.

'I am, Darjee,' she said softly.

'If your mother were here, she'd be very proud of you,' Darjee said, his voice breaking.

Darjee saw Himani's chin quiver, and he wondered if she would cry, but Himani didn't, and Darjee felt a sense of pride. This was a girl toughened by circumstance. *She will make something of herself one day*, a voice in his head assured him. But he also knew that for that to happen, she needed some help. Now.

The next morning, before he left, Darjee sat Harpreet and Keerat down on the maroon sofas in the living room. 'I think Himani is old enough to be married,' he said without preamble.

Harpreet rolled her eyes. 'Darjee, she is too young,' she began, 'not even twenty.'

Darjee nodded; he had expected Harpreet to say something like this.

'I've spoken to some people, but no one is interested. We'll speak to more people, Darjee, and find a match,' Keerat said dismissively.

'That is good, Keerat. The right place for a grown-up girl is only in her husband's house,' Darjee said. 'Also, when possible, do let her go to school.' Acid dripped from Darjee's voice and Harpreet stared at her father-in-law in surprise.

'We do, Darjee, we do! In fact, we insist!' Harpreet replied at once, shrugging her heavy shoulders helplessly. 'But Himani *puttar* doesn't really like it.'

Darjee tried hard to force a smile on his face as his son and daughter-in-law bent to touch his feet. '*Jeete raho, puttar*,' he said, putting a hand on each of their heads. He promised himself that if he was going to do one thing before he died, it would be to get Himani married to a nice man.

∼

In a cluttered, small two-bedroom apartment hundreds of miles away in Bombay, the city of dreams, Nayantara Joshi—Amma to most—clad in a well-draped, crisp, cotton sari sat in her rocking chair. Her son Dr Om Joshi, thirty-one years old, sat by her feet. She had made tea exactly the way he liked it—generous quantities of chai masala and ginger and then simmered for a good twenty minutes, poured lovingly into china mugs that were older than Om. A plate of onion bhajis, freshly made obviously, accompanied it.

It was July, and the monsoons were lashing their annual fury on the city, the trees bent double in obeisance. The downpour had been harsh enough to have drenched the heart surgeon on his short walk home from the hospital. His white shirt clung to him in wet patches, providing a sneaky glimpse of his well-toned body.

Amma put a towel over her son's head and gently massaged his wet hair. 'I cannot believe that you were once so little that you fit in my lap,' said Amma in a lilting voice filled with affection. 'And look at you now. Six feet tall—just like your father.'

Om knew exactly what would come next.

'He was fair like butter and cream, with eyes so black that they looked like licked stones.'

'And I look *exactly* like him, Amma! I know, the colour of my eyes and hair and face and nose!'

Amma laughed. She was happiest in the company of her son. 'So,' said Amma, patting her hair that was scraped back in a tight bun, making her delicate features appear even more bird-like, 'Panditji has sent me a picture and horoscope of another girl.'

'Oh, Amma,' said Om, smiling indulgently. 'I've had a busy day in the hospital—can we talk about this later?'

'At least look at this picture. The girl's name is Himani. She lives in Delhi with her father who owns a shop in Gaffar Market. Panditji has known her grandfather for decades and can vouch for the family. This girl's grandfather is very keen she marry you, Om.'

'Amma,' Om said, glancing at the picture cursorily at first and then pausing to look at it more carefully. The girl was fair with large, dark eyes. Her hair was tied up in two plaits, and she was beautiful in a uniquely innocent way.

Amma watched as Om tilted his head to one side and stared at the picture. 'She is eighteen, almost nineteen, and has finished studying until the ninth—she's not very educated, but she is a nice, loving, obedient girl. She will make a good wife and, one day, a good mother,' Amma added. She looked at the photograph again.

Himani was Sikh and not of their community, but Amma was wise enough to know that it didn't matter. What mattered was that the girl was young enough and looked naïve enough to allow her to continue to rule the house. Amma had invested all her life in Om—she was not going to be relegated to the background like most of her friends had been upon the arrival of their daughters-in-law. That she was motherless was a bonus.

Om nodded, looking thoughtful.

'Will you consider it? Shall I go to Delhi to meet her?' Amma's voice was becoming shrill with excitement.

'Yes, Amma—find the daughter-in-law you like,' Om said, a rare smile touching his face. There was little in this world that he wouldn't do for his mother.

19

Aqua Limited Office, Vauxhall, London

February 2019

'That fucking bloody bastard should be hanged in Covent Garden. And then fired at. Those ... those ... you know those people with faces painted in metallic silver, who pretend to be statues ...you know the ones near the Apple Store,' Francesca paused to stuff some more Nutella croissant into her mouth, chewed it noisily for a bit, one hand patting her bump and then added, 'they should stop pretending to not be real people and cheer when the bullets hit Fredrick Heisenberg. And ... and ... that, that is what fucking *DailyMail* should cover. Not his fucking engagement to that fucking American actress.'

Francesca drew back and let out a deep, angry breath, oddly satiated with the swearing. She scrolled down her phone, glaring at the stupid forty-one images that accompanied the *DailyMail* article. Who needed forty-one more pictures of Ava Smith?

'"How my life changed under the cherry blossoms", actress Ava Smith captioned a photo on her Instagram that shows her and her London-based billionaire boyfriend Fredrick

Heisenberg in a passionate embrace in Tokyo. It is believed that Mr Heisenberg proposed using a ring that cost £400,000,' Francesca read out. 'Ugh. More like cheating, lying bastard decides to destroy the life of a delusional, semi-written-off actress who has more plastic on her face than what ends up in the whole of the Atlantic Ocean.'

'Do you wish to go into labour right now?' Ika asked, calmly taking a sip of her coffee. She tucked her tee into the waistband of her Zara Mom jeans out of habit.

'No!' squeaked Francesca, looking around Vauxhall Beer and Food Garden guiltily. A lady walked past them, and Francesca looked hungrily at the four glasses of beer she was carrying. 'I need one to get over Fredrick and Ava's engagement,' she said, slurping her lips.

'Why the anger about the engagement, Fran? I have not even heard from him since the day he vanished. It's not like—'

'Oh,' said Francesca, angrily drumming her fingers on the wooden table, 'don't get me started on that. So, you called him, what a hundred times in that first week? Two hundred times? Did he pick up even once? You sent him messages? How many? Thirty, forty? Did he even send you one two-word reply? TO FUCKING AT LEAST END IT? Did you not deserve an explanation? Is that the way to treat a woman you say you love? Love? LOVE? FUCKING LOVE?'

The elderly lady at the table next to them raised her eyes at Francesca and Ika mumbled a hurried apology on behalf of her friend.

'Does he,' now Francesca leaned in and whispered through gritted teeth, 'know what you went through after that? You were a mess, Ika. A mess! Diagnosed with depression! On antidepressants, which you like an idiot did not even take! And on top of that, you worked at some shitty job! He left you so alone ... that idiot,' Francesca's voice quivered now, 'I will kill that man with my bare hands. I kid you not. I'll joyfully rot in prison for killing him for the rest of my life. Because, now, now when you are just about finding your way out of that darkness, his fucking billionaire highness is back? With a fucking stake in your company? What the fuck? FUCK!'

'Pimple mentioned Fredrick is in London, though hopefully I won't need to see him,' Ika said weakly letting her head fall into her hands. Francesca drew back and looked at her friend, feeling a lump form in her throat.

'How ridiculous of that Pimple of yours to ask you to get involved in this shit with HE.'

'He does not know anything about Fredrick, Fran,' Ika said, 'though I think he is very suspicious.'

'Don't get me started on that moron. He thinks he is fucking James Bond and Sherlock Holmes rolled into one pimply-gingery mess,' Francesca breathed out heavily and looked disdainfully at her lemonade. 'How's the other man in your life?' Francesca asked.

'Veer?'

'Not the one I like...' Veer's godmother replied, 'the moron.'

'The one you like peed on Rox's head last night.'

'Rox? Some kid?'

'The neighbour's dog. I'm not even sure how that happened,' said Ika with a shrug, and Francesca giggled.

'How's things with the other man I need off this planet, aka Vivaan?' Francesca asked, stirring the lemonade angrily.

'The usual. Screaming-shouting,' Ika replied, smile vanishing.

'I hope you are retorting with equal screaming-shouting?'

'I hate it, Fran, that's not me. But I can no longer take any more of Vivaan lying down. Getting trampled all over is surprisingly exhausting.'

'Good for you.'

'He said I've become very obstinate in the last few years.'

'That idiot misses the doormat.'

'It takes a lot of my energy, Fran. It's not me.'

'Oh, my delicate, gentle soul,' said Francesca smiling a small, sad smile, 'whatever are we going to do with you?'

∼

Ika hitched up her grey jeans and tucked in her pink M&S top. She walked to the meeting room, her head hung low enough for her to hear her own breathing—laden and nervous—like you do when snorkelling. She wished she was snorkelling, actually, far away in the corals somewhere. Anywhere but here.

It's just Jacob. You like Jacob. And Ellin. You like her too. Just sit in this meeting for a bit and then leave. Pretend you are not well or something. Don't—

'Hullo, Ika,' came Pimple's Scottish drawl and Ika looked up, 'Pink and pink.' He winked, pointing first towards her and then at himself. Today the fashion guru was wearing a pink shirt with watermelons in a darker pink printed on it. Where, Ika wondered despairingly, does he do his shopping from?

Ika tried to smile but managed only a grimace, turning instead to focus on the people in the room.

'Welcome to our first meeting with HE, exciting, eh?' Pimple exclaimed, his pimples bristling. 'See some familiar faces?'

Ika recognized many faces from the HE HQ and nodded her acknowledgements, stilling when she saw Jacob. Blue suit and grey glass rims today, still Joe Biden-y, suspiciously less grey, the familiar air of competence and kindness surrounding him. Jacob caught Ika's eye, and he gasped dramatically, got up, and in quick long strides, was next to her.

'Golly gosh! Ika,' he exclaimed softly and wrapped his arms around Ikadashi, 'I couldn't be more pleased to see you.' Ika allowed herself to sink in Jacob's embrace.

'I've missed you,' she heard herself whisper to him in a teary voice.

'As have I, my beautiful girl, as have I,' mumbled Jacob tightening his arms around her.

'I'm sorry I didn't stay in touch. I couldn't bear to...' Tear-filled eyes looked up at Jacob, and he shook his head dismissively. That she hadn't taken any of his calls or responded to his texts somehow no longer mattered. He understood then, and he understood now. Jacob leaned in to kiss the top of Ika's head. She looked different, beautiful still obviously, but different. Like she'd weathered a few storms, like she was stronger from braving them. Her eyes—was it just his imagination or did they shine from a newfound strength?

'Did anyone miss me? Little bit? At all?' Ellin said coming up to them and putting an arm around Ika. 'It feels so good to see you, Ika,' she said gruffly.

Preston took his seat, chewing the end of his Minion pencil and watched the little reunion from a distance with growing distaste. Ika's entry into the room seemed to have shifted the air.

Ika had never mentioned that she was this close to Jacob Carmen. *The* Jacob Carmen. Preston watched Jacob hold Ika's hand and lead her to the chair next to him. Like she was HE. She wasn't HE, was she, Preston wanted to point out to Jacob.

In the next hour, as discussion between HE and AL heated up, and tension in the room rose to peak level, Preston noticed that

Jacob was repeatedly looking at Ika like he could not quite believe that she was there. Every few minutes he would lean in and mumble into her ear. Once, to Preston's utter horror, he even put a hand on her head. Ika looked uncomfortable—overwhelmed and emotional—like she would much rather be inside a space shuttle hurtling towards an unknown destination in space than be sat next to Jacob. All this made little sense, unless ... unless...

Did Ika need saving from the dirty old man? Preston's pimples quivered as the revolutionary idea came to him.

At that moment, before the machinery in Preston's brain could properly digest the idea, the doors to the meeting room burst open. A man in a well-stitched black suit, brown leather briefcase in one hand and the other jammed in his pocket, walked in and Preston found himself staring at the new arrival with an open mouth. The air around this man buzzed with electricity. The man walked like he owned the world. The man's eyes, blue-grey and razor-sharp, scanned the room and stopped at him. Preston gulped and hurriedly got up. Almost everyone in the room, Preston noted, straightened up as well, collectively alert in the presence of such magnificence.

'Mr MacLeod?' the man asked in a silky voice, and Preston stared at him transfixed—another thought, revolutionary and life-altering, crystallizing in his brain. This man, whose mere presence commanded full attention of everyone in the room, was the man Preston wanted to be like. Look like. Walk like. Speak like. The watermelons on his shirt looked stupid now; he should have worn the shirt with the grinning whales.

'Mr MacLeod?' came the voice again, and Mike nudged him. Startled into life, Preston proceeded to nod his head furiously.

'Fredrick Heisenberg,' the man introduced himself.

Of course. Fredrick Heisenberg. *The* Fredrick Heisenberg.

'Glad to meet you. Thanks for your patience, my morning meeting overran,' Fredrick said, extending an arm.

'I dinnae know you were coming,' Preston fumbled and then reddened and blinked a couple of times, 'I mean, you're welcome of course, I just didnae, maybe the email—'

'That's fine,' Fredrick said dismissively, looking a bit annoyed, 'let's continue the meeting. I'll catch up with Jacob,' he said nodding at Jacob, still frowning.

Preston exhaled deeply and sat down with a thud. Such was the magnificence of the man that even exchanging a few sentences with him was exhausting, Preston concluded, even more impressed.

Fredrick was, in the meanwhile, walking purposefully towards Jacob. Preston saw his eyes fall on Ika, who was staring at her hands. Preston wondered if he was imagining it or had Ika really turned white like the proverbial ghost. Jacob was still, too, watching both Fredrick and Ika. The moment, Preston thought, tilting his head to one side, a wee bit perplexed, felt like it was made of glass, and if anyone moved, it would break into a million little pieces.

Fredrick stilled. Preston saw him gulp. He looked away from Ika but his eyes flew back to her the next instant. For one quick moment, the expressionless face gave way to immense pain. Preston, watching from a distance, wondered if he was imagining all this.

'Jacob,' Fredrick nodded curtly at Jacob who responded with a slight nod, and Preston noted a slight wobble in his voice, 'Ellin,' said Fredrick looking at the white-haired police-inspector-type lady who also nodded without a smile. The HE lot did not smile a whole lot, thought Preston sliding further into his chair.

Preston focussed his attention on Ika now.

He saw her let out a deep, ragged breath and Preston's heart lurched. He got up.

'Let me introduce our team to you, Fredrick,' Preston heard himself say, mentally applauding his own bravado. Preston quickly introduced the legal teams and Mike, and then, with a grand flourish of his hands, he said, 'And there, next to Jacob is sat our Head of Sales, Ikadashi Kumar. I understand you are all familiar with her,' he concluded with a grin that no one returned.

As Ika continued to stare at her hands, Jacob put an arm around her like this was somehow an emotional moment for her. To Preston's confusion, Ika looked like she was ready to cry. 'She's just da best,' Preston said loyally, looking around.

'Good morning, everybody,' Fredrick said, his voice curt, pausing to glare at Preston but avoiding Ikadashi completely, Preston noted.

A shiver ran through Preston. Was he imagining it, or had icy coldness gripped the room?

A scenario was fast playing out in Preston's head, the only one that explained everything. Jacob, the creepy, dirty old man, desperate to get into Ika's pants, must have made a move on Ika while she was at HE. Ika, the firebrand, must have outed the scummy bastard to HR. Jacob was Fredrick's right-hand man—well-known fact—so Fredrick would have stood by him. That would have left Ika with no option other than to resign. No wonder she never wanted to talk about her time at HE!

Excitement bristling out of his barely there whiskers, Preston banged his fist on the table in front of him. Mike, sat next to him, shuddered.

White haired police-type lady leaned over to glare at him. Hmm, thought Preston, rubbing the pimple on his chin with the back of his Minion pencil, the weird inspector-type white-haired lady? Probably worked in collusion with Jacob and brought girls to him. That disgusting woman.

There, he thought jubilantly, he had figured it all out.

And with that, Preston realized he needed to get Ika out of the clutches of the creep immediately.

'Ika, love,' Preston said out loud. He never called her 'love' but doing so now would assert that Ika was cherished at AL, unlike, he thought pointedly at HE. 'I know you have a deadline with the Memphis Account. You can leave if you wish to?'

Ika looked at Preston, her face expressionless. Were there tears in her eyes, Preston thought with immense concern. That crummy, sick bastard, he thought angrily, shooting a glare at Jacob who was holding Ika's hand. Wonder what he tried to do to Ika. Preston watched Ika get up, brush past Fredrick Heisenberg and leave the room without a word.

Preston saw Fredrick turn to look at Ika's retreating back. That immense yearning came back to his face again, the sort that left Preston a bit breathless, but just for a moment. Just for one fleeting moment. Confused, Preston glanced at Jacob. He was staring, his eyes unblinking and accusing, at Fredrick.

Maybe—thought Preston, rubbing his hands—Jacob was angry that Fredrick let Ika go.

20

Bombay

February 1987

'*B*ahu! Where is Om's stethoscope? He is getting very late for hospital!' Amma's shrill voice rang through their small Bombay flat.

Startled, Himani sprang up from the bed where she had almost dozed off. She hastily grabbed her dupatta and threw it around her neck. She pushed her feet into blue rubber slippers on the floor just under the bed. As she left the room, she glanced once again at the wooden *palna*, the crib that had been used in the Joshi family for generations. Her three-year-old daughter lay inside, sleeping peacefully.

'And her name?' Panditji, the family priest, who had come to perform the eleventh-day prayers and rituals for the newborn, had asked Amma all those years ago.

An incense stick had gently puffed dark aromatic smoke at the pictures of a variety of gods and goddesses, and Amma had smiled, folding her hands respectfully. 'Born on the eleventh day of the lunar cycle, on the day of *ekdashi*, this is Ikadashi Joshi, who will one day be a doctor—just like her papa.'

Om, his hair beginning to show the first hints of grey, had smiled, and so had Himani.

'Ikadashi—Ika,' Himani had said to herself slowly. 'Beautiful.'

It had taken Himani three long years to conceive. In the beginning, Amma had asked Himani every month if there was any news. But month after month, Himani's only response had been an almost imperceptible shake of her head till one day, when Amma had asked, and Himani had burst into tears. Amma wrapped her arms around the young girl and held her as Himani's body shook with sobs.

'I miss Mataji, Amma,' Himani said between sobs. 'I really want a baby in whom I can see a bit of my mother.'

Amma was silent for a bit, resting her chin on Himani's frail shoulder. 'The grief of losing a parent is like the ocean, Himani—big, huge, dark and scary. With no end in sight. The only way to survive it is to learn how to swim in it. Exist with it. Embrace it,' she said, a faraway look in her eyes.

'Amma,' said Himani pulling back, 'you never talk about *your* parents.'

Amma smiled a weak, sad smile. 'My mother died giving birth to me, Himani *bahu*. Very common in those days to not survive childbirth, you know. And then my father passed away two years later. I never knew them, but...' said Amma, '... what I do know is the pain you feel.'

Himani stared at Amma.

'You know Om's toe, the one that twists like the Vasuki Nag around Shiv ji's neck?'

Himani smiled at the description. Yes, she knew that toe.

'I tell myself he gets it from my mother. I don't know it for sure, but I tell myself that, and I spend hours looking at it, marvelling at how my mother continues to live on in us. That is what you need to do, and maybe... we can do that together whenever the time comes?' she finished as Himani looked questioningly at her mother-in-law.

'Look for our mothers in your child?' Amma said, smiling, and Himani found herself smiling back.

With this incident, two things happened that day. Amma stopped asking if Himani was pregnant, and Himani realized that perhaps lurking inside the strict, bird-like Amma was the mother she had longed for her entire life. That day, a friendship emerged, one that continued growing in strength for as long as Amma lived.

'Where in God's name is the stethoscope?' came Om's annoyed baritone, bringing Himani back to the present.

'Himani bahu, come quickly!' Amma shouted again, and Himani, with one final glance at her peacefully sleeping daughter, ran out of the room. Respectfully, she covered her head with the dupatta when she reached the living room. The living room was mostly occupied by a large bed, usually occupied by Amma, who now sat cross-legged on it, chewing paan.

'It's here,' Himani said, quickly opening the steel cupboard in the hallway and pulling out Om's stethoscope.

'Why did you keep it here?' asked Om in irritation, and Himani turned to look at her husband of seven years. His broad frame occupied the hallway, blocking out the light. He touched his moustache now, as he was wont to when annoyed, his dark eyes staring at her. He had never hit Himani, or even shouted at her, and yet Om scared her.

One of Himani's greatest loves was reading, and she met different people in each book. Jane Eyre and Mr Rochester. Elizabeth Bennet and Mr Darcy. Scarlett O'Hara and Rhett Butler. She read about these women and their stories wistfully. Of late, a quiet longing for the love they experienced had begun to consume her. Her own story, Himani had come to realize very soon into her marriage, was destined to be starkly different.

'Should we go out for dinner?' she had nervously asked Om as a new bride.

'Why?' Om had looked up from a thick book. 'Don't you like the food at home? Also, Amma will be left alone, and I don't want that,' he had said and had gone back to reading.

On their first wedding anniversary, she had spent hours picking out a red sari and decorated her hair with flowers. 'Do I look nice?' she had asked hesitatingly after he had come home in the evening.

'Eh?' Om said, looking up from the file he was reading.

'Umm... I... am I looking...' she faltered and saw his eyes narrow. 'Would you like some tea?' she heard herself ask finally, her shoulders slumping in defeat and disappointment.

'No, but I would like to finish working in peace.'

Himani would look at couples holding hands or kissing on Marine Drive and wonder how that felt. How, she wondered, did it feel to have your husband sneak up from behind and wrap you in his arms? For him to lay his head in your lap and tell you that you were beautiful. For conversations to last hours. To fall asleep in his arms. For the beating of his heart to be your most favourite sound in the world. For him to be your most favourite person in the world.

Om was all about grocery lists and chores that needed doing. He neither desired nor needed love. Himani knew that what she dreamt of was just that—a dream—that would never be her reality.

'Very few people are destined to find real, true love,' she mumbled to herself as she kneaded the chapatti dough. 'The rest just plod along, making the best of what the universe doles out to us. Yearning and longing, constantly underwhelmed, unable to fill the void in our lives, fearful that we may never be able to fill it. Searching but never finding.'

'Why did you keep my stetho here, Himani?' Om repeated, the edge in his voice noticeable. Himani looked at her husband; he was wearing a blue shirt and black trousers, the stethoscope around his neck now, giving him a distinguished air. He was well respected and good at his job, but she felt devoid of any love for him. She wanted to tell him that she had not put his stethoscope in the steel cupboard—*he* had. She had seen him put it there. Yet, years of being told, directly and indirectly, that she was inferior dictated that she remained silent.

'Should I pack your dinner?' she asked instead.

His brow furrowed in response.

'Okay, I will do it now,' Himani answered hurriedly and quickly made her way to the with the kneaded dough in her hand. She packed him chapattis, dal, some vegetables and a salad of cucumbers and tomatoes.

Following her inside the kitchen, Om bustled around filling his water bottle. 'Don't forget,' he said, 'you have to bring Ika to the hospital for her vaccination.'

'*Ji*,' she nodded.

'And you have to take your vitamins—give Amma hers too. And her diabetes medicines.'

'*Ji, ji.*'

'If you have another headache tonight, try to not take paracetamol you have taken three already this week. Tell Amma. She will give you a head massage,' he said and then poked his head out of the kitchen. 'Amma,' he said, 'If Himani—'

'She is my daughter too, beta,' Amma said, smiling from her bed. 'But come here both of you, we need to talk.'

'Amma, I am getting late,' Om replied as the two dutifully walked out of the kitchen back into the living room. The annoyance in Om's voice not lost on Himani. It always made a weird kind of hollowness appear in her stomach.

'Just two minutes,' said Amma. Om grudgingly came and sat at his mother's feet, and she put a hand on his head. 'Himani *bahu*, come sit with me.'

Himani obliged, wondering where this was going.

'Tell her, Om, what we discussed last night,' Amma said.

'*Aah*, that!' Om said, nodding.

'Yes, *that*,' Amma smiled.

'Himani,' Om said, turning to face his wife, 'some time ago, you told Amma that your biggest regret was not being able to complete your education…'

'And I've seen how keenly you read the newspapers and magazines, always hungry for more,' Amma said, eyes twinkling.

Himani settled the dupatta on her head and nodded, her heart beginning to beat faster. The last time anyone had spoken to her about school was her beloved Darjee, gone for six years now. An ache, visceral and sharp, ran through her chest as it always did when she thought about her beloved grandfather. Everyone, thought Himani, everyone she had loved, was now gone.

'I was wondering if you would like to complete your education and enrol for a bachelor's degree? It's up to you obviously,' Om asked.

Himani stared at him open-mouthed. Go back to school? Read? Write? Get a degree? Her heart somersaulted, and Himani looked around, unsure. Was that still possible? 'Ika?' she said, her heart sinking. Who would look after her?

'*Arre!* What are grandmothers for? I will take care of her when you're at college.'

Himani gasped in surprise and joy. 'Amma, will you *really*?' she said, clutching Amma's knee.

Amma laughed, dimples showing. 'Yes, yes! Of course, I will!'

'So,' said Om, a hint of annoyance appearing in his voice again, 'would you like to study?'

'Yes, please!' Himani said hurriedly, her voice quivering with excitement.

'All right, I will get the paperwork sorted.'

'Thank... *thank you!*' Himani said breathlessly in a whisper to Amma and then to Om, not sure what to do next.

A loud wail from the bedroom cut through the moment. Ika had just announced that she was awake and needed to be the centre of everyone's attention.

Himani ran to her daughter. Even though Ika was just three, Himani wanted to share the news. She was sure that Ika would understand.

21

Knightsbridge, London

March 2019

'Now that the engagement is done,' Ava said, chasing a truant piece of organic Chinook salmon on her plate, 'and dusted,' she cast a happy glance at the humongous diamond sat on her finger, 'maybe we can think about a baby?'

The Instagram post about the ring had three hundred and twenty-five thousand likes. The numbers still took her breath away.

Fredrick looked up and delicately wiped his mouth with the corner of a napkin. Estelle, his housekeeper of more than two decades, appeared magically by his side and picked up his plate. While it was delightful to see Fredrick after the long hiatus, it was exhausting to have Ava around, Estelle thought.

The entourage, her assistants in particular, who were stuck to Ava's backside with super glue, made life hell for Estelle with their demands for the actress. Six candles—Archipelago Black Forest—in the bedroom for Ava. White tulips (without leaves) in clear, round vases (not square—never, *ever* square) to decorate each table in the house. Leafy floor plants that had as much foliage at the top as they did on the bottom inside the house. Each meal to be served with a portion of Garcia Blue Corn Tortilla Chips. Only Fiji Water. The drapes in the room could only be blue or white. The list was endless. And draining.

Just that morning, Ava had been frantically walking to and fro in her bedroom, getting her steps in, flailing her arms around and breathing out noisily. Her 'chakra healer', flown in especially from Argentina, was behind her swaying her arms like a woman possessed, supposedly clearing Ava's chakras. 'Through the nose, through the nose, only through the nose,' the chakra healer chanted, and Ava nodded, speeding up. Ava's Löwchen, unoriginally named 'Star', was following the chakra healer and right when the chakra healer said to Ava, 'Your chakras have healed, my angel,' in a faraway, spooky voice, on cue, Star sunk her teeth into the healer's ankles. Healer yelped and doubled down in agony.

Don't know about your chakras, but your ankle definitely needs some healing now, Estelle had chuckled to herself, rushing towards the healer with first aid.

However, Estelle thought, taking a deep breath, the actress herself was harmless. There was a naiveté to Ava that appealed to Estelle, like she was almost oblivious to her own stardom. And she was clearly madly, madly in love with Fredrick. Sometimes, Estelle wondered, as she took her place behind Fredrick's chair and dissolved into the shadows, if Fredrick loved Ava half as much as Ava loved him. If asked, Estelle would have said someone very different from Ava would be the one for Fredrick. Someone…Estelle struggled for the right word…someone whose world was…simpler. Who got Fredrick's silences better than his words. Who Fredrick truly opened to.

'We've discussed having a baby many times, darling.' Fredrick frowned. 'I'm good without one.'

'You'll make a super Pa, Freddie. Just 'coz your folks did what they did—'

'I don't want to talk about my birth parents, Ava,' Fredrick said quietly. There, see, Estelle thought, Fredrick clamping down again with Ava.

'You've worked your ass off trying to track them, don't ya think it's time to move on?'

And there again—not what Fredrick wants to hear, Ava, Estelle said silently to the actress. Tell him please that he will find the answers to questions that torment him through the night and that they will bring him peace. Estelle sighed deeply. That woman needed coaching on how to be with Fredrick. Maybe, sighed Estelle, Fredrick deserved someone who understood him more. No one saw this more clearly than she did, but who was she to speak up.

Fredrick stared at his plate, a thousand words springing to his tongue, none of them kind.

'I know,' he said finally.

Ava put a hand on his. 'Do you feel like I don't get you?'

'No,' lied Fredrick.

'Sometimes I feel like I can't reach you…'

'That's not true,' Fredrick lied again, with a small smile. And as always, with Fredrick's smile, the order in Ava's world restored itself. She grinned happily. If only she could somehow convince him. A little baby girl. Ava sighed deeply and then beckoned for Fredrick's Head Housekeeper—whatever her name was, Emma, Elliot, whatever, she never could remember even after all these years—to clear her plate.

~

This is a terrible idea, Fredrick mumbled to himself as he reached out to press the bell for Flat 26. He sucked in a breath when the door opened, and Himani appeared.

'Fredrick,' she gasped, bringing her hand to her mouth in surprise, 'you are in London!' Ika's angry outbursts and the very unexpected sobs in the last few days suddenly made perfect sense now. *Poor, poor girl.*

'Hi Himani,' said Fredrick shifting uncomfortably.

'Ika is not home,' said Himani still a bit dazed.

'I know.'

'Oh,' Himani paused, 'would you like to come in?'

'Thank you,' said Fredrick and stepped inside and almost tripped over a kid's tricycle. 'Is he old enough to use this?' he asked, surprised.

'Time is a thief. They grow up very fast,' Himani replied and then nodded towards the dining table, the same one where they had sat the day Fredrick had left for LA two years ago.

'Can I get you some—'

Fredrick surprised himself by grabbing Himani's hand. 'Please sit?'

Himani looked at the long, artistic fingers around her wrist and then at the anxious eyes that looked at her. She smiled a small smile and sat down. Fredrick followed suit. Himani watched Fredrick fidget with his watch for a bit. The ticking of the cuckoo clock in the corner of the living room was the only sound that surrounded them.

'You must hate me,' Fredrick said finally.

'No, actually I don't,' Himani said and then tilted her head, surprised at the answer.

'Why?'

'We all have our reasons, Fredrick, for doing the things we do. Even if those things hurt the very people we love.'

Fredrick stared at Himani and then looked away.

'I think sometimes you have to choose between duty and love. And sometimes you have to choose between love and love,' said Himani, shrugging. Her shoulders slumped now, and she sank into her chair.

'I see you think I loved her,' Fredrick said staring at his hands, thinking hard.

Himani smiled and waited for Fredrick to again look at her. 'I think you *still* love her.'

Himani cupped her chin in the palm of her hand, her elbow resting on the table and watched a deep red blush rise on Fredrick's face.

'Why would you say that?' he asked.

'Because you are here,' Himani said quietly. Fredrick looked down and seemed to be struggling with his emotions. Himani leaned in and gently patted his arm.

'I asked Ika to leave Vivaan and come to me,' he said, wincing at his own words, 'she decided against it.'

An icy cold hand gripped Himani's heart.

'A mother is a mother before she is a woman,' she said cryptically.

'I …I wanted to say sorry to you, Himani,' said Fredrick, getting up to go. 'That's all I came to say—sorry.'

Before Himani could reply, the door burst open, and a little storm entered, laughing and shouting. It took a moment for Fredrick to deconstruct the madness that had just made an appearance. Ika was carrying her laptop bag on her back, three overflowing Waitrose bags in her hands and Veer at her hip.

Veer was clutching onto her hair, laughing like a maniac, and Ika was screaming.

'Get off my hair! It's hurting me, you little—' Ika shouted at Veer who giggled and responded with a 'Mumma shouting. Rude. Rude.' His dimple, exactly like his mother's, appeared and Fredrick stared at it transfixed. Veer shook his head, and his curls—identical to his mother's—danced around his little face.

Fredrick watched Ika as she tried to put Veer down, but he clung to her legs like his life depended on it. Ika groaned and picked him up again, setting the grocery bags down.

'Veer bit two boys today at nursery, Mummy,' said Ika looking exasperatedly at her mother, 'one of the other mums wants to speak to the mum of the 'biter'. I mean, come on. I am sure this is a breach of his human rights; labels at three? Veer would ne—'

Her eyes fell on Fredrick, and she stilled, her expression changing.

'Who this, Nani?' the glib 'biter' asked, expertly sliding down his mother's legs and walking towards Himani and Fredrick.

'Fredrick, Mummy's... friend...' Himani ventured slowly.

'Mummy's friend. *Hiii*,' said Veer to Fredrick, who despite the awkwardness of the moment, could not help but smile.

'Why are you here?' Ika asked, now taking a step towards Fredrick, the vitriol in her voice contrasting with the excitement in Veer's. Her chin quivered. 'Get out of my house.'

'Ika, I...'

'What should I ask you first? Huh?' Ika took another step closer to Fredrick, anger rising by the second. 'Why did you not return my calls? Why did you not get in touch? Why did you not think for one moment that you were leaving behind a girl you…' she faltered now, tears—helpless and angry—appearing in her eyes.

'I…'

'Why did your company buy a stake in AL two weeks after I signed paperwork?'

'Ika…I…'

'After all that you have done to me, Fredrick, why can't you do me the kindness of just leaving me alone?' Ika was shouting now, and Veer ran first to Himani and then once he reached her arms, he changed his mind, pushed them away and ran to Fredrick. The 'biter' stretched out his arms in anticipation of being picked up.

Fredrick looked at Ika. At the angry tears and the quivering lips and his heart lurched. He bit the insides of his cheeks lest tears appear in his own eyes.

'Pick me up,' the three-year-old tyrant ordered with authority.

Fredrick bent and picked up Veer.

'Put my son down,' Ika ordered, her voice dripping with acid, the vulnerability from a few moments forgotten.

'*No Mumiieee,*' howled Veer and wrapped his arms around Fredrick like they were bosom buddies being separated by a cruel dictator, 'No Mumiiieee, NO!'

'Hey, little guy,' said Fredrick gently, looking at Veer, 'I need to go, buddy. Let's listen to your mum, shall we now?'

'Leave my son. Leave equity in AL and leave London,' Ika said, her voice now dangerously calm.

Fredrick looked at Ika, his eyes hardening.

'I'm not going to do any of that.'

'You want me to resign from one more company because of you?'

'Your life. Your career. Your choice.'

'I hate you, Fredrick Heisenberg,' Ika said, rubbing the fresh bout of tears that appeared at Fredrick's words with the back of her hands. She took three long strides so that she was standing right next to Fredrick. For a moment their eyes met. She looked different from before. More real. More beautiful. Like she had been through things that had taught her lessons. He desperately wanted to see her smile. More tears rolled down her cheeks.

Ika pulled Veer away, who shrieked dramatically and kicked like he was being kidnapped.

'I will submit my resignation,' Ika said bitterly to the background of Veer's howls, tears streaming down her face, nose red and eyes wide with anger. 'You can do what you want with this godforsaken company. Please show yourself out.'

Carrying a screaming, kicking Veer in her arms, Ika walked out of the living room into her bedroom and slammed her door shut.

In the safety of her bedroom, Ika sat on the edge of her bed, her tiny body shaking, taking deep, unsure breaths. On seeing Fredrick two weeks ago at the AL meeting, Ika had run out of the meeting room and once outside had gulped mouthfuls of air, unable to get enough oxygen inside her. In the following days, tears unwelcome and unbidden, seemed to just flow down her cheeks at the oddest of times—in meetings, while eating, as she watched the telly. It was as if all that she had buried inside for two long years—the conversation, the laughs, the friendship, the love—had come out, drenching her in angst that was both alien and exhausting. Now, in her room, as she waited for Fredrick to leave, the tears came back, refusing to stop. They came from deep within her, like her body was in immense pain. Her heart hurt, physically hurt. Hurt in a way that made her wonder if a paracetamol would help. She could sense a darkness, a feeling of utter hopelessness approaching her, ready to engulf her just as it had when Fredrick had left. No, she could not allow herself to fall down that chasm again. Himani did not deserve that, Ika, Veer did not deserve that, Ika. She had to do what she needed to protect her sanity. And with that, tears still streaming down her face, she picked up her phone. Outside, she heard the door close.

Meanwhile, Veer sat on floor, threw his hands and legs around and cried too.

Both mother and son, Ika realized, were crying for Fredrick.

'Hi Preston,' she said into the phone, her voice breaking.

∽

Preston slumped into the grey, doughy sofa in the living room of his Brixton apartment and felt his hands shake as he put his iPhone down.

He tugged at the neck of his Marvel print T—a habit of many years and thought how terrible life would be if there was no Ika at work. True, he was nosy and felt inexplicably curious about her life, but she was also a great asset to the company, wasn't she? Why should AL lose someone like her because of someone like Jacob Carmen?

She had been crying, he was sure about that, he thought, his heart sinking lower.

The rumbling of Victoria Line stopping at Brixton station reached him through the open window, but Preston ignored it.

Ika had agreed to stay the notice period, so he had her for another three months. She had also rather unwillingly agreed to remain the main person in charge of managing the whole AL, HE case. It was a strategic move on Preston's part. He had to see Ika around Jacob to understand what may have happened. He had only three months to figure it all out and if possible help Ika stay back.

He narrowed his eyes at the telly in front of him. David Walliams was wrapping himself around Simon Cowell in a rerun of BGT. Preston loved the unlikely comedy double act of Simon and David, but for the moment, he barely noticed anything.

He needed to be clever about this if he was to have any hope of getting Ika to change her mind, he thought to himself. He went and poured himself a glass of milk. He stirred in some Nutella. And then he dunked a jaffa cake into it. He counted till three and then pulled out the soggy cake and hurriedly plonked it into his mouth before it broke into the milk. It was his favourite thing to eat.

22

Bombay, India

June 1993

Himani stepped out of the auto rickshaw and handed the driver ten rupees, blissfully unaware of the glorious storm waiting for her.

Himani walked into Bombay College, noticing neither the intricate flower design on the Mughlai arches nor the temples carved into the thick pillars. She walked watchfully and quickly, the pallu of her soft pink sari swishing behind her, keeping time with her long plait. She walked to the Teachers' Room to gather her belongings and to have a cup of tea before she faced forty fifteen-year-old girls and tried to explain Shakespeare to them. Outside the Teachers' Room, the names of the staff were printed on the door.

Himani Joshi, English, BA, MA

If all went well, she would soon be applying for a PhD. A delightful tingle ran through her body. Dr Himani Joshi. How amazing would that be! And maybe then, when she was a doctor like her husband, Om would stop seeing her as a little girl, thirteen years his junior, who needed to be looked after. Even Ika had started saying, 'Baba knows everything, Mummy knows nothing.'

Himani took a deep breath, touching the oxidized metal earrings she had chosen to wear that day and opened the door. And then she stilled. Her chair was occupied and sitting in her spot was a man. All she could see was a crop of wavy brown hair bending into a book.

'Excuse me!' Himani exclaimed, walking in, her eyes flashing. 'That's my seat! Please get up.'

'English Madam is here,' hissed Mr Wahal, the head of the geography department, his sneaky, beady eyes narrowing at the sight of Himani.

Ignoring Wahal, Himani glared at the man sat in her chair, who now got up slowly and turned to face her.

'How dare y—' Himani started and faltered. And then she stared. And then she blushed.

Standing in front of her was the most handsome man she had ever set eyes on. The man was tall and broad, with brown wavy hair. There was an exquisiteness to his features that was hard to describe—his Grecian nose and bow-and-arrow-shaped lips were almost poetic. His eyes were green and reminded Himani of the ocean and skies—of leaves and clouds. Himani was transfixed.

The thing was, so was Iqbal. He stared unblinking at Himani for a long moment. And then he turned to Mr Wahal.

'*Husn waalon ko sawarne ki zaroorat kya hai?*'

'*Woh toh sadgi mein bhi qayamat ki ada rakhte hain,*' came perfect Urdu in a golden, velvety voice.

'What does that mean?' Mr Wahal asked, continuing to chew his paan, looking first at Himani and then at Iqbal.

'Those with beauty do not need adornments; their simplicity is enough to bring the world to a standstill,' Iqbal replied, and casting one final look at Himani, left the room.

Mr Wahal patted his belly and tried to not blush. Surely a handsome man like Iqbal sprouting poetry while staring intently at him must mean something, he reasoned. Not that he...err... was interested in men...

Himani shook her head and hastily got herself a cup of tea. No one had ever called her beautiful. She rubbed her arms, willing the goosebumps to go away. She plonked herself into a pink plastic chair, her own forgotten now, and took her first sip of the piping hot tea. It was, as always, too sweet.

∼

Expectedly, the arrival of a handsome male teacher created quite a stir in the all-girls institution that was more used to the likes of the pot-bellied Mr Wahal. Hushed whispers in the college corridors dissected and analysed everything about the new professor—from his sharply pressed trousers and crisp white shirt to how his eyes looked in the sunlight.

His name, Himani was told, was Iqbal Sultan Ali Sheikh. The girls repeated it dreamy-eyed and agreed that it sounded like the name of a powerful general out to fight a bloody war. Rumour had it that his parents were from Afghanistan. Amitabh Bachchan had played the Afghan Badshah Khan in the recent Bollywood hit *Khuda Gawah*, and at the moment, all things Afghani held an unmistakable allure. Iqbal Sultan Ali Sheikh included.

Girls whispered about how clever he was—after all, doing a PhD in chemistry couldn't be easy—and Iqbal was teaching the junior classes at the same time. What a genius, the girls agreed over paper cones of laiyya, spicy puffed rice, bought from the vendor just outside the college gates. Students who had taken up arts asked if they could switch to chemistry 'just for a few days.'

In about a fortnight of Iqbal's arrival, Himani knew that it was a matter of time until one of the girls fell madly in love with him and a scandal hit the college. In fact, she was thinking about this while walking up the stairs to a class, already a few minutes late, when she saw him coming down the stairs.

'Excuse me,' she said, hurrying past him, annoyed at how her heart had started beating faster.

Iqbal raised his eyes and stared at her. '*Arz kiya hai*,' he said, a slow, charming smile appearing on his face, his voice a low baritone that thrilled Himani. He stepped down trying not to look at her, as if she were the sun, and yet he saw her, like the sun, even without looking. Iqbal brought his cupped hand to his forehead in an exquisite adaab.

Something acerbic. Something sharp. Something from a fancy book. Quick. Quick.

'Umm... I... you... I think,' Himani mumbled, eyes darting everywhere before finally meeting his when she heard him chuckle. 'I need to go,' she said and walked past him.

'Ah,' he said loud enough for her to hear, 'leave me not to pine, alone and desolate; No fate seemed fair as mine, no happiness so great.'

Himani's cheeks were red, and she broke into a run, crashing a minute later into a group of sixteen-year-olds who were incidentally scrounging the college campus for the elusive Iqbal Sultan.

'Can't you see where you are walking,' Himani shouted angrily at the girls, fully aware that it had been her mistake.

∼

A few days later, Himani walked up to Iqbal Sultan to get his signature on the General Teachers' Meeting notes, ignoring the thudding of her heart. A few teachers (and some flies) occupied the Teachers' Room on that hot, humid summer day. The fan, once beige in colour and now a dull grey from the layers of dirt, laboured slowly.

Himani stopped a few feet away from Iqbal, unsure. He looked up, his eyes finding and then focussing on her with delicious laziness.

'Please can you sign this?' she asked softly, a tad angry that she was feeling this shy.

With studied movements, Iqbal took the notes and the pen. Their fingers touched lightly. Himani looked up, startled. He didn't blink.

'Something wrong?' Himani asked.

'Why would anything be wrong?'

'What are you staring at?'

'You,' he said, his eyes boring into hers.

She opened her mouth and then closed it. 'Listen,' she started hotly, 'I... I...'

'Yes?'

'I am married. And a mother.'

'So?'

'So... umm...' she said as redness crept up her face. 'Umm... I mean...'

Iqbal chuckled. 'I should not stare at you?'

'Yes, exactly, you should neither stare nor go around sprouting poetry or *shayri* when you see me.'

'It's your fault, really.'

'How?'

'You're too beautiful for me not to stare at.'

Himani rolled her eyes and tried hard to not smile but failed.

'But I am sure you're too used to compliments for any of mine to matter.'

'I hardly ever get compliments,' Himani said, cocking her head to one side, puzzled at Iqbal's assumption.

'Bizarre,' said Iqbal, trying to not smile at Himani's innocence. 'You know what, I have some *kadak* masala chai here,' he said, bending to pick up a blue thermos that he now placed in his lap with great fanfare. 'I would be happy to share with you if you sit down.'

Himani's eyebrows shot up. She put her hands on her hips and let out a deep, dramatic sigh.

'I won't sign if you don't sit,' Iqbal tried again as Himani narrowed her eyes at him. 'And you will have to explain to Principal Ma'am why you couldn't get all the signatures,' Iqbal chuckled.

'Like I care,' said Himani, but she was smiling, and Iqbal pulled out a chair next to him and patted it invitingly.

'Tell me about yourself,' Iqbal said as soon as Himani sat down. A fly buzzed past them, and Iqbal, with great bravado, batted it away from Himani. He got up to pick up two Styrofoam cups from a stack of cups on a plastic table in the corner.

'You mean apart from my husband and my daughter?' Himani asked as she watched Iqbal pour tea into the cups. His fingers, long and artistic, wrapped around the white cups were an oddly beautiful sight.

He paused at her words and turned to face her. 'I want to know about everything, including the husband and daughter.'

Himani scoffed. 'Why should I tell you anything?'

'Because I care,' he said softly, dropping his hands into his lap.

Himani stilled, her eyes fixed on Iqbal's face.

'I am married,' Himani tried as the attraction she had felt for Iqbal from the very first second tightened its grip around her.

'I know you're married. I would much rather you were not,' he continued with a quick smile and a wink. 'But you are, and I am okay with that. I just want to get to know you. I promise to respect your words and your story.'

Himani felt cracks appearing in her defences, and it scared her. She bit her lips and fidgeted with her fingers. 'I don't understand you,' she said finally, slumping back into the plastic chair.

Iqbal puckered his lips to sip the tea and then beamed as if he had just tasted the best thing on the planet. Himani laughed, pushed back a strand of hair and picked up her cup.

'What little I have to tell isn't all very happy,' Himani said thoughtfully.

'Begin from the beginning?' Iqbal said, placing his elbows on his thighs, leaning in with interest.

Himani wondered why she was about to tell her story to someone she had only just met. But she went back to that day all those years ago when she had woken up to the death of her mother. And as she did so, speaking almost without stopping for the next hour, Iqbal leaning forward towards her, listening intently to every word that came out of her, she realized that she liked being around Iqbal and she *wanted* to tell him her story.

It was as simple and as scary as that.

~

Later that night, Iqbal sat on a rickety chair in his room in the teachers' quarters and thought about Himani, a heady mix of foreboding and longing overcoming him. The purple of her sari had contrasted with the white of her blouse. White jasmine flowers had peaked mischievously from behind the bun she had tied her hair into.

She was a wife. Forbidden.

A mother. Forbidden.

A Hindu. Forbidden.

Was all of this adding to the allure? Or was it *the* allure?

He shook his head in frustration. His feelings for Himani, a woman he had just met, were getting too big for him. This was unlike anything he had ever felt before. This, he poked his chest to remind himself, might destroy him. And her.

23

HE HQ, Knightsbridge, London

April 2019

Preston was, Fredrick thought, looking sideways at him, sitting way too close to Ika. In a breach of both privacy and personal space, Preston was staring over Ika's shoulder at her phone. The AL team was at HE HQ twice every week now, and Fredrick had noted, with growing annoyance, that Preston rarely left Ika's side. The one time Fredrick had seen Preston leave Ika, he'd also heard him tell Ika that he was going to the gents. Nature's call, he had added with a grin. But don't worry, it's just a number one, Preston had finished, and Fredrick could only stare.

'Why were you at the Kensal Green Cemetery yesterday?' Fredrick heard Preston ask Ika.

Kensal Green.

Fredrick stilled, straining his ears.

While walking towards his father's grave on Saturday, Fredrick had spotted a lady in black bending down to place a flower. The black form had seemed vaguely familiar, but the lady vanished by the time Fredrick reached the grave. Wondering who she was, Fredrick had picked up the white lily, his father's favourite flower and pocketed it. It now lay in his father's library, pressed between the pages of a thick book.

'Are you stalking me again, Preston?' Ika asked dryly as if she was quite used to this kind of behaviour, opening her laptop, not bothering to look at her boss.

'Only on Insta,' Preston replied with a sickening grin. He was an odd mixture of brains, creativity, Harry Potter glasses, creepiness and pimples, thought Fredrick. 'Either tell me why you were at the cemetery or tell me exactly and truthfully why you are leaving AL,' Preston was saying.

'Or else?' asked Ika, now looking at her boss.

'You will be my plus one for the Marketing Events Awards later tonight,' Preston grinned. There were times, Preston thought, when he could be both clever and cute.

Images of Preston, clad in a neon pink tee, hobbling around stepping on her toes on the dance floor, his pimples glistening in the disco lights came to Ika. Some battles, Ika concluded, were best not fought at all.

'Why does anyone go to a cemetery, Preston? To visit a grave,' Ika said breathing out.

'Whose grave?'

She hates you, as she probably should. Nothing about her concerns you anymore. Nothing about her should concern you anymore. Fredrick looked at Ika. She was dragging a hand down her face.

'Someone I used to know…he—' she hesitated. Her eyes flew to Fredrick a few seats away. Their eyes met. He looked away, caught red-handed.

'How did he die?' Preston asked and then trailed off, worried. Why, he wondered, was Ika looking so uncomfortable all of a sudden? He raised his neck and looked around. No sign of Creepy Jacob. Fredrick was sat a few seats away, staring at his computer screen like his life depended on it, the tips of his ears red, which was also oddly beautiful. About twenty-odd HE folks sat around him, on high alert, disbelieving that *the* Fredrick Heisenberg was amongst them. Preston allowed his eyes to linger on the exquisite beauty that was Fredrick Heisenberg (like he often did these days). Last night, in front of the full-length mirror in his Ikea wardrobe, Preston, face covered with a thick layer of benzoyl peroxide for his pimples, had jammed his left hand in the pockets of his H&M joggers and attempted to walk straight and erect like Fredrick. He had to admit, grudgingly though, that the effect was not quite the same. He had blamed the benzoxyl peroxide.

'Are you okay, Ika?' Preston asked Ika.

'Eh?' Ika responded, looking very distracted. Preston saw her look at Fredrick again. Maybe she was also, like him, in awe of the majestic Mr. Heisenberg. A twinge of jealousy rushed through Preston, but he doused it with a little shake of his head. First, Fredrick was, well, Fredrick Heisenberg. He belonged to a different world that neither he nor Ika inhabited. Second, Fredrick was dating an actual actress. Ika could look at Fredrick all she wanted, but nothing was ever going to happen.

'Are you okay?' Preston asked Ika again.

'I need to go,' she said finally, shutting down her laptop with a bang.

'Are you mad? Fredrick's here. D'ye know how important AL must be for HE for him to be here?' Preston exclaimed and yanked Ika back down into her seat.

'You are such an idiot, Preston,' Ika mumbled. She opened her laptop again. The meeting started a few minutes later.

Fredrick sat still, spoke only when spoken to and when Ika stood up to present, he got up and left.

~

Preston, that idiot!

Ika mumbled angrily to herself when, just as she was about to sit next to Jacob for the AL-HE dinner, he called her away. This resulted in Ika, much to her chagrin, finding herself sat next to Fredrick Heisenberg.

Ika expected waves of anger, frustration and discomfort to lash at her unstopping, especially given how she had reacted to Fredrick's presence in her house. To her surprise, and even as they purposefully avoided any contact, speaking intently to people on the other side, their backs towards each other, it felt, if anything, reassuring to be this close to Fredrick. He felt soothingly familiar, like a well-worn blanket or a familiar shirt. His smell, his touch, his presence, all of it reminded her not of the agony of their separation but oddly and surprisingly of the comfort of his friendship.

And with that, the tense initial minutes passed, and Ika found herself relaxing, allowing her shoulder—the one that sometimes touched Fredrick—to finally relax. And then, as she discussed with Preston, who was sitting on her left, in excruciating detail how she'd managed to hurt her thumb over the weekend, she tried to memorize the feeling of being this close to Fredrick.

Preston then moved on to the super fascinating topic of a trip back to Scotland to meet his 'faither and mither' and Ika concentrated on cutting her steak, her injured thumb making this task almost impossible.

'Please take this,' came a familiar voice, just as Ika was about to throw up her hands in exasperation.

Ika looked at him, startled. Without waiting for her response, Fredrick replaced Ika's plate with his. In the new plate, the steak was cut up into bite-sized pieces.

'No, I—'

'Please, I insist.'

'Thank you,' she said not looking at him.

And with that, he went back to talking to others at the table.

Preston kept a close eye on Fredrick and Ika. They did not speak at all except for that weird bit where he cut food for her— like, come on, who does that? And also, why in the name of God did he not think of doing it? Was it, Preston wondered, chewing his steak so noisily that it made Ika glare at him, just his imagination or post the food chopping, were Ika and Fredrick really sitting closer, almost huddled together, but not looking at each other or talking?

Weird. Weird. Weird.

Everything, Preston concluded with a sigh, everything about this dinner was weird.

Food done, the mood of the little party changed dramatically. Music grew louder, and Ricky Martin's "Livin' la Vida Loca" filled the air around them. Some thus far high-nosed and composed executives began to gyrate to the beats with flailing of arms and thrusting of pelvises.

Restless, Fredrick found himself walking towards Ika and Ellin, who were standing in a dark corner, away from the dancing, deep in conversation. In an olive-green shift dress that hugged her toned body, Ika was more formally dressed today than he had seen her recently, Fredrick noted. Fredrick was unsure about what he wanted to say to Ika—no, he had no idea, and perhaps there was nothing left to say, but he knew he needed to be closer to her. Somehow. Even if just for a few moments.

Had her eyelashes always been this long, he wondered? Eyes this black and sad? Face always this innocent?

Ika saw Fredrick walking towards them, and she felt her heart begin to thud. Something between them had shifted. Had it, or was she imagining it? Had her harsh words ruined any hope of …of…Ika's mind drew a blank. There was no hope of anything between them anymore, not even friendship. They were going to be strangers for life. The thoughts cut through her heart. Nervously, she looked everywhere, twiddling her fingers.

Fredrick saw Ika twiddling her fingers and felt an urge to take her hands into his. 'I—' Fredrick began coming up to the girls, feeling nervous.

'Heisenberg,' an American voice cut Fredrick short and Ika turned around to look at the man who had just walked through the doors.

'Stiller,' Fredrick stared in surprise. The air around them shifted instantly, the warmth and lightness of the pub evaporating in an instant.

Taller than Fredrick's 6'2" by an easy three or four inches, Harry Stiller commanded the space he walked into. His skin, red in the light of the pub, like it was burnt from too much sun, added a roughness to his face that Ika disliked immediately. His facial features, tiny and bird-like, sat asynchronously with his humongous frame.

'And to what do I owe this pleasure?' Fredrick asked, his voice at its politest—and coldest.

'Your stunning receptionist told me that the office was at the pub when I told her I was a childhood friend looking for best buddy Freddie.'

Ellin stiffened visibly.

'Lemme deal with this for you, Freddie,' she said fixing her eyes on the American, her voice dripping with contempt.

'Excuse us please, Ellin,' Fredrick said instead, without looking at her. Ellin opened her mouth to speak but then shook her head and left.

Ika waited for Fredrick to ask her to leave, but he didn't. The two men had locked their eyes.

'I wanted to ask ya, my old friend,' said Harry, grinning slyly, 'what does it feel like to cheat a man into buying a company? Dubai, remember?'

'Three years gone by and still smarting, are we? Eh?' Fredrick grinned, but the mirth did not reach his eyes. 'Sometimes, you have just your own stupidity to blame for bad business decisions, Stiller.'

'Someone pissed their pants a little bit when I tried to acquire Aqua two years ago, right after this lady,' Stiller nodded at Ika who drew back in surprise, 'took up the job.'

Ika stared at Stiller, his words sinking in.

'And why exactly were you trying to acquire Aqua, Stiller?' Fredrick put his hands in his pockets, his voice acidic.

'So Fredrick, it's the women in your life, isn't it? Always the women? Causing all the problems, breaking your heart?' Stiller drawled, grinning, and Ika felt a coldness grip her insides. 'First your mother. Then you fall in love with a married woman who decides she's better off without ya. All I was trying to do was to take care of her when she wouldn't let you,' and with that Stiller nodded at Ika again, a sickly sweet smile playing on his lips.

Ika stood there stunned.

'Take care of Ika?' Fredrick scoffed.

'You do not trust me around your married ex?'

'You would've made life hell for her. She has been through enough to—' Fredrick left the sentence midway, looked at Ika and reddened.

Stiller laughed.

'Devastated that you don't trust me, my friend,' Stiller pouted, and Ika felt repulsed. 'So Ika,' said Stiller turning to face her, 'this—us—wasn't probably meant to be, I guess. The first time we tried to get your company, Freddie here bought a majority stake and stalled the acquisition. So, we had to try again. And when he did, he got super antsy and ran all the way from across the pond to protect his lady love. *Ex* lady love,' Harry said grinning sickly. 'And that reminds me, congrats on the engagement, my friend. Look forward to attending the wedding. Love that you are in love with one girl and marrying another. Epic.'

Ika stared at Fredrick.

'Leave Ika out of this, Stiller,' he growled, his brow furrowing.

'Now,' said Stiller, chuckling and continuing to stare at Ika, 'that you are leaving AL. So,' he looked at Fredrick with a shrug, 'we are no longer interested in this stupid company. We are pulling out,' he said with a smirk. 'However,' Stiller's smirk widened into a grin, 'you bet we'll keep an eye on where the lady chooses to work next.'

'Is that a threat, Stiller?'

'I don't really want to have to fight you, Fredrick. You come from filth, but somehow I enjoy it very much,' Stiller continued.

Ika looked at Fredrick waiting for his response, but she saw him take a shaky, nervous breath.

'There is an institution in Texas for poor little knocked-up prostitutes that I hear you support,' continued Stiller, 'that Stiller Group can look at now that AL is gone. It can be my new pet project.'

'So that's why you're here,' Fredrick whispered, his face turning white.

'If not Ika, then why not Mummy?' Stiller drawled. 'Your women, Fredrick, their love for you, their betrayal, and your helplessness in the face of that betrayal... fascinating.'

The sides of Fredrick's jaws clenched as did his fist, Ika noted. Yet, he said nothing. Was it just her imagination or was a shadow of helplessness darkening Fredrick's face?

'And maybe, in the process of looking after the American prostitutes, I can find out a little more about a particular lady from many years ago...' Stiller continued, his beady little eyes narrowing at Fredrick.

'Leave. That. Alone,' Fredrick said, his voice a sinister whisper. The din of the pub seemed to have vanished, and the world consisted just of these two men, animal-like, angry and ready to pounce on each other.

'And if I were to tell you, Heisenberg, that I know what you are, you piece of shit—'

'Don't you *dare*,' Ika heard a voice say authoritatively and realized, with a fair amount of surprise, that it was hers. She had stepped sideways so that she was now standing between Fredrick and Stiller, shielding Fredrick from the American. 'Don't you *dare* utter another word, Mr Stiller.'

'Ooh!' said Stiller mockingly, making a show of looking down at the much smaller Ika. 'The other little lady. Do you know his dirty little secrets?' Harry narrowed his eyes at Ika, who fixed an unflinching glare at him. 'I can tell you things—'

'Will you leave, or should I call security?' Ika's voice was dangerously calm.

'You're asking *me* to leave?' Stiller repeated, stilling. He looked at Fredrick, who was staring at Ika, looking as surprised as Stiller felt.

'No,' Ika shook her head. 'I am *telling* you to leave. You can do it on your own, or security will drag you out. The choice is yours—the pleasure will be mine.'

'You'll pay for this,' Stiller said, his eyes boring into Ika's, his face red with anger.

'With pleasure,' said Ika, and she grabbed a stunned Fredrick by the elbow, turned, pushed the doors of the pub open and walked into the darkness of the blustery winter night.

A few moments later, when the cloud of anger dissipated a bit, and Ika began to get her bearings back, she realized she was walking very fast. She stopped, turned and saw Fredrick staring at her. He looked surprised, but there was also something else on his face. Ika's shoulders slumped, and a million thoughts raced into her head. What they could have been, what they had been and the mess that they were now.

Snow was falling around them in soft white petals forming a layer of delicate white powder on the cobbled street. Ika realized with a start that she was still holding Fredrick's arm and she immediately let go. For a moment, neither spoke. 'I...I...' she tried, her voice shaking, eyes darting everywhere. 'I need to go,' she said finally and about turned to leave before tears that simmered dangerously just below the surface let themselves out.

A hand, firm and familiar, clasped her wrist.

'Ika...' Fredrick said, his breath pluming in the cold of the dark night, and Ika turned around to face the man she loved. They stared at one another. He saw her chin quiver as a mist of tears appeared in her eyes. A cold knot appeared in the pit of his stomach.

'I need to go,' she repeated helplessly. 'Please let go of my hand.'

Fredrick tightened his grip on her wrist. He looked like he was about to say something, but he closed his mouth and released her.

Ika began walking away, her heels clacking against the stones.

'Ika, please wait!' Fredrick said. He jogged up to Ika, yanked off his black jumper and placed it around Ika's shoulders. 'It's cold,' he said softly, his voice, his words, a whisper in the night.

Ika's shoulders sagged.

What we had was so beautiful, she wanted to say, why, oh why did we throw it away? The tears were coming, she could feel them. Without another word, she turned and began to walk away from him. She clutched onto his jumper, pulled it in tighter around her as she broke into a run, desperate to put as much distance between them as possible. His jumper. It smelled of him and, wrapped around her, it felt as if Fredrick's arms were embracing her. But that was something that would never happen now.

And then Ika began to cry. She cried harder than ever before, her heels clicking on the cobbled streets. She cried for herself, for him, for them, for what could have been and for what was now never going to be.

~

Climbing into bed that night, Ika's heart felt all kinds of heavy from the revelations that had come to light that evening. There were so many questions she wanted to ask Fredrick but was there any point in knowing anymore?

'What the fuck is this?' came Vivaan's voice and Ika felt the familiar sinking feeling start to consume her insides whenever he began to swear. Clearly, and yet again, she had done something to upset her husband. And that's when it hit her. A simple thought that shook her.

She hated being around Vivaan with all her heart.

I hate being around him, she said to herself, silently chewing on the words, absorbing them. Understating the huge significance they carried.

I hate being around him.

I hate being around him.

'What happened?' She said nevertheless patting the pillow behind her, pretending that his tone did not make her heart palpitate. Vivaan, handsome even while angry, in his black silk pyjama set that set off his dark eyes, sat on the bed and threw a piece of paper at Ika.

'You invested in these stocks? Without asking me?'

'It's my money,' she said, hoping her voice sounded nonchalant. She hated how her heart thudded.

Vivaan scoffed. 'What makes you think you have the brains to figure out which stocks to invest in?'

Ika stared at him, sitting upright on her bed. He was laughing. No, jeering. Killing any confidence she had inside her.

'Just leave this money business to me. You do your sales,' he said putting sales in air quotes like it was not a real job, 'or better still, find another job that pays you less. Like you did when you left HE.'

'I've left AL too, actually,' Ika heard herself say.

'You have what?'

Ika stayed silent now.

'Why?' he asked, getting angrier, his black eyes staring incredulously at her.

Ika remained silent.

'Same reason as HE?' he mocked, thumping his fist onto the white pillow.

Actually, you are right. The exact same reason—Fredrick Heisenberg.

Ika remained silent.

'Such an idiot,' Vivaan hissed, turning away from Ika and picking up his phone listlessly.

And with those words—not the meanest, not the angriest that Vivaan had said to her—something inside Ika gave way. Like a bridge just about holding on finally gives way under the footfall of a little girl and rumbles and tumbles into oblivion into the river that rages below.

Why, she asked herself, should she live with this cruelty? Why did she have to pretend like she was strong, and it did not matter? Perhaps being strong was owning that it mattered and doing what was needed to change it?

'*How dare you call me that?*' Ika thundered. 'Don't you dare, ever fucking dare, call me an idiot again.'

Vivaan stared at his wife. Her nostrils were flared, eyes wet, angry tears streaming down her face, a wildness in her eyes that scared him for a moment.

'I am going back to India, Vivaan,' said Ika after a moment's pause, surprised at the words coming out of her, 'I think we both need a break from us. I need a break from this constant line of abuse that I no longer have the strength to listen to every single day. Every. Single. Day.'

'What are you doing?' Vivaan asked, taken aback.

'What I should have done many years ago. Standing up for myself,' Ika said, her heart still achy from the evening with Fredrick, beating fast, 'and booking tickets to India.'

Ika got out of her bed, snatched her laptop from the table and with quivering fingers opened the BA website before the voice inside her head told her to be logical about things, put family first and stay back.

London spelt heartbreak of many kinds for her at the moment. She needed to go back home to mend her heart. Away from Vivaan. Away from Fredrick. Away from it all.

To breathe. To collect. To strengthen.

24

Bombay College, Bombay

January 1994

'*Meri jaan*,' Iqbal said, expertly flicking a roasted peanut from a paper cone into his mouth, and Himani blushed.

Meri Jaan. Urdu for 'my life'. Beautiful, intimate and poetic. She loved it when Iqbal called her that.

For the moment, Himani and Iqbal had stepped out of the college gates into a colourful cacophony. Hand-drawn carts of all shapes and sizes surrounded them, selling peanuts, aloo tikki and pani puri. The sun shone bright and strong. The world was abundant in colour, hope and love.

'What if,' Iqbal paused, turning to face Himani, his smile vanishing, and said, 'I say I'm falling in love with you?'

Himani stopped walking and gripped her handbag tightly, her expression changing instantly. In a turn of events that had completely gobsmacked Himani, she had found herself matching every advance Iqbal made with one of her own. She had batted her eyelids, smiled seductively, let her hands carelessly brush his thigh. She had already done things that she would have not imagined herself capable of seven months ago.

But here was the thing—Iqbal was not married. *She* was. Iqbal was not wrong in loving her. *She* was. And what was she supposed to do about that?

'What would you say to that?' Iqbal asked, the lightness from a few moments back evaporating.

'Auto!' Himani hailed a three-wheeler a few feet away, determinedly looking away.

'What are you running away from, Himani?' Iqbal asked, squinting, bringing his hands up to shade his eyes from the sun. His white shirt shone brightly in the light, contrasting with the blue of his jeans.

Himani craned her neck, willing the auto rickshaw to come to her that instant.

'You're running away from the love you feel, aren't you?' Iqbal prodded with a gentle smile. 'But you understand that you can't, don't you?'

The auto stopped next to Himani.

'I need to leave,' Himani said hurriedly, gathering her sari and getting into the auto rickshaw.

Iqbal put his palms on the roof of the vehicle and peered inside, his eyes boring into Himani's. 'You can outrun me and my love, but you can't outrun yourself—remember that,' he said.

Himani stared into his eyes and felt a heady concoction of sorrow and joy erupt inside her. 'Let's go, *Bhaiya*,' she said to the driver who was eyeing the two with ill-disguised disdain in the rear-view mirror. 'Let go, Iqbal,' Himani said, brushing her forehead with her palms.

Iqbal's eyes didn't leave hers, but he took his hands from the top of the auto.

∼

A few days later, when Himani opened her locker, a note fell out. 'I do love nothing in the world so well as you—isn't that strange? *Much Ado About Nothing*, William Shakespeare.'

Himani clutched the note to her heart and looked around surreptitiously. Guilt, excitement and fear coursed through her, consuming her in a weirdly delicious, dangerous way.

There were many things Om was not, but he was enough. Or, thus far, had been. He was not physically or emotionally abusive, and he was a good father to Ika. He didn't go out spouting poetry at the drop of a hat; he didn't tell her relentlessly how beautiful she was, and her heart didn't start galloping like a stallion when she saw him enter a room. Why did she feel this way about Iqbal, she asked herself hopelessly, tossing and turning all night, trying and failing to understand her own emotions.

Ridden with guilt, she worked doubly hard at home, kept the house spotless, made extra food even where it was not needed. She washed and ironed Amma and Om's clothes. She sat for hours with Ika, playing with her dolls, all in the hope that it would somehow make up for her feelings for Iqbal Sultan.

She was in love, and foolish though she knew it was, nothing had ever felt like being with Iqbal. Himani didn't know what she could do to stop herself. Tea in the cafeteria had led to clandestine meetings in the park where for the first time, Iqbal, hesitatingly at first, wrapped his fingers around hers.

Then a few weeks later, sitting in the corner-most seats of a darkened cinema hall, Iqbal had turned to face her. The movie was halfway done, but Himani could not tell anyone who asked, who the actors were, so consumed had she been with Iqbal's physical proximity.

'Meri jaan, I can't focus on this movie,' he had whispered.

'*Sshh*! I don't want to miss a second,' she had whispered back.

'All I can think of is you, Himani.'

Himani had turned around to face him, and their eyes had met in the darkness.

'What I feel for you,' Iqbal had said, gently pushing back a strand of Himani's hair, his touch making a shiver run through the length of her body, 'is mad, passionate and extraordinary—the only way love should be.'

Himani had stared at him in the dark, and her eyes had flown to his lips. Suddenly, all she had wanted was to kiss him. Himani had never known passion like this. Sex with Om was mechanical and often painful. It almost always started with his desire and ended with him coming all over her. In this sweaty, dingy cinema, she had surprised herself by putting a hand on Iqbal's neck, pulling him closer.

It was scary. It was liberating. It was wrong. But also, nothing had ever felt this right.

And with that, on cue, Iqbal's lips met hers greedily at first, but then he slowly, softly, explored every bit of her mouth in a way that Himani had never known was possible.

Yet, it was not just this passion that began to define them. What was even more frightening was the friendship that began to take shape. Himani found herself sharing things about her past that she had never discussed with anyone. She finally gave voice to the nagging suspicion that her father had a role in her mother's 'suicide'. She told him how she'd spent years being Keerat and her stepmother's house help. For the first time, she told someone about how she'd continuously been told that she was lesser, not enough, unworthy. He listened to how she'd got married to a man thirteen years her senior who had never told her that he loved her. But all of it was bearable because of Ika.

Thoughts she didn't even know existed in her brain found an outlet in the presence of Iqbal's tender love, and Himani began to discover her true self.

Iqbal was gentle. With his words. With his actions. With his expressions. And Himani, who had lived her life—a life that had largely been dictated by tragic events—mostly untouched by gentleness of any kind, thrived in it.

He caressed the thoughts she shared with him as if they were precious. They mattered. *She* mattered. He treated her like a clever, modern, ambitious woman with a mind of her own and that alone was alien and exhilarating.

Trips to deserted industrial estates where they could kiss, after which Himani would reach home drenched in guilt but delirious with happiness, became common. Sometimes, Himani would sit and wonder if she even knew what she was doing. Wasn't it all going to end in tears any which way? Wasn't this always, from the very start, doomed?

Yet, being with Iqbal changed her. The changes were subtle but unmistakable. Himani hummed when she cooked. She laughed when she played with Ika. And when she thought no one was looking, she danced.

Amma observed it all and smiled. She had always wondered if Himani and Om were truly happy, but now she knew.

And so, in the February of 1994, Himani's relationship with Iqbal took a turn that she both dreaded and desired. Amma and Om were going out of town at the same time, one to a wedding and the other to a conference.

Her One True Love

'Should I take Ikadashi with me?' Amma asked. 'She has not been to a wedding in a long time…'

Himani, sitting at her mother-in-law's feet, cutting okra for dinner, didn't look up. Her heart was thumping. She pursed her lips and tried not to let any emotion show on her face.

'We will be gone only one night,' Amma added. 'I know you don't like being alone, *Bahu*.'

'That should be fine,' Himani said casually, expertly slicing the okra into two. 'A colleague from college, Mr Iqbal, will be coming to pick up a book, but other than that, I will keep the door shut and stay inside.'

'Iqbal?' Amma asked, crunching up her nose in distaste. 'Mussalman?' she asked as Himani nodded.

'Make sure you give him the book at the door. Don't let him inside our house,' Amma warned, and Himani nodded obediently. 'Don't let him touch anything in our house. A Brahmin's house.'

'How many chapattis, Amma?' Himani hurriedly changed the topic 'Shall I make two for you?'

The 'Mussalman' finally came home, but he didn't bring a book and they didn't have tea. Himani and Iqbal began to kiss the moment she shut the door behind him and with their clothes flying everywhere, they ended up on Amma's bed in the living room within minutes.

∽

'Oh, I forgot to ask,' Amma asked a few weeks later. 'Did your Mussalman professor come to pick up his book?'

Himani furrowed her brow like she didn't quite understand what Amma, sitting on the same bed that Himani and Iqbal had made love on, was talking about. '*Ji*, yes! Mr Iqbal.'

When Amma looked up a moment later, Himani had disappeared. 'Where did she go now?' Amma mumbled, annoyed, and carried on sorting clothes.

Himani, meanwhile, had rushed to the toilet. Restlessly, she stood by the wash basin, staring at the thin sliver of soap by the tap, waiting to throw up. Nothing happened, but when after a few minutes, she stepped out of the bathroom, her mind was racing. The nausea had been going on for far too long for it to be related to food, and she wondered if she should talk to Om about it.

But then another thought struck her.

'*Haye, Rabba,*' Himani gasped, bringing her hand against her mouth in shock. She slumped into the wall of the bathroom. It was a rather jarring shade of blue. The paint was chipping in many places, she thought listlessly. They should call someone to give it a lick of paint in time for Diwali. She slid down and sat on the floor, letting out a deep breath.

Her periods were at least two weeks late.

25

HL Office, Vauxhall, London

May 2019

'That *eejit*…err…Jacob called to tell me that you have been made exempt from your three-month notice period,' Preston said, running a hand through his ginger hair, looking like he was ready to cry. 'Apparently, I need to do as he says.'

'Sorry, Preston, it's a small world. I'm sure we will work again together someday.'

'We need to at least be in the same country for that!' Preston whimpered. 'When do ye leave for India?'

'Tomorrow night,' Ika replied, thrusting her fist into the pocket of her black bomber jacket. She bit her lower lip tersely.

'And when do ye come back?'

'Not soon,' Ika said and watched Preston's lips turn into an inverted U.

'And yer husband's okay with it?'

'When has he been okay with anything I've done? I'll risk this one,' Ika said. Preston nodded absently; he had had time to get proof against Jacob, but he had blown it. Time, treacherous and whimsical, was up. His nanna used to say—whit's fur ye'll no go past ye—what if the universe needed him to try once more?

There are moments in one's life when one has to muster all the courage one has, thought Preston, gulping with difficulty. He took a swig of Red Bull from a can kept on the table. It went in the wrong way, and Preston coughed and wheezed for an eternity while Ika watched, shaking her head slowly.

'I need you to know that I know what Jacob did…' he said, looking intently at Ika. It was important these things came out. Women need to speak up. And if they needed the help of men like him, brave and solid, he was there for womankind.

'What did he do?' Ika asked, feeling bewildered.

'You don't need to pretend in front of me, Ika. Not anymore,' he said, his face serious, the pimple on top of his nose quivering with emotion. 'The worst is over now.'

'What?'

'You are safe with me,' Preston said, imagining the camera panning to focus on his eyes. He has just pulled the pretty girl out from the clutches of a serial rapist, and she is clinging to him, more thankful than she has ever been. He is wearing a police vest and looking devastatingly handsome. Even more handsome than Fredrick Heisenberg. The girl looks up at him with adoring eyes and says—

'Shut up, Preston,' Ika said.

'Wha—' Preston looked at Ika, startled. Ika put her hands on her hips and had opened her mouth to speak when Becca, her hair flaming red today, ran into the meeting room.

'Ika! Why the fuck are you not picking up your phone, man?'

'Wha…?'

'Your mum has been trying to call you.'

Ika hastily pulled her phone out of her pocket. Eleven missed calls from Mummy seeing which a coldness gripped Ika's insides.

'Is everything—?'

'The flat...the flat.' Becca paled, throwing up her hands, 'caught fire.'

Blood drained from Ika's face.

'Everyone is okay, *don't panic*,' Becca added hurriedly.

'Okay, okay, okay. I'm okay,' Ika was breathing heavily and looking anything but okay. She pushed away Preston, who had jumped to Ika's side and put an arm around her.

'Your mum called some Fredrick, and he has taken your mum and Veer to Chelsea and Westminster Hospital.'

'Hospital?' Ika repeated weakly.

'Fredrick?' Preston repeated even more weakly, 'who is Fredrick? Some old friend? Some—'

'Shut up, Preston,' Ika mumbled, rushing out.

'Who is this Fredrick, Becca?' Preston asked, feeling more curious than he had ever felt in his entire life. Did Ika have a secret boyfriend? A Fredrick?

'Shut up, Preston,' Becca said unhelpfully and rushed out after Ika.

∽

'This is Room 305,' Jacob said, gently pushing the door open. Ika had bumped into Jacob at reception in the hospital, and they had rushed upstairs together, Becca following them closely. 'Why don't you go in and check on everyone, and I'll go speak with the doctors?' Jacob had added, taking Becca with him.

Taking a deep breath, Ika entered the room. Once Ika's eyes adjusted to the darkness, she spotted Himani lying on a couch in the corner. Himani stirred when Ika walked up to her, her hands flying to the small bandage on her forehead. 'Are you okay, Mummy?' Ika whispered. 'Where is Veer?'

Himani sat up, smiling gently at her daughter in a way that told Ika that she was okay, and pointed to the bed.

Many machines surrounded the bed, but none of them were in use Ika noted, her shoulders sagging with relief. Veer was on the bed, fast asleep, blissfully unaware of all the drama around him. A quick check confirmed that he seemed unharmed. Lying next to him, a hand under his head was Fredrick.

Ika let out a deep, shaky breath, feeling fragile, like a dried-up autmn leaf.

Veer had turned sideways so that his face was buried in Fredrick's chest.

'Mummy,' Ika whispered as she turned and crouched next to her mother, 'what happened?'

Himani rubbed her eyes wearily and put a tender hand on her daughter's cheek. 'I was at home when I sensed something burning. They are saying the fire began on the fourteenth floor and moved down. I grabbed Veer and made a dash for it,' she said, shaking her head. Then Himani smiled and said, 'I did manage to get our passports out though.'

'How clever of you, Mummy!' Ika said, grinning through her tears, feeling relieved to just be in the same room as Himani, Fredrick and Veer.

'I tried calling you so many, times but when I couldn't get through to you, I called Fredrick,' Himani shrugged. 'I hope you're not upset about that, puttar?'

Ika shook her head. 'I am just glad, Mummy, that you are all okay.'

'I decided to not call Vivaan. What, I thought, could he do from Lucerne?' Himani added indignantly.

Ika shook her head. 'There is no need to call him anymore,' said Ika, not sure of what that even meant at this stage, but the words came instinctively.

'Fredrick took Veer from me once I was out of the building, and that little boy has not left his side, Ika,' said Himani. 'It's like the two of them have some kind of bond.'

In the darkness of the room, Ika stared at the sleeping form of Fredrick, feeling hopelessness overcome her.

Ika sat next to her mother for a few more minutes, lost in thought.

'I need to stretch my legs. I'll take a short walk and come back. You can lie down on the couch,' said Himani, casting one final look at Veer, getting up and leaving the room.

Slowly, Ika got up and walked to the side of the bed closest to her son and put a hand on his chest, feeling the familiar rise and fall. Ika lightly rested her head on Veer's arm, and with every cell in her body, she thanked the universe for taking care of her baby.

Then, she walked to the other side of the bed. Fredrick was on his side, his body turned towards Veer, his back was towards Ika. She sat on the little blue stool next to the bed and slowly leaned into him so that her head was resting against the back of his shoulders.

Fredrick stirred and gingerly turned his head. He stilled when he saw her face just a few inches away from his.

'Thank you,' she whispered in the darkness.

Tenderly, he withdrew his arm from under Veer and turned around to face Ika. He propped himself on one elbow.

In the dark, sterile hospital room, as doctors battled to save lives outside, Ika and Fredrick stared at each other for a long time.

'You took care of Mummy and Veer,' she said finally.

'Of course,' Fredrick said softly.

'Why?'

'*Why*? Because they matter to me. Because *you* matter to me. Because no matter what, you'll always matter to me.'

'I told you I hated you,' Ika said in a small voice.

Fredrick watched Ika's face crumple and tears roll gently down her cheeks. Her dimples, unmindful of the feelings of their owner, appeared now, and Fredrick stared at them.

'I know you don't,' Fredrick said in a whisper, putting a hand on her head and then letting it slide so that it rested on the nape of her neck.

'I'm so, so tired, Fredrick,' she said, her shoulders slumping.

Fredrick sat up and pulled Ika into an embrace. He could feel her hesitate, but then she wrapped her arms tightly around him, sinking into the embrace. 'It's okay, Ika,' he whispered.

'Nothing is okay,' she said and brought her hands to her heart. 'My heart, Fredrick,' she looked up at him. 'My heart hurts… I… I feel like something has sucked all the happiness out of my life. Like time is refusing me any joy.'

Fredrick opened his mouth to speak, but the door opened, and Himani and Jacob walked in. Ika withdrew hurriedly. Fredrick continued to stare at Ika, unblinking.

Himani's face was expressionless as she walked up to the two. 'All clear from the doctors,' she said, her voice a tad too bright.

'Okay,' said Fredrick, still unable to peel his eyes off Ika. 'Let's get going. I want us home.'

'There is a hotel I know in Chelsea—let me call them and see if we can spend the night there. I am guessing we can't go back to the flat just yet,' Ika said, wiping her tears and pulling out her phone.

'Ika,' said Fredrick. 'You are *all* coming to mine. No arguments—not a single one.'

'I will call ahead to make sure Himani, Ika and Veer have the things they might need for the night,' said Jacob, who had followed Himani in, nodding vehemently.

'Fredrick, no—' Ika started, but Fredrick raised a hand to cut her short.

'No, Ika. For once, *please* will you just listen to me?'

She recognized that hard, shuttered look on his face. There was no winning with Fredrick now. To his home it would be.

An hour later, it was an odd group that walked towards Fredrick's car in the underground car park of the famous Chelsea and Westminster Hospital. Himani and Jacob led the pack in silence while Fredrick carried a sleeping Veer on his shoulder, one hand wrapped around Ika's waist.

'Thank you for everything,' Ika mumbled, feeling the safest she had felt in a long time, looking up into Fredrick's blue-grey eyes.

'This little guy,' Fredrick replied, nodding towards Veer, 'has my heart in a way only his mother ever has had.'

Ika stilled. A red Volvo drove past them. Fredrick stared into Ika's eyes and tightened his grip around her. Her beautiful face held a million questions. For a second that seemed to last an eternity, he wondered if there was any point in saying it out loud. *No, don't do it, you idiot. There is no point in saying anything— there is no future in which you can be together. Don't say it. It will just cause more hurt and more pain.*

'Ika?' he said in a barely there whisper.

'Hmm?'

'I love you,' he said softly, slowly. The words swam in the air around them, lingering lazily in the haze, enveloping them both.

Fredrick watched as Ika's little nose began to turn red. It made him smile.

'I always have and always will,' he finished, his voice still a gentle whisper.

At Fredrick's words, words she had in some corner of her mind always known to be true, a million thoughts erupted inside Ika's head. She shushed them. She wanted one moment, this one precious moment of being honest with Fredrick.

'I love you too, Fredrick,' Ika said simply, her voice a soft whisper that vanished into the magic of the warm night. 'I always have and always will.'

Earth had shifted on its axis for Ika and Fredrick, and it seemed implausible that all around them, life carried on as usual. A woman shouted in the background. A boy laughed. A car honked. A very pregnant lady waddled past them, grimacing.

Fredrick tightened his arm around Ika, and she slid an arm around his waist. They both smiled.

'Quack, quack,' Veer mumbled on cue, asleep, nuzzling deeper into Fredrick's chest, as always, making his presence felt.

'He is dreaming of ducks,' Ika giggled through her tears, and Fredrick laughed.

'They look happy—like a family,' Himani whispered to Jacob, having just stolen a backward glance.

'They *should* be a family, Mrs Joshi,' said Jacob, his face serious, and Himani shrugged helplessly.

'Some things are just not meant to be, Jacob *ji*?' Himani asked with a sigh, her heart heavy for her daughter and her mind wandering to all that had happened decades ago.

'No, Mrs Joshi,' said Jacob slowly, his own mind going back years and a wistfulness creeping up his chest. 'Some things are just not meant to be. It's most sad.'

'Indeed,' said Himani.

Himani and Jacob sighed in unison, both thinking about loves they had lost.

Many miles away, Preston also allowed himself a sigh and slumped into his grey sofa. It was correct to say that, for once, he was gobsmacked. He cracked open a bottle of beer and took a large swig. He read the message from Becca again.

Fredrick is Fredrick Heisenberg. The Fredrick Heisenberg. Ika and Fredrick are an item.

He could not believe it. Fredrick and Ika? *The* Fredrick Heisenberg and Ika? An item?

Preston took a generous swig of beer and hoped he looked cool and brooding doing it. It was time for some hard questions, wasn't it, he wondered.

Why had Ika always fascinated him so much? Why had he always run around Ika the way he did? Why did a smile from her make his day erupt in colour?

Preston shook his head.

Fredrick Heisenberg. God, *the* Fredrick Heisenberg. He had not seen that one coming.

26
Ballard Estate, Bombay
March 1994

The trees, lush and green, on either side of Sprott Road in Ballard Estate, drooped with the weight of the water and winds. The sleepy government buildings, their colonial architecture and the wide, tidy roads, even quieter on the weekend, came together to create a charming nook that had always held a unique charm for Iqbal. But not today.

All Iqbal had on his mind was Himani.

Iqbal had a niggling doubt that something was not quite right. He had seen her almost daily since their little adventure in her house a few weeks ago, often clutching a book—*Villette* by Charlotte Brontë these days—to her chest, eyes cast down, an air of worry clinging to her. And then, last week, she had vanished. General assumption was that she was unwell, and that made Iqbal very restless. He was about to go to her house when she reappeared, looking pale and distraught.

Iqbal could only imagine what his parents, the devout Muslims that they were, would say when he told them about the married Hindu mother he had fallen so hopelessly in love with. He had tried, Allah knew he had, to stay away, but the pull had been stronger than anything he had ever felt before. He was ready to give up everything for this love. There was no doubt about it in his head or heart.

With these thoughts running amok in his head, Iqbal stepped inside Britannia & Co, one of Bombay's most beloved Parsi restaurants and looked around. The faded paint and paintings added charm to the restaurant he knew had been set up in the early 1920s to cater to the British palate. His eyes scanned the room and only stopped when he spotted Himani at a table at the far end. Finally!

'*Adaab,* mohtarma,' he said by way of greeting, smiling as he sat down opposite her at the small table, bringing his hand to his forehead.

Himani, he sighed. She was wearing a yellow sari with a well-fitted, sleeveless black blouse. A small black bindi adorned her forehead, and her hair was tied into a bun clasped by a gajra of jasmine flowers. Bits of the white flowers poked out from beneath Himani's ear, and Iqbal stared at them, mesmerized. They were delicate and beautiful—just like his Himani.

He focussed on her face now, and his brow furrowed. She looked drawn and pale, and his heart lurched. Something had definitely happened in the past few weeks.

'Hello,' Himani said, a little shyly, putting a hand on her stomach.

'How are you, meri jaan? We have not had the chance to speak properly since… er… since…' he faltered.

Himani smiled shyly, colour rising up her cheeks. 'I know—things have been busy,' she said softly.

'Are you okay?'

'Yes,' she lied.

The waiter came to their table, and Iqbal said distractedly, 'Bun maska and teas, please, for two.' As the waiter left, Iqbal said, 'I've been thinking, Himani.' He covered her hand with his own, his green eyes blazing.

She looked questioningly at him, letting her fingers twirl around his. *It feels so good to just be able to hold his hand*, she thought.

'We need to get out of here.'

'But we just got here—'

Iqbal laughed despite himself. 'I mean, we need to leave Bombay…'

Himani stared at Iqbal, her mouth open.

'I've worked out all the details. I have a scholarship to Berlin, and I will leave by the end of the year. Come with me to Agra—I have friends there, and I can start the visa process for you too. And for Ikadashi, too, obviously. I have enough money to take care of us till we leave for Germany. We can start afresh, away from everything here, together, as a family of three.'

'Iqbal… I—' Himani gasped, her hand tightening around her stomach, around her secret. Her big, heavy six-week-old secret.

'Himani, just answer this question: do you love me?'

'Yes,' she said, looking down at his fingers entwined around hers.

'Do you love Om?'

'No, I don't, Iqbal, but a lot of women are not in love with their husbands.'

'That's fine, Himani, *meri jaan*, but we've been given a chance at true love. Are you going to throw it away just because other women don't have this chance? Can you imagine what it would be like to be able to live our lives openly and not meet in secret like this? For you to be my lawfully wedded wife? For us to be a family one day? Himani?'

'I don't know, Iqbal—I just don't know,' she said, withdrawing her hands from his fingers and holding her head in her hands.

'Find the courage in yourself, Himani—I know your heart wants this. Why are you letting society curb your happiness? You're answerable only to yourself.'

'My heart wants nothing more than to be with you, Iqbal, but—'

'There are no buts then. I've already bought three tickets for you, me and Ikadashi. We take the 4 p.m. Rajdhani from CST. Just bring a few sets of clothes for you and Ika, and I will take care of the rest.'

'Iqbal... I...'

'Stop thinking—if you think, you will never be able to do this.'

'Iqbal... I... have...' Himani looked around wildly, her heart thudding. *I need to tell you something. I should tell you. I don't want to tell you.*

'Just say yes—say yes, Himani! Either we do this now, or we live without the one big love the universe has been generous enough to give us.'

Himani took a deep breath, closing her eyes, trying to shut out the noise. Iqbal would make a good father to Ikadashi—there was no doubt about that. And the new baby, well, once Iqbal found out about that, he would simply go crazy with joy. He loved her. She loved him. It made sense, right? 'Yes,' she said, after what seemed like an eternity.

'Thank Allah!' Iqbal breathed out, shoulders slumping in relief. 'Now don't think any more,' he said, grinning, 'and be there with Ikadashi at 4 p.m. sharp. I will meet you at the station—trust me with it all, please.' He nodded at the waiter who put two plates of bun maskas in front of the lovers.

Himani smiled weakly in return, disbelieving the turn of events. Had she just agreed to elope with Iqbal, she wondered in utter amazement as she stared at the food on the table.

When Himani reached home, she threw her purse to one side, switched on the ceiling fan, which did little to ease the humidity the monsoons always brought, lay on the bed and began to think. Did she have the gumption, the madness, the courage that this love now seemed to demand, she wondered, her pulse quickening?

27

London

May 2019

At about 2 a.m., after having put Veer to bed in one of the many guest bedrooms (which, to Ika's surprise, had been miraculously equipped with a child's cot, clothes and some toys), Ika walked into the living room of the palace that was Fredrick's apartment. She vaguely recalled reading about the ten-bedroom Knightsbridge penthouse in some fancy magazine a few months ago. If memory served right, they had called it one of London's most sought-after addresses.

And not for nothing, too, thought Ika, looking around in amazement. Everything was done up in shades of grey and steel. Various murals, grey and abstract, occupied large walls. Ika stared at the seemingly harsh brush strokes and wondered if Veer could paint something similar at... erm... a much lower cost. The rugs, grey and washed out, appeared expensive like they belonged to a queen's palace somewhere in the hills of Europe.

The house was mostly bare, but even the starkness somehow, grave and silent, added to the opulence. A humungous piano, stately and authoritative, occupied a large part of the living room. A well-thumbed book of musical notes lay on the piano stool.

'I didn't know he could play,' she mumbled, struck by how well she felt she knew Fredrick but how little she knew about his life.

'Himani's settled in her room,' came a deep voice and Ika turned around, startled.

Fredrick had just emerged from a room and was walking towards her, the top button of his shirt open, sleeves rolled up, hands in his pockets—looking deliciously sexy. 'I *think* she understands how the shower works,' he added with a doubtful smile.

Ika touched her bun consciously. Without any makeup, she was sure she looked like something the cat had dragged in. In the rains. Ugh.

'Veer go to bed okay?' Fredrick asked and came to stand by Ika.

'He only spent about thirty minutes trying to break your exclusive, state-of-the-art, eye-wateringly expensive bed,' Ika said, her face serious. 'And then he tried to break the cot and then tried to kill himself by jumping off the bed into the cot.' Ika waved her hands dismissively, and Fredrick's smile widened. 'All the while crying because he'd been separated from you. But other than that, it was perfect.'

'I think I might have heard the screaming,' Fredrick laughed.

'The Queen in Buckingham Palace may have heard it too, Fredrick,' Ika smiled.

Still smiling widely, Fredrick walked closer to her and held her by her shoulders. The air around them felt different now that they had both confessed their feelings for each other, Ika thought. Lighter. Like heavy curtains had drawn apart, finally, revealing the truth. Like they, for once, for a little bit, did not need to pretend. And how liberating this felt, Ika mused.

'Hey,' he said softly, bringing her attention to him. Ika allowed herself to lean into him, her forehead touching his chest. She could hear the thudding of his heart, and Fredrick took her in his arms. 'You okay? It's been a long day…' he asked in a whisper, his chin resting on her head.

'My house may have burned to ashes for all I know, and as of tomorrow, I don't have a job, and I'm going to soon be leaving someone I love behind,' she said and looked up and smiled. 'But here, right now, I am, oddly enough, absolutely okay. Happy. The happiest I have been in a long time actually.' Ika shrugged.

Fredrick smiled. 'Come with me,' he said, holding her hand.

He walked her to a room that seemed to be his and shut the door behind them. There was a low bed in the centre, dressed in white and framed by floor-to-ceiling windows on two sides. There was a side table with a few iPads carelessly strewn across it and a huge TV on the wall. 'Let me get you some comfortable clothes,' he said.

Fredrick opened a door and walked into his closet. He came out with a white T-shirt which he handed to her. Ika sat down next to Fredrick, close enough for their shoulders to touch, shirt clutched in her hands. 'Do you love her?' she finally asked.

She heard him take a deep breath. 'Had I been truly in love with Ava, I wouldn't have fallen in love with you.' He paused for a minute and then asked, 'Does this feel wrong to you?'

'No,' she said, 'even though it probably is.'

'Who decides what is right and wrong?' Fredrick asked and leaned in to kiss the top of Ika's head. He slid an arm around her waist, and they sat like that, unmoving, lest the magic that surrounded them evaporated.

'Why did you disappear?' she asked staring ahead, her voice almost a whisper.

'Mostly because I was a coward,' he said, 'but also because I couldn't be around you while you let a man trample all over your spirit. I had to leave to be able to breathe.'

Ika let out a deep sigh.

'And also, while I may not love her the way she thinks I do, I couldn't leave Ava when she needed me the most... That night, as I waited for you to text, Ava called. I picked up the phone to tell her that I needed to end the relationship, but she was crying.' Fredrick's eyes had a distant look in them. 'Her latest movie had flopped, the reviews were terrible, and she was spiralling downwards. She has a history of mental illness—she was in rehab for anorexia for many months a few years ago—and she was scared she was headed that way again. I...I just couldn't... you know...break up with her then,' he said with a shrug. 'She needed me, you'd decided to stay with Vivaan, and I couldn't bear to be here. So, I left, Ika. It wasn't black or white, just all a dark, scary grey. A grey I couldn't deal with and decided to run away from,' he finished.

Ika tightened her arm around him.

'I'm sorry,' he said, staring ahead, 'you have been due an apology for a long, long time.'

'I wish you'd spoken to me once. Just once. To explain it.' Tears pooled in her eyes.

'I too wished you'd spoken to me once before deciding to stay with Vivaan,' Fredrick said, his voice heavy, giving Ika her first glimpse into the hurt she'd caused him.

She stared at his face lined with sadness and a coldness gripped Ika's insides.

'I'm sorry, Fredrick, I was so consumed by my own pain that I never realized that you got hurt too.'

'I should've explained myself, I know, at least when the anger subsided, but somehow I couldn't,' Fredrick said shaking his head. 'I'm really sorry for not responding to your texts and calls. Really, really sorry.' Frederick looked at her, his face sincere and lined with pain and remorse. 'If I could go back in time and change one thing, I would change that, and respond,' he said.

For a few moments, they both stared at the mural on the wall in front of them.

'Did you ever think about me?' she asked.

'Every single day, every waking hour, all these years,' Fredrick said with a small smile. 'Did you?'

'Every single day, every waking hour, all these years,' she replied nuzzling in, wrapping her fingers around his. 'Did you really come back to London because of me?'

'Absolutely,' Fredrick said simply. 'Harry tried to get his hands on AL the day you signed their offer letter. He goes for the jugular with me, and he figured out that you were my weakest spot. He would have made life hell for you. Jacob was able to thwart that attempt, but when he tried it again, I knew I had to come and get his hands off your company...' Fredrick's voice trailed off, 'and also perhaps I was just looking for an excuse to see you.' Fredrick turned his head so that his lips rested on Ika's forehead. 'I really missed you, Ika.'

'And you got engaged a day before coming to London?'

'I was scared. So,' Fredrick shrugged his shoulders helplessly.

'Protection?' Ika pointed to the ring on his finger.

Fredrick chuckled. 'Perhaps.' And then he paused. 'But still, look at us.'

Ika giggled into Fredrick's shirt.

'What is it now?' Fredrick asked, smiling already.

'Bad one.'

'Go on?'

'Even protection is only 98 per cent effective. I guess we are the 2 per cent,' and with that, Ika dissolved into peals of laughter. Fredrick tried to not laugh, 'Not funny!' he said, but seeing Ika tumble into a mess of giggles, he joined in too.

'Why are you leaving for India?' Fredrick asked a few minutes later once the giggles had stopped. 'Things with Vivaan?'

'He begged for forgiveness when I suggested divorce two years ago, and things were a bit better for a bit, but,' Ika shook her head, 'mostly, they have been the same. Screaming, shouting, putting down—the usual. I don't have any patience for it now, actually. I shout back too most of the time and hate it, but I don't take it lying down…'

'Good for you,' Fredrick replied.

Ika rested her head back on Fredrick's shoulders. 'I feel deeply unhappy,' she said in a small voice, 'I want to take a break from being with Vivaan. Think it all through. I desperately want Veer to be with his father though.'

'Even if he makes you so unhappy?'

'How does my happiness matter?'

'Your happiness matters the most, Ika,' Fredrick said quietly. 'Will you come back from India?'

When Ika did not answer, Fredrick shook his head. 'Sometimes, you have to be brave and leave,' he said, shrugging.

'And sometimes, you have to be brave and let go,' she said.

'When do you leave?'

'Tomorrow night.'

'So, we have tonight together?'

'One night together,' she smiled.

She lay on the bed on her stomach and rested her elbows on a white silk pillow, fingering the 'FJH' monogrammed in royal gold on it. Fredrick lay down next to her on his back so that he could look at her and take in the dimples, the olive skin, the dark black eyes for their first and last night together. He stared at her for a bit and smiled when she looked away with a shy smile. 'Come here?' he asked pulling her in. They wrapped their arms and legs around each other, trying to get as close as possible.

'Once,' Ika said, 'you said to me that you don't feel like you belong.'

'Hmm...' Fredrick pushed the hair back from her forehead.

'I want you to know that some part of you will always belong to me,' Ika said taking Fredrick's handsome face in her hands. 'In some weird, illogical, incomprehensible way, even though we may never see each other again after tomorrow, you will always belong to me.'

'I'm sorry I caused you so much pain,' Fredrick said gently kissing her forehead.

'When I met you, Fredrick,' Ika replied, 'I'd lost myself. In being with you, I found myself again. There have been hard times, but I'll always look at us with immense love in my heart. Always.'

Fredrick wrapped his arms tighter around her. 'And I've opened up to you in a way I've never opened up to anyone before and don't think will ever again. I've faced my demons and realized that some were not as scary as I'd feared. You taught me to live better, Ika. And love better.'

'What do I do with all that I feel for you, Fredrick?' Ika asked, helplessly.

He shrugged. 'I don't know, Ika. I've asked myself the same question so many times. This is the hardest thing I've ever done.

I love you, and even though we may choose to not be together, I'll always continue to love you.'

'I'll always love you too,' she said softly, smiling, a wetness appearing in her eyes. 'Please live your life knowing that there is someone far, far away who only wishes the best for you, who loves you,' Ika's voice faltered here, 'more than you will ever know.'

Fredrick looked away. 'This is hard, Ika,' he said biting his lower lip. Ika put a hand on his face and gently tugged at it so that their eyes met again.

'I love you. I love you. I love you. I love you,' she mumbled, smiling, her eyes shining with tears. 'I'll keep saying that even when I'm in India.'

His eyes fixed on Ika's, with one deft movement, he flicked a strand of hair off her face and then took her face in his hands. His eyes traced her face and then lingered over her lips. They reminded him of rose petals.

'You're beautiful,' he said and watched with a smile as a blush rose on her face. 'I think I'm going to kiss you now,' he whispered, smiling.

And with that, Fredrick wrapped his arms around Ika, lightly at first but with urgency a moment later, pulling her as close as he could. Time stood still. His lips found hers, and very slowly, the world around them began to dissolve into nothingness. It was just the two of them. Together. For one night. Their first and last.

28

Bombay Central Station

March 1994

Sometimes, love demands a courage that borders on madness. The kind of courage that Himani clearly didn't have, thought Iqbal as he watched the train chug out of sight. He let his suitcase fall on the platform with a thud.

Iqbal looked at the train tracks, and even from a distance, he could see the rats scurrying about. A little shiver ran through his body at the sight of them. A very old man, bent double with age, walked past him carrying a basket of *murmura* on his head. A little boy cried and his mother, squatting on the platform, smacked him into silence.

Another train arrived at the platform and planted itself firmly in place of the train that would have taken Himani and Iqbal to their future together—the old replaced by the new. Iqbal picked up his suitcase, turned around and walked out, the cacophony of the station helping him think.

What if something had gone wrong? What if she'd wanted to come, but someone or something stopped her?

Iqbal stared at his watch and immediately brightened. It was going to be 6 p.m., and the annual teachers' get-together was scheduled for 6.30 p.m. at the college. Himani would know that he would come there when he didn't see her at the station. He believed in his heart that Himani would be there, waiting to tell him how desperately she'd tried to get away and had been unable to. And in hushed tones, they'd make another set of plans to build a future together. They would try, again and again, till they made it work.

With renewed purpose, Iqbal hurried out of the station, pushing aside the crowd, hailed a taxi and jumped into it. 'Bombay College!' he said breathlessly. 'As fast as you can!'

~

The sounds of teachers laughing and talking reached him as soon as he walked through the main door. His steps quickened, and by the time he burst through the room, he was almost running.

'*Arre, Iqbal Miyan*, where are you coming from?' Mr Wahal asked, walking towards him. His mouth was red from the beetle leaves he was always chewing, and Iqbal couldn't help the wave of disgust that hit him.

Sugary red Rooh Afza was being passed around in Styrofoam cups, and paper plates laden with oily samosas and bhajiyas, generous dollops of ketchup on the side, sat on every table. These smells hit Iqbal and his stomach churned.

'Mr Wahal,' said Iqbal, forcing a smile and taking the Styrofoam cup he offered. 'Mrs Himani Joshi left a register I need to return to her—have you seen her today?' he asked, trying hard to keep his voice casual.

Mr Wahal's eyes grew big, and his face beamed. 'Oh, you've not heard, have you?

'Heard what?'

'Mrs Joshi resigned this morning.'

Iqbal stilled. '*What?*'

'Yes, yes,' said Mr Wahal chattily, blissfully unaware of how every word he uttered cut through Iqbal's heart. 'All very sudden. She came and met Principal Ma'am this morning. The family has decided to go back to… to wherever they come from,' he said, waving a hand dismissively. 'She has not been keeping well and wants a change…'

'What?'

There were a million thoughts running through Iqbal's head. *Did she say anything? Did she leave a message for me? Did she—how could she?*

'I… I should go… I…' Iqbal trailed off, walking out of the room in a trance. Mr Wahal stared blankly at the retreating form of Iqbal Sultan and thought that one could be good-looking as hell but what use were good looks if you didn't have any manners.

'Did it mean nothing to her? The love? The words? The promises?' he whispered to himself. 'Was she just playing with my feelings?'

The din surrounding him muted itself into non-existence and Iqbal slumped against the wall, all energy leaving him. His body felt numb. He closed his eyes. *Why, Himani, why?*

Iqbal put his face in his hands, and when he felt the tears come, he rushed to the gents toilet. And with that, for the first time in his adult life, the irreverent, once carefree ladies man found himself huddled in a corner in the gents, his body racking with sobs, sounds guttural and animal-like coming out of him that he did not quite recognize. Iqbal cried for a long time that day. He cried for the heartbreak he would always live with, and for the courage that Himani didn't have.

∽

The mood in the Joshi household could have best been described as cautiously happy. That morning Amma had seen a pale-faced Himani rush to the bathroom to throw up and had immediately called her son with the happy news.

Om, who had just come out of a three-hour surgery, felt like his heart would leap out of his body, so immense was the joy cascading through him. Another baby to love and cherish! A little sister or brother for his precious Ika? What could possibly be more wonderful? But to his great surprise, he came home to find Himani—pale and thin—crying.

'She has not stopped crying the entire day, Om—she's been walking around the house like a pitiful cat,' Amma whispered as soon as he put his briefcase and coat on the sofa. The TV was on, and Ika was sitting cross-legged in front of it, her mouth slightly open, her front two teeth conspicuous by their absence, watching *Tom and Jerry*. She gurgled with laughter, and Om looked distractedly at her before focusing again on his mother. 'Amma?'

'I don't know why she is behaving like someone died.'

'It's the hormones, Amma,' Om whispered back.

'What can we do to cheer her up, Om?'

'I don't know, Amma,' Om said. He got up and went to Himani, wrapping his arms around her awkwardly. Himani jerked away, and Om drew back in surprise. 'It's the hormones, Himani—that's what's making you feel low. Try being happy. You know, if the mother is sad, the baby gets affected too.'

'I don't care!' Himani shouted at her husband for the first time. 'I don't care. Why am I the one giving up on all my happiness for the sake of everyone else? It's killing me, Om, it's killing me. I want to die.'

'Himani! What's wrong?' Om looked at her, aghast at her words and anger. 'Let's get some food and go shopping to buy you something nice.'

Om had expected Himani to look brighter at the suggestion, but Om's words seemed to push Himani over the edge instead. Her whole body heaved with emotion, and big, fat tears started rolling down her cheeks.

'I am horrible, Om—I am a wicked person! I hate myself.'

'Himani, no! These are just changes in your hormones—you're nice, you're very nice,' he said, looking around helplessly, feeling very much out of his depth.

'I don't want to go to college anymore. I don't even want to see the building. I don't even want to pass by the building ever again.'

'Don't then!'

'I don't want to stay in Bombay anymore,' she sobbed. 'Everything in this city will remind me of what a terrible person I am.'

Amma, who had been watching the scene with some surprise, now got up. She walked slowly to where Himani was standing. 'Om,' she said to her son, 'my daughter-in-law doesn't need to work if she doesn't want to. Take her to Principal Ma'am today and have her resignation submitted.'

'Yes,' said Himani, wiping away her tears. 'I want to do that now.'

'And,' continued Amma, 'we have always talked about going back to Almora. You were talking about the new hospital opening there? Didn't Bishnoi Uncle ask you if you would consider taking a job there? Maybe it's time to think seriously about that.'

'It might be better for Ika also to grow up in the hills, away from the filmy culture of Bombay,' mused Om, looking at his wife—her face was wet with tears.

Over the next two days, Amma remained a mute spectator to her son's failed attempts at getting through to his pregnant wife. Resigning seemed to somehow make things worse; Himani paced around the house restlessly all evening, looking again and again at the grandfather clock in the living room, eyes welling up every few minutes.

'Why are you looking at the clock like this, bahu? Do you have to get on a train?' Amma asked lightly, putting a hand on her daughter-in-law's head.

'I don't have to get on a train,' said Himani, her bloodshot eyes blank as Amma shook her head. 'I can't get on that train!' she cried and broke into a fresh bout of the most pitiful sobs.

Amma shook her head and wondered what else she could do to calm the girl down. Himani was no longer making sense. A few days later, Amma watched as Himani called Ika and got the little girl to put her hand on her stomach. 'That's your brother, Iku,' she said to her little daughter.

'Really, Mummy?' Ikadashi asked, sounding awed. '*Inside* you?'

Amma craned her neck to look at the two of them and shook her head when she saw Himani break down again.

With Himani being so unpredictable and fragile, it was with immense reluctance that Om left for a conference in Delhi three days later. It was while he was there that he got the news of his wife having miscarried. Amma had gone to meet a friend that morning, and when she came back, Himani was in bed, crying like a baby, screaming that she had killed her baby boy.

In the weeks that followed, Amma and Om had tried everything to cheer Himani up, but nothing seemed to work. All Himani talked about was the baby and how it should have lived and how she was responsible for its death.

'I killed him, Amma,' Himani said yet again, her eyes filled with tears.

Amma sat on the bed in the living room and chewed on some paan before speaking. 'You didn't kill your baby, Himani,' she said. 'God took him back.'

'Why? Why did he make me kill him?'

'Maybe because he wanted him—just like he wanted your mother. And my mother.'

Himani paused. 'God wanted my baby...' she said softly, slowly.

'Yes,' said Amma, a faraway look on her face.

'Why?'

'Maybe because he decided that he needed that baby more than we did.' Amma shrugged.

'Maybe I should go to God too and see my baby,' Amma heard Himani mumble as she got up to go to the kitchen.

That one sentence made Amma sit up straight. *This girl needs a change of scene*, she thought, her heart thudding, *or she will kill herself. We need to get her away from here.* With that, she picked up the bright blue landline phone to call Om at the hospital.

A few days later, Om found himself sitting across the dining table from Himani, having just finished dinner. The roti on Himani's steel plate was largely untouched. She was crying less these days, but there was a vacant, dead look in her eyes that was even scarier.

'I've spoken to Bishnoi Uncle. If you want, we can go to Almora—I have a job there,' he announced.

Himani looked up at him, her brows furrowing under her red bindi. Wisps of hair had escaped the low bun she had tied her hair into that morning. Her kajal was smudged, making her dark circles more pronounced. Her sari didn't match her blouse. Ika was in front of the television, like she had been more often than not in the past few weeks, gaping at some Bollywood song that had the hero thrusting his pelvis everywhere with a silly grin on his face.

'We can put all this behind us. A fresh start?' Om watched in surprise as for the first time in what seemed like a really long time, a small smile appeared on Himani's face.

Yes, thought Himani, taking a tiny step out of the trance she had been in since she had found out about the pregnancy. It would be good to get as far away from Bombay as possible. To leave everything that reminded her of the happiness Iqbal brought to her life. To forget that life had once offered her a great love that she had refused. To somehow try and forget that a few days ago, she had walked into a shabby clinic, and a woman who smelled of cheap alcohol and wore blue plastic gloves had helped her get rid of the child that she loved with all her heart.

To somehow try and forget that she had chosen to not bring her own child into this world.

29

The Steps Leading to St Paul's Cathedral, London

May 2019

Francesca: *I am crying, like literally crying. Real tears crying. Snot running down my face crying. Not sure if that's because this little beast is chomping down on my nipples or because I have not slept in a month or because I cannot deal with your plight or because you are leaving.*

Ika: *Just give baby Viv a bottle, for God's sake, Fran.*

Ika scrolled down WhatsApp. There were 147 messages from Preston; there was no way she was reading even one of them. There were twenty-three messages from Vivaan.

A few furious messages from Francesca now popped in along with many links to articles on why breast is best. Ika shook her head in wonder. How her erstwhile weed-snorting best friend had morphed into Mother Earth with the arrival of a purply, squishy little thing was mind-boggling at the very least.

Ika looked up and stared ahead, breathing in the beauty of London.

The crowds leading to St Paul's Cathedral were, like always, a mixture of the smartly dressed office goers briskly walking to and fro from the office looking important and the wide-eyed tourists desperate to click selfies with the 'building' where Princess Diana got married. Sat on the stairs leading up to the cathedral, a half-eaten Pret falafel wrap in her hand, Ika acknowledged that there was a lot going on in her mind. In the last twenty-four hours, her family had escaped a fire, she had confessed her feelings for a bazillionaire who, lo and behold, returned them—firmly planting them in the category of star-crossed lovers—and by the time night fell, she would be on a plane to go back to India. That was the plot of a Bollywood movie right there, Ika thought.

She had always known, through Vivaan, how a relationship should not be, but in the last few hours with Fredrick, she had gotten a precious glimpse into how beautiful love *could* be. How love *should* be. Fredrick and Ika were not meant to be, she knew, but was the suffering that came to her through Vivaan worth it?

The sun shone, and the London spring—flowers everywhere peeping through—stared back at Ika in all its glory, teasing her, asking her if she was ready to leave London behind just yet. Spring, thought Ika, a new cycle of life, she mused, was that a sign? Ika bit her lower lip and allowed memories from the previous night to play through her mind for the hundredth time. Fredrick had touched her like she was the most delicate, beautiful thing he had ever held in his arms. His eyes had blazed with love, and she had found it difficult to peel hers away. 'I've never loved anyone the way I love you, Ikadashi,' he had said, and she had wordlessly curled around him, the brown of her skin against the white of his, both deliciously happy and unbearably sad.

Ikadashi sighed and took a sip from her bottle of water.

It had taken her thirty-odd years to find the love of her life, and she had allowed herself one night, just one night, with him. That was almost cruel, wasn't it, she mused wistfully. Unfair. Heartbreaking.

Ika and Fredrick had agreed that they would part ways that morning. She would be out of the house by 5 p.m. to get on her India-bound flight scheduled for departure at 9.20 p.m. from Heathrow. Fredrick promised he would not return before then.

The farewell. *Oh gosh*, thought Ika, the very emotional, heartbreaking farewell.

They had clung to each other, taking in as much of the other as possible. They had stared at each other, kissed each other, touched each other's faces and tried in many futile ways to make time last longer.

'I should go before Mum comes looking for me,' Ika had said, looking at her watch. It was 7 a.m.

'Let me kiss you one last time,' Fredrick had said, and Ika had smiled, tiptoeing close to him. They had shared a long, lingering kiss which had ended with Ika sobbing into Fredrick's chest and Fredrick biting the insides of his cheeks to keep himself from breaking down.

'I need you to give Veer something when he is a bit older,' Fredrick had said into Ika's hair. He drew back, leaned towards the desk by his bed and pulled out a small golden bag.

Ika had peered inside and found a well-worn Rubik's cube. She had gasped, touching it like it were the most precious thing in the world. 'Is this … this is the cube you were playing with when you met James for the first time?'

'This was the only possession I had for the first twelve years of my life. I clung to it, Ika. It was my respite from the ugliness around me. It was my hope,' he had said. 'You don't need to tell Veer about me, but if you're okay with it, just please let him have this. I'll feel happy knowing a bit of me is with him.'

'You don't want me to tell Veer about you?'

'How will anyone benefit from that?' Fredrick had asked, and Ika had felt her heart sink.

'I like to think that in an alternate world, you two would have been best friends.'

'An alternate world?' Fredrick had smiled weakly, leaning in to plant a chaste kiss on Ika's forehead. 'Where I get to love you both?'

'Hey,' came a rough voice, bringing Ika back to the cathedral and the sun. Vivaan stood in front of her, suitcase in hand. His white tee, blue jeans and black cap should have made him look younger, but he looked worn out. Older. Meaner.

Around his feet, pigeons pecked on the grey step. The sun shone brightly. A lady walked past them and leaned towards the ground to take a picture of the cathedral. Tourists chatted excitedly.

'Hey,' Ika replied squinting in the sun, bringing her hands to cover her eyes.

'Are you fucking kidding me?' Vivaan began, 'You are actually going? Just cancel those tickets. I'll find us a hotel to stay in till we find an apartment.'

'I'm leaving tonight, Vivaan.'

'What rubbish!' he exclaimed and let go of his suitcase, which fell with a thud onto the ground. He charged towards her. 'Let's get going, don't waste my time.'

A young girl sat next to Ika, munching on a bag of low-calorie vegetable crisps, looked up at Vivaan, alarmed at the tone of his voice. She shuffled away.

'I'm leaving for India,' Ika repeated.

'Without my permission?'

'Permission?' Ika scoffed, shaking her head.

'You can't do basic things, Ika. For all I know, it was your carelessness that caused the fire in the effing building. How do you think you will manage in India? Stop this childish behaviour and come with me.'

Ika's heart fluttered. The all-too-familiar nervousness gripped her heart. Maybe Vivaan was right—how *will* she manage things in India? And then another face loomed in front of her. Fredrick's. His kindness. His love. His words. No, scratch that, he is gone now, a voice said to her. But he trusted you with his biggest projects, Ika. He valued your judgment. There were occasions when you were his strength. You were the one who stood up for him in front of Stiller. *You.* He may be gone, but in loving him and in being loved by him, you realized your true self. Maybe you should not have needed that to know your worth, but you did, and now you know.

'This constant disparagement. I will not put up with it anymore,' Ika heard herself say.

Vivaan grunted. 'Then stop being a constant disappointment. Now shut up and come. I'm not going to ask you again.'

'You will never change,' Ika said quietly, letting go of the scarf she had been twiddling with nervously for some time, feeling a kind of calmness descend upon her. 'And I refuse to put up with this anymore. I'm leaving.'

'If you leave now, I'll not take you back.' Vivaan looked threateningly at Ika.

'If I leave now, I promise, I'm not coming back,' Ika surprised herself with her reply.

'You know we have Veer too, don't you?'

'We deserve better than this, both Veer and I.'

'You think there is some man waiting there for you, ready to marry you?'

'That's exactly it, Vivaan, there's nobody,' Ika said. 'Because there doesn't need to be another man. My son and I deserve not just a husband or a father. We deserve a good husband and a good father. And if you can't be that, we are better off without you.'

Vivaan stared at Ika.

She got up and dusted herself.

'Jacob's helping me manage the flat. I'll let you know what I decide to do with it.'

Vivaan opened his mouth to speak.

'No.' Ika shook a warning finger at him, her face expressionless. 'Don't tell me what to do with the flat that I bought with my money. While I may not have love, I know now what it looks like, Vivaan,' Ika said calmly, 'and it's not this. We don't love each other. We probably never loved each other. I stayed because I let you eat at my confidence. I believed somehow that you were what I deserved—a man who disparaged me every second I was with him. But I now know that I deserve better. Every woman deserves respect, and if you cannot give that to me, you're out of my life.'

'You will be all alone, Ika.' Vivaan said threateningly.

'I've been all alone these eight years, Vivaan. That's one thing I do not fear. My lawyers,' Ika said, getting up and putting her Ray-Bans back on, 'will be in touch. Let's not make it messy for us.'

And with that, Ika swung her Coach bag across her shoulder, heaved her backpack on her shoulders and began to walk away from the cathedral, feeling lighter than she had in a decade.

Vivaan was shouting in the background, waving his arms threateningly, but it did not matter, not anymore.

There it is, this is me, walking, literally, out of my marriage. I have no money and no job. I have a mother and a child to look after. Things will be hard, very hard, and I will be on my own. But I am strong and will find a way. I will live in respect. And I will be happy. And that matters. Finally, it matters. My own happiness matters.

Himani was standing a few feet away, two Costa coffees in hand. She had heard everything, her heart thudding. Tears, unashamed and unabated, were streaming down her face. With her arms, she wiped them away. Ika was being brave, and the least she could do was try and be brave too.

Ika had finally found her courage. Himani wanted to roll her tongue and whistle her loudest. She wanted to throw the coffees to one side and clap nonstop for her daughter. But this was a rather posh part of London where coffee throwing and whistling might not be appreciated, she thought and decided against it.

Instead, she walked up to her daughter and wordlessly but with her widest, happiest smile, handed Ika her cup of coffee.

'Let's get on that plane?' Himani asked gently.

'Yes, Mummy,' Ika replied, managing a small smile. Himani noted that her daughter's lips were white and that her hands were shaking. 'Let's get on that plane.' And with that, Ika slipped her hand through her mother's.

30

St Paul's, London

May 2019

Himani cancelled the call, put the phone in her bag, and as she got back in the car, she found herself thinking hard. It was, she knew, time to make a decision. Could she share the truth with Ika, she wondered? The driver turned on the ignition.

'Knightsbridge, please,' Ika said to the driver and then slumped against the seat, exhausted, and closed her eyes.

London sped past them as they drove towards Fredrick's apartment one last time to pick up Veer, their stuff and then head out for the airport. The two women sat in silence, both wrapped up in their thoughts.

'Why can't Fredrick and you be together, *puttar*?' Himani asked finally.

Ika allowed her head to roll towards her shoulder so that it faced her mother. Her eyes remained shut.

'Well,' she mumbled, 'Ava. And Vivaan.'

'Vivaan is out.'

Ika opened her eyes, surprised.

'Well, yes,' she said sitting up as if it had just struck her, 'can you believe it?' and then she slumped against the seat again, 'but Ava.'

Himani said nothing and went back to staring at the cars passing them by. River Thames appeared now, grey and petulant against the backdrop of the London skyline as their cab sped past Blackfriars Pier.

'Ika *puttar*, I need to tell you something,' Himani said finally, decision made.

'Hmm?'

'Many years ago, I met a man called Iqbal Sultan... and I fell madly in love with him,' Himani said, her voice even, like she was telling Ika something casual about her day.

Ika bolted straight up, spilling her coffee, and then spent the next few minutes furiously wiping it off the seat, apologizing to the driver who looked less than pleased.

'You what?' she managed, gulping once the damage had been undone.

'We were living in Bombay then,' Himani said.

'So that was when Baba...an affair, Mummy?' Ika's eyes had grown to the size of saucer pans.

Himani shrugged. 'It's hard to put a label on some relationships. Incorrect even.'

'And?' asked Ika, her mouth hanging open.

'And?' Himani repeated, her voice carrying some of the disdain she had always felt for her actions all those years ago. 'I did exactly what you're doing—I chickened out.'

∼

Fredrick stared at the screen in front of him, but nothing registered. He got up and then sat down. He put his hands in his pockets and then took them out. He sprang up from his chair with a grunt, paced the office and then plonked himself back into his chair.

'*Arrghh!*' he groaned into his hands, frustrated. Image after image from the previous night swam in front of his eyes, blurring the reality around him. Her smile. Her caresses. The way she kissed him. The way she looked at him. The way she loved him.

'*Arrgh! Arrgghh! Arrgghhh!*'

He had been unfaithful to Ava, and yet this didn't feel like cheating. The guilt could, and would, come later, probably, who knew, but what really felt wrong was the fact that he was letting Ika go. A cacophony of emotions rose in his chest again, and he wondered how he could put the night, the last couple of years—and Veer—behind him.

'May I come in, son?' Jacob's voice asked from a distance. Fredrick looked up, startled, sat up straight, fixed his expression and nodded.

'How are you, my boy?' Jacob asked, walking in and sitting down in front of Fredrick. Jacob stared intently at the handsome young man he had known for twenty-odd years.

'How can I help you?' Fredrick asked distractedly, looking at his watch. It was 11 a.m. He wondered what Ika was doing. Was she also thinking about last night? Had it meant as much to her as it had to him? She had tears in her eyes when they had kissed, of course it meant—

'Many years ago, Freddie,' said Jacob, taking off his glasses—rimmed with a bright orange that matched perfectly with his orange loafers—and putting them on the table in between them, 'I fell in love with a girl.'

'Florence,' Fredrick smiled weakly, thinking about Jacob's most devoted wife of many decades.

'No,' said Jacob, shaking his head, 'not Florence.'

Fredrick stared at him in surprise. 'So, before Florence?' he asked, sitting up straight.

Jacob shook his head slowly. 'She was the most beautiful burst of sunshine I could have ever imagined. I was a different person when I was with her. But…' said Jacob, pausing, 'she was not my wife. I was too scared to let go of what I had, to accept who I was and acknowledge what I wanted.'

'So … it was an extra-marital affair?' Fredrick asked incredulously.

Jacob shrugged. 'Call it whatever you want—simply put: it was the biggest love of my life.'

'And?'

'And nothing. I scampered back to a loveless but stable marriage and never looked back.'

Fredrick stared at Jacob. Jacob leaned in, put a hand on Fredrick's hand and whispered, 'To this day, every day, I regret not having the guts to own up to the love I had for that girl. Don't make my mistakes, Freddie. Don't let Ika go.'

~

Ika could only stare at her mother, open-mouthed. 'Mummy… I—' Indignation raced through her body, her heartbeat quickening as she struggled to find the right words.

Mummy had been dishonest with her Baba, her beloved Baba. Cheated on him. Dishonoured him. How terrible it—but then she paused, and her shoulders slumped.

'Oh god,' Ika mumbled weakly, dragging her palms down her face in frustration. Baba had been her best friend, but Ika also knew that stern words, words he would never use with Ika, had unceremoniously been hurled at Mummy with shocking regularity. It was an uncomfortable truth that Ika had shoved into a dark corner of her brain.

'I only ask you to not judge me,' said Himani, her face set, her heart beating fast. She wanted to tell Ika about her baby brother—she wanted to give that little boy the dignity of at least acknowledging his existence, but shame held her back. That, Himani realized with a broken heart, was her unborn son's destiny.

'I won't, Mummy.'

'Baba may have been a good father, but as… as a husband—'

Ika nodded. 'I know, Mummy.' And then she paused and asked, 'Do you regret it, Mummy?'

'Iqbal?'

Ika nodded.

Himani scoffed, 'On the contrary, it hurts,' she said.

'What does?'

'The letting go.'

'Why did you let go?

'Actually,' said Himani, breathing deeply, 'he suggested we elope. And I said yes.'

The cab driver, getting his money's worth from the conversation felt so shocked at Himani's confession that he sped through a red light. 'Damn!' he grumbled and then glared at Himani through the rear-view mirror like it was her fault.

'Oh my god!' Ika gasped, bringing her hand up to cover her mouth. 'Then?'

'I let him wait for me at the station, and I never turned up.'

Ika closed her mouth. 'Oh wowzers, Mummy!' she said after a bit, digesting the information.

'Wowzers it definitely was, puttar,' Himani mumbled distractedly.

'And?'

Himani smiled, shaking her head. 'And nothing. Do you know why I'm telling you about Iqbal, Ika? Why now?'

Ika bit her lip. *Yes, she knew.*

'I think you should find Fredrick and tell him that you're leaving Vivaan. Have left him. Do it before we leave for India. Give your love a chance, Ika.'

'It doesn't matter, Mummy. He has Ava, he won't—'

'And that's fine. You do what you should do. Leave the rest to,' Himani raised her hands.

'God,' chipped in the driver and Ika and Himani turned to stare at him.

'Fredrick is at the HE headquarters in Knightsbridge,' said Himani, looking questioningly at Ika. 'Should we go there now?'

'Yes, I think so,' interjected the cab driver even before Ika could reply. 'I am updating the sat nav now; give me the postcode, Mummy,' he said frowning, turning towards Himani.

∼

It was about 4 p.m. by the time Ika found herself running into Fredrick's office at HE HQ without knocking, her hair—no longer tamed by copious amounts of product—billowing around her like a black, wild halo. She stilled when she opened the door. The walls and furniture stared back at her. Her heart sank. 'Where is Fredrick?' she asked Ella, the HE HQ receptionist, who had followed her in.

'He had a meeting with Jacob this morning and has basically vanished since. I've—' Ella replied, gesticulating with her hands, but Ika dashed off before Ella could finish her sentence.

Ika dramatically barged into Jacob's office a few minutes later, again without knocking. She found him standing in front of a discreet, grey metal safe, and when he saw Ika, he stumbled in surprise.

About thirty envelopes, all identically white, fell from Jacob's hands onto the floor. Ika rushed to him, mumbling an apology, getting down on her knees to help him gather them.

She glanced up at the safe and drew back in surprise. It was filled with hundreds of similar white envelopes.

'Where's Fredrick, Jacob? I've been looking everywhere for him—he's not even answering his phone,' Ika asked as the two shoved envelopes hurriedly back into the safe.

'I had a bit of a chat with him, Ika, about you two. Pushed him a bit, and I think he got upset with me. He asked me to stop my "incessant interfering in his personal life" if I recall correctly,' Jacob shook his head, getting up. 'He got up and just left after that.'

Ika's face fell. *Of course.*

'I wish things had ended differently for you and Fredrick,' Jacob said, his voice small and sad.

'Me too.'

'Ask Fredrick to leave Ava, Ika.'

'I can't do that, Jacob, but what I can do, have done actually is that I've left Vivaan.' It was queer to say those words. *She had left Vivaan.* Wow.

'Golly gosh, Ika!'

'Golly gosh it is, Jacob,' Ika had to agree.

Jacob looked intently at Ika. 'So, you found the courage,' he said softly with a smile.

'Do you think it was the right decision?' Anxious, large eyes looked at Jacob.

'No one gets a medal for staying in an unhappy marriage.'

'Soon-to-be single parent,' she said, jabbing a finger in her chest.

Jacob now put an arm around Ika. 'You may be leaving HE and London, darling, but I don't let go of friends.'

'We're friends?'

'Of course,' Jacob nodded, grinning. 'You both are a little bit pathetic, you know,' Jacob quipped, adjusting his glasses. 'You and Fredrick.'

Ika rolled her eyes. Pathetic was the last thing the majestic Mr Heisenberg was.

'You are here because you just want to see him again—one last time. Isn't it?'

'No!' Ika shook her head vehemently. *Too* vehemently.

'Liar.'

Ika's shoulders slumped. 'I already miss him, Jacob,' she said pouting, her voice small, 'and I have not even boarded that godforsaken plane yet.'

'Don't look at me with those sad eyes,' Jacob said sternly, 'to leave is your choice.'

'Better to have loved and lost than to not have loved at all, etc etc?' Ika asked, shaking her head.

The two of them stood like that for a bit. His arm around her slim shoulders, both lost in thought.

'If it helps, I don't like Ava,' Jacob said. 'Never liked her. Unimaginably annoying, don't know how Freddie puts up with the incessant whinging.'

'That's a bit harsh, Jacob, come on!'

'It would be a pleasure to put little red ants in her tea.'

'Wow! What a mature way to deal with your disappointment.'

'I particularly dislike her entourage. Especially that bat shit crazy life coach who keeps talking about my chakras not being aligned with my heart or liver or spleen or whatever organ they are supposed to align with.'

'Who knows, maybe you do have faulty chakras. What else would make you want to put ants in someone's tea?'

'I am certain Ava will make Fredrick turn vegan. That boy loves his bacon.'

Ika guffawed. 'Maybe that's not a bad thing!'

'And make him sip lava water from New Zealand. And force him to eat only three grains of farro from the right side of his mouth at 5:53 p.m. each night. And make him wear tights and do some yogic-tantric Zumba.'

Ika giggled. 'Fredrick in tights. Doing yoga tantric Zumba.'

'Deeply disturbing image.'

And the two of them sat there, hips resting against the edge of Jacob's crowded table, hanging out one last time like friends, smiling, clutching onto the moment.

'To find love is rare, Ika,' Jacob said after a pause. 'Throwing it away is foolishness.'

'Jacob?'

'Yes, my darling?'

'Don't tell Fredrick I came looking for him again?'

Jacob slowly nodded.

'Jacob?'

'Yes, my darling?'

'I love you,' Ika said simply.

Jacob felt tears pool in his eyes, and he brushed them away hurriedly. 'I love you too, my poppet,' he mumbled, 'come on here,' and with that, Jacob pulled Ika into one final embrace.

Ika was so lost in untangling the mess that currently seemed to be her life that she realized she was clutching one of the envelopes from Jacob's safe only when she was back in an Uber on her way to Fredrick's apartment to pick up Himani and Veer.

Ika stared at the envelope and turned it over. 'Isla, 18.02.2005' was printed on it in Jacob's sprawling handwriting.

'*Isla*,' Ika whispered the name. There was a ring to it that she immediately liked, and Ika distractedly wondered who the girl could be before her mind drifted back to her own situation.

She was getting a divorce.

She was going to be a single mother.

She was leaving Fredrick.

She was never going to see the man she loved again.

How, she wondered, had she gotten her life into this mess?

31

Fredrick's Penthouse, Knightsbridge, London

May 2019

Ika's heart beat fast as she walked into Fredrick's apartment one last time. This was it.

The end. The closing of the proverbial door—the final and the forever.

Fredrick's head of staff, Estelle, who let her in, stood by the entrance waiting patiently and expressionlessly, her hands clasped in front, as Ika looked around the unoccupied living room.

'I'm just here to pick up Mummy and Veer,' Ika said awkwardly to Estelle, who nodded with a small smile.

Now this girl, Estelle thought with a sigh, *this* girl, I like. Really like. Perfect for Master Fredrick. She had spent the night here, hadn't she? If only…

Ika wondered distractedly why Estelle was staring at her, but then her eyes wandered across the living room to the door to

Fredrick's room. On cue, images from the previous night came rushing back. A longing for the love she was turning her back on seared through her, burning and visceral, and Ika clasped the head of the grey sofa for support.

'This is so, so, so hard,' she mumbled angrily, hot tears stinging her eyes. 'Why did I have to go fall for a man that everyone and their dog knows is dating a world-famous actress? I *deserve* this pain.'

Just then, her phone pinged, and she pulled it out.

Francesca: *Just get on the bloody flight. You will have nine hours to sob pitifully into your fugly beige economy-class blankie. Follow their wedding on the DailyMail as punishment. Hashtag FreddiewedsAvie!'*

Ika: *You have stopped swearing on text too?*

Francesa: *What if the baby, you know…*

Ika: *No, I don't know Fran. Viv is one month old. She does not read. She does not pick up a phone. Hell, all she does is loll her head from one side to the other.*

Fran: *Hey, she cooed last night. And almost half, no, quarter smiled. She is a $%%$£%$£ genius for her age.*

Ika grinned and put the phone back into the pocket of her red trousers. She tugged at the cream polo neck and cleared her throat. There was no evading it. She had to leave. And leave now if she wanted to get on that plane in time.

'Mummy,' Ika hollered, walking towards the room that had been assigned to Himani. 'Mummy?'

The door to Fredrick's room clicked open. Ika turned around sharply and stilled when she saw Fredrick.

His suit, navy today, was razor sharp, his eyes shining. With one hand in his pocket, he stood tall and broad. He looked resplendent, Ika thought, like someone had scrubbed him extra hard in the bath today.

Great, I am now hallucinating as well.

'Hi!' he said.

Wow, the hallucination speaks too, thought Ika, mildly amused. She blinked a couple of times to see if blinking helped hallucinations disappear. No, it didn't, she mumbled to herself a moment later.

'Ika!' Himani said as she walked out from behind Fredrick, Veer clasped to her chest.

Ika stared at Himani, Veer and Fredrick.

'Hi, Mummy!' Ika said, eyes still focussed on Fredrick. Himani affectionately patted Fredrick's shoulder. The pair exchanged a smile.

'You can see him?' Ika asked drawing back in surprise, looking at her mother.

'What?' Himani asked.

'You're not a hallucination?' Ika asked, tilting her head to one side and looking at Fredrick.

'What?' came Fredrick's baritone.

'Oh god, you're real.'

'What's wrong with you, Ika?' Fredrick asked, laughing.

'S—sorry. I thought… no, nothing,' she mumbled and looked around helplessly.

Fredrick ran his fingers through his hair, and for one fleeting moment, he looked unsure. He took a faltering step towards Ika and said, 'I know I am not supposed to be here.'

Act casual. Act casual. Act casual. 'It's okay.' She shrugged. 'It's your house—you're allowed in it.' Veer, always the one for picking the right moment, proceeded to thwack his grandmother in her face for no apparent reason. When Himani yelped and glared at Veer, he turned red and began to cry indignantly like he had been grossly wronged.

'I will take this monster away. You kids have loads to talk through,' said Himani and quickly walked into the room she had just emerged from, carrying a wailing Veer.

Ika now focussed her attention on Fredrick. 'My flight is at 9.20,' Ika said, glancing resolutely at her watch. *His being here doesn't change anything.*

'I'm very aware of the departure time of your flight.'

'I don't want to miss it. I came to take a shower and pick up Mummy and Veer,' Ika blabbered.

'Really? So keen to get away from me?'

Ika rolled her eyes and then smiled. A small, sad smile.

'Jacob is worried you will go vegan and attend *chakra* healing classes soon.'

'He is perpetually worried,' Fredrick smiled.

'Don't attend *chakra* healing classes.'

'I can't promise. Who doesn't want their chakras healed by a mysterious woman in harem pants?'

'Take care of yourself,' she said.

'Okay.'

'Don't work very long hours. Don't open any company in the Nordics.'

'Why?'

'Ellin told me you got voted sexiest something there.'

'Of course, in that case, I won't,' Fredrick replied solemnly.

'Don't wear a black shirt with a black jacket.'

'Why?'

'You look far too handsome to be allowed in those.'

'Of course. Noted.'

'Stay happy with Ava and don't miss me too much.'

Fredrick traced his temple with his forefinger, as if thinking.

'Neither of those is now possible, sadly,' he said, his face serious. He took a step closer to Ika. Perplexed, Ika took a step backwards.

'What do you mean?' she asked.

'Himani told me you had a chat with Vivaan?'

'Yes,' Ika took a deep breath. *So, he knows.* Her heart thudded.

'And?' Fredrick prodded Ika.

'I am getting a divorce.'

Fredrick raised his brow. 'So I've been told.'

'I… I…' Ika threw up her hands defensively. 'It's a decision I took independently of us. I won't become an obsessed stalker that you and Ava need to go to the police to keep away.'

'Exactly what I was worried about,' he said, taking another step closer.

'I will be in India—far, far away,' Ika said, taking another small step backwards.

'Come sit with me?' he asked, taking a few steps towards her, grabbing her hand and pointing to the sofa.

'I need to go,' Ika said, trying to wring her hands free of Fredrick.

'Just for a minute. Please?'

Ika let out an exasperated sigh and walked to the grey leather sofa. She sat upright, uncomfortable. Fredrick unbuttoned his jacket and sat next to her, half turning so that he could look at Ika properly.

Ika looked at him. His nose. His eyebrows. His lips.

His lips. She felt heat creep up her face. How delicious Fredrick's lips had felt on her bare skin. A little shiver ran through her and Ika shook it away.

Fredrick watched Ika stare at him; he watched the sudden blush come on, and he saw her shake her head. He smiled. What he would not give to find out what had just gone through her mind. 'You're fidgeting,' he said, smiling as he watched Ika sit on her hands.

'No, I am not,' Ika replied hotly.

Fredrick's smile widened. 'Why did you ask Vivaan for a divorce?'

'No one gets a medal for staying in a bad marriage.'

'You *almost* sound like Jacob.'

Ika grinned.

'Are you scared?' he asked.

'A little bit.'

'Of what?'

'Many things. But mostly the labels. Divorcee. Single mother,' Ika said, her brow furrowing. 'And of moving on.'

'From the marriage?'

Ika shook her head. 'From you. From us. From what could have been. You know, I need to go now,' she said, getting up, feeling the heat rise up her cheeks. 'If I don't, we'll miss the flight and, also,' she paused and stared at Fredrick, 'being around you is hard at the moment.'

As Ika turned, she felt long fingers grasp her wrist. She turned back to look questioningly at Fredrick. 'What?' she asked, her shoulders slumping. 'I really need to go now, Fredrick. Please don't make this harder than it already is.'

'You didn't ask me why I'm here,' he said, tugging at her hand, making her sit down again.

'Why are you here, Fredrick?' Ika asked with a frown, slumping back into the sofa.

'To tell you something.'

'What?'

'I had a chat with Ava.'

Ika's body stiffened at the mention of Ava's name.

'I told Ava about us.'

Ika brought her hand to her mouth. 'Why?'

'Why? Because that's the right thing to do. To not lie to everyone and carry on with this farce of being in love with Ava.'

'But ... we *just* talked about this last night.'

'And Jacob made me see sense.'

'Oh god!'

'Ika, I don't want to spend the rest of my life regretting, you know, us…'

'Did my decision to leave Vivaan make you do this?' she asked, her heart sinking.

'I found out about you and Vivaan when I came home to see you and tell you about Ava.'

Ika took a deep breath. 'You said that you've been betrayed by a lot of people and you don't want to betray Ava.'

'And how is lying about being in love with her not a betrayal?' Fredrick asked, his eyes dark.

Ika breathed out slowly, spreading a hand over her forehead. 'Are you sure?'

'That I do not love Ava?'

'Yes.'

'I don't love her,' he said. 'Maybe I would have been happier to marry her if we'd not met, but I can't spend my life with her feeling the way I do about you.'

'So, I essentially broke you guys up?' Ika asked.

Fredrick shrugged. 'I broke us up, Ika, no one else,' he said. 'I've been living a lie and don't want to do that anymore. I'm going to be selfish and choose love—the love I want.'

Ika looked at Fredrick, her mind numb.

'What's wrong in wanting what I want?' Fredrick asked, shrugging.

'Nothing,' said Ika after a pause. 'Nothing,' she smiled. 'What did Ava say?'

Fredrick let out a deep breath. 'It was actually very... I don't know... sad, I guess? There were a lot of tears, a lot of "Please tell me what I did wrong"s',' Fredrick rubbed his forehead and then dragged his palm down his face. He continued, 'Ava said she knew my heart had not been in our relationship for the past few months. That she appreciated the honesty, and while it would take her a long time to get over what could have been, she would much rather face the truth than live a lie.'

'Ava and I, you and Vivaan—these were both broken relationships, Ika...' Fredrick continued, staring straight ahead. 'We could have tried to fix them, maybe we did, maybe we could have tried harder—I don't know, and I guess we'll never know. But what I do know is that what we have here is beautiful...'

'It would've been easier had Ava ranted and raved,' Ika said.

'Yes,' Fredrick nodded, 'a lot easier. Jacob called to tell me that the word is out already that we've broken up. Apparently #AvaBreaksUpWithBillionaireBoyfriend is trending.'

Ika's eyes grew large. 'She has 35 million Instagram followers, and it may get ugly,' he warned and smiled at Ika's terror-stricken face. 'For a bit only. Jacob and I will look after you, don't worry.'

The two became quiet, sitting on the grey sofa, shoulders touching, looking straight ahead, both lost in thought. They sighed in unison and then looked at each other with a smile.

'Long day,' Fredrick said.

'Long day,' Ika replied with a wide smile.

'So?' His eyes turned sideways to face her, eyes twinkling now.

'So?'

'You're getting a divorce, and I am single.'

'Yeah,' said Ika slowly. 'How did *that* happen?' she asked as she splayed her hands across her cheeks. They felt hot.

'Should we cancel your flight to India?' Fredrick asked, leaning in.

'What?' said Ika in surprise, 'and not eat aeroplane food and not sleep on a chair with a screaming three-year-old for nine hours?'

'Despite its many obvious attractions, would you consider it, please?' Fredrick asked, grinning. 'For my sake?'

Ika smiled, and then the smile turned into a giggle.

'I love you more than I've ever loved anyone, Ika. And *finally*, I'm free to love you,' he said. Fredrick pulled Ika close and kissed her forehead. 'We'll ride this storm together.'

Ika buried her face in his chest. There was a lot to think about, to process, to understand. To forgive. To forget. But all that could come later. For the moment, she only focused on how much she loved the man in her arms.

'Do we have happy news?' came Himani's voice as she gingerly stepped out of the room, holding on to Veer's chubby arm, her heart thudding with excitement. For the last thirty minutes, she had sat listlessly on the bed, staring at the walls, distractedly minding Veer, her fingers crossed.

The sight of the Fredrick and Ika, their arms wrapped around each other, happy smiles plastered on their faces, was a good indication, she thought as she grinned, her eyes shining with tears.

Children, she thought as she and Veer ran to Fredrick and Ika for a group hug, *need help. Oh god, sometimes, they really do need help*. And thank god, *she* had had Jacob's help. As she wrapped her arms around Fredrick and Ika while still somehow managing to hold Veer, her mind went back to the many phone calls she'd had with Jacob since the fire.

It had been his idea. A two-pronged attack was what he had called it. 'You,' his emphatic voice had boomed over the phone, 'pick examples from your life. I am sure there are some,' he had said, and Himani wondered if he knew. 'Tell Ika why she needs to get out of that joke of a marriage. And I will manage Fredrick. They will behave like our words don't matter. There may be banging of doors, cancelling of calls, but soldier on, Mrs Joshi—our words will have an impact. They always do,' he had said.

Fredrick took Veer from Himani and planted a kiss on his cheek. Veer responded with the latest salvo in his vocabulary, 'Silly sausage!'

'Fredrick and Ika should be together, shouldn't they, Jacob *ji*?' Himani had asked on the phone earlier that day, right after Ika had asked Vivaan for a divorce, just before stepping into the taxi with Ika.

'The world won't be right if they aren't, Mrs Joshi. All they need is a bit of our help.'

When finally the group pulled apart, all tears and happy smiles, Himani drew to a corner, pulled out her phone and sent Jacob a text. 'The world is all right, Jacob *ji*,' it read.

A few miles away, Jacob, staring at the grey safe filled with letters, looked at his phone when it beeped. His face broke into a smile when he read Himani's text. The occasion deserved a letter, he thought to himself—this *definitely* deserved a letter. And with that, he pulled out a fresh sheet of paper and picked up his pen.

'Dear Isla, you will not believe what happened today...' he began writing in his neatest cursive.

32

Café Concerto, Knightsbridge, London

May 2019

The large windows embraced the summer sun that peaked in through them joyfully. Women in colourful clothes and men in shorts and shades sat in the café, drinking and eating. Smells—sugary and heady—of the strawberry gateaux and chocolate mousses wafted around plush chairs, chunky glass chandeliers, and mirrors rimmed in gold. The world happily soaked up the sun, oblivious of the storms that raged inside Himani's heart.

After much discussion with Ika, Himani had finally selected a blue dress that just about skimmed her knees. Scandalous, if you asked Himani.

'Don't you know? Sixties is the new forties, Mummy,' Ika had said, squinting at her mother, hand on her hips, handing her mother a light pink Dior lipstick. 'To go with the sun and the dress!'

Ika's strength in finally stepping away from her toxic marriage had inspired Himani, she had to admit, and given her the courage to reach out to Iqbal.

Though now, as Himani fiddled with her phone, then with the menu, distractedly fingering it, she wondered if the idea wasn't entirely mad.

'What the hell are you even thinking Himani!' Himani mumbled to herself as panic began to rise in her chest. She was about to get up and run out of the café when a tall, broad man appeared at her table. Himani looked up at him distractedly, her mind still contemplating how best she could avoid meeting Iqbal.

He's a professor was the first thought that came to Himani. The gentleman's shirt, a light blue linen of the same shade as her dress, was open at the neck and paired with beige trousers. His hair was mostly white, but his skin was youthful like it had decided not to age. When he smiled, as he did now, his eyes—a glorious shade of green—crinkled at the sides.

As recognition dawned upon Himani, she gasped and got to her feet, her hands suddenly feeling cold and wobbly. In the past few weeks, Himani had practised this precise moment innumerable times, often like a teenager in front of the bathroom mirror. But now that it was happening, she found herself unaware of what different parts of her body were doing. The hands that she didn't know what to do with, the eyes that darted everywhere, the smile that came and went and then came back again.

'Himani?' Iqbal asked, his voice wearing the hint of an accent, and Himani nodded.

Himani and Iqbal stared at each other. They were again in their thirties, and London was replaced by the little lanes of humid Bombay. She was wearing a cotton sari, her hair in a braid that swished about when she walked. He was a young teacher, naïve and madly in love, yet to explore the world and its wonders.

Iqbal took a step forward and unexpectedly pulled her into a long, tight embrace.

Himani let him hug her, closing her eyes. When she finally pulled back a few minutes later, they were wet. 'Let's sit down,' she said sniffing, looking everywhere but at him.

'Yes, let's do that,' said Iqbal, not taking his eyes off Himani, registering their wetness. 'How are you?' he asked gently.

Meri jaan. He used to call me 'meri jaan'.

'I'm good. You?' Himani said, smiling weakly. That fluttering in her stomach—that was the butterflies, wasn't it?

Iqbal stared into her eyes. 'I'm well too, Himani. Can't believe I'm actually seeing you after all these years—I'd long given up hope.'

'Thank you for coming to London to meet me,' Himani said.

'Nothing could've stopped me,' he replied softly, and they held each other's gaze before he spoke again. 'I was surprised you asked to meet me.'

'My daughter felt it was high time we did.'

'Aah, you told her about us?' Iqbal asked with a smile.

Himani nodded and then sat silently, nervously fiddling with the napkin on the table. 'I don't know what to say,' she said finally.

'That's all right,' said Iqbal, his voice even, his eyes not leaving her face even for a moment. 'We can just be silent—look at each other for a bit. I for one have an amazing view.'

Himani smiled, shaking her head. *Such a flirt even after all these years.* 'I heard you got married?' she tried again, feeling a little less knotted up.

'And had two daughters.'

'How lovely!'

'And then got divorced two years ago.'

Himani raised her eyebrows in surprise. 'Two years ago? Why at this stage in your life?'

'What do you mean *this* stage? I am in my early sixties and have a good two decades ahead, at least, if not more,' said Iqbal, touching the little flowerpot that decorated their table. 'Actually, I looked for you soon after my divorce was finalized ... but could not muster the courage to reach out, I guess.'

Himani looked quizzically at Iqbal. 'You divorced your wife of thirty years and then looked for a girl you spent less than a year with three decades ago?'

'Yes,' he said, his eyes twinkling. 'Something like that. The last time around, you were in a relationship, and when I met you this time, I didn't want to be in one.' He paused. 'I am assuming you're not in a relationship?'

Himani smiled. *This time.* 'Well,' said Himani, her face serious, 'there *is* this forty-year-old man I really like…'

At her words, Iqbal's face lost its colour, making Himani break into peals of laughter. 'No, Iqbal… there has not been anyone since Om… passed away,' Himani said, her face sobering up.

'I'm sorry, Himani,' Iqbal said earnestly. 'No matter what happened between us, I always wished you happiness with Om. I was very sad when Mr Wahal told me about Om's passing.'

'You remained in touch with Mr Wahal—of *all* people?' Himani asked, barely able to hide her surprise.

'Life has its own way of surprising us, doesn't it?' Iqbal said with an easy smile.

Himani nodded and fiddled with the menu on the table, a thousand awkward thoughts running through her head. How could she start to say all the things she needed to?

'I forgave you, you know,' Iqbal quipped softly, breaking her line of thought.

Himani looked up, startled. Relieved. 'Did you?'

'Yes,' he smiled. 'As I grew older and somewhat wiser, I realized that what I'd asked of you came at a very big price. At that time, in the throes of my anger, I doubted our love, trashed it, in fact, and I blamed you for many things. But I realized that the madness, the tempestuousness of love, came easily to me because I didn't have to think about a child being taken away from a parent she adored. You carried a much heavier burden.'

Himani slumped back into her chair and closed her eyes. 'You may have forgiven me, but there are many things for which I've not been able to forgive myself.'

She could stay silent, avoid the confrontation that her words would bring. But she wanted to speak. She'd been silent for far too long. 'Had it not been for Ika, I would have been at the station,' she said finally, her voice low.

Iqbal smiled. 'You were in a no-win situation—you didn't do anything wrong, Himani. You were being a mother, and there are few things greater or more noble than that.'

Himani looked at Iqbal, tears brimming in her eyes.

Iqbal saw them, and he stiffened. 'Now that the apologies are out of the way, let me look at you.' When Himani smiled in return, relief washed over Iqbal.

'Look at a sixty-year-old grandmother?' Himani asked.

'Look at the most beautiful woman I've ever seen is more like it, I'd imagine.'

'Even now? With the wrinkles?'

'Especially now. Especially with the wrinkles.'

Himani said nothing for a few moments, staring at the man she'd thought about every day for the last thirty years, and then she smiled.

'How's Ika?' he asked.

'Doing well and is a mum now. I live with her and Veer in London.'

'And with a certain Mr Heisenberg?' Iqbal said, his eyes twinkling. 'The tabloids are full of the Ika-Heisenberg-Ava angle.'

Himani smiled.

'I was never able to forget you,' Iqbal said as a sadness crept up on his chiselled face. 'Believe me, I tried but failed. Were you happy with Om in the years you had him with you?'

Himani looked at her hands and thought hard before she answered. 'Honestly? No.'

Iqbal pondered on Himani's reply for a moment. 'I'd imagined this would make me happy, Himani, but it just fills me with great sadness.'

'You showed me a love so glorious, Iqbal, that nothing ever could compare—I never stopped thinking about you either. There is, though, something important that I've needed to tell you all these years,' Himani blurted out before the courage that she held on to with all her might deserted her.

'Go on?'

'There was a baby,' she said in a rush, hurrying the words out before she changed her mind.

'A baby? Whose baby?'

'Our baby,' Himani replied quietly and watched the colour drain from his face for the second time that morning.

'*Our baby*?' he repeated slowly, aghast.

'You know... know...' Himani hesitated. 'That day in my flat...'

Iqbal shook his head. Of course, he remembered that day in Himani's flat, but a *baby*? 'Where is the child? Does he live with you? Did you give him up for adoption?'

Himani stared at Iqbal, suddenly scared as Iqbal's green eyes blazed with emotion. 'I had an abortion,' she said softly, hanging her head.

Iqbal stared at Himani. He opened his mouth but didn't know what to say. 'You…' he tried, but no words came out.

Himani watched in distress as Iqbal processed this information. He got up from his chair, sat down again, tried to open his mouth, shut it, paced the restaurant for a bit, his face dark with thoughts that swirled noisily in his head.

'Our baby?' he said finally, sitting down. Himani could see a film of water in his eyes, and tears pooled in hers. 'Were you pregnant when I asked you to come with me to Berlin?'

Himani nodded, and Iqbal breathed out heavily.

'Amma found out that I was pregnant and told Om, who thought it was his. And I couldn't live with that. I just could not. There was no way… it was the only way to… I don't know, Iqbal. I wish I had the courage to bring the child into this world, God knows I do, but I didn't.'

Himani stayed silent for a while, hands clasped together on the table in front of her. As tears chased one another down her cheeks, she said, 'I betrayed Om, and then to not betray him and Ika any further, I betrayed you and our son. You should hate me now even if you didn't earlier.'

Our son.

Iqbal, who had been staring outside the window, his eyes glassy, now looked at the tear-soaked face of the woman he had spent the last three decades loving. He got up, walked to the other end of the table, pulled his chair close to hers and sat down so that their shoulders almost touched. She looked at him in surprise as he wrapped his arms around her in a sideways hug.

'How scared you must have been,' he said finally to the top of her head, his voice a whisper.

At those words—unexpectedly kind and gentle, far away from the accusing, berating, angry ones she had feared—Himani's body sagged and slumped into the chair in relief. Sobs from deep inside her, coming from the hole in her heart that the abortion had left, broke forth, the long-buried pain bubbling to the surface.

'You know,' Himani said, between the sobs, 'Fredrick's mother gave him up for adoption, and I can see how that has broken him. And what course did I choose?'

And with that final admission, Himani's crying intensified. Words that she'd never uttered now found a voice, and her grief, stifled for so long, ballooned in front of her eyes. Iqbal held her tight, and she sobbed into his chest. A few moments later, she realized that Iqbal was silently crying too. His shoulders heaved, and with each heave, Himani felt her heart break again.

'Do you hate me?' she asked, looking up after a while.

'I've loved you far too much and for far too long to ever hate you, *meri jaan,*' said Iqbal.

Meri Jaan. Meri Jaan. Meri Jaan. His life.

Earth stopped. The sweetness of the two words drenched Himani in a kind of gentle joy she had never dared to imagine she would experience ever again. The two words told her far more eloquently than any speech ever would have that she was forgiven. That she was loved. That she was longed for. That she was desired.

There was little Himani could do to stop the fresh onslaught of tears that came from deep within her.

A bit later, once they were both calmer, Iqbal took Himani's hands in his.

'I'm really sorry, Iqbal,' she said, sniffing away the final tears.

'Shush, Himani.'

'I think about our baby every day. He would have been thirty-one now and perhaps even married…'

'Don't torture yourself, Himani,' Iqbal said gently. 'Allah didn't want him to come to Earth; we will ask Him questions when we meet Him. I'm sure He had his reasons.'

'I went to a shady clinic and some illiterate—'

Iqbal gently began to tell Himani to not go there, but then he stopped. Himani needed to grieve, and so did he, he realized. And with that, he nodded, encouraging her to complete her tale. Get it all off her chest. Speak the memories out to dull the sharpness of their edges.

Himani told him about how she'd found the clinic and how scared she was. She told him how she stood outside the blue, decayed door of the sidey hospital and how once it was all done, she cried for days—for their baby, for him, for herself. She told him how she grappled with suicidal thoughts that refused to let go of her and how Ika's innocent love saved her. She told him how she still loved and longed for the baby she had lost.

Iqbal listened, and he felt Himani's pain like it was his own. He held her hand, wiped her tears and cried with her. They sat huddled like that, for the first time, as parents together. Parents to their unborn child. They spoke about the baby for many minutes and agreed it would have been a boy—a boy with Iqbal's green eyes and Himani's love for storytelling.

'Do you see them, meri jaan,' Iqbal asked finally, 'the many loose ends to our story, hanging over the cliffs of destiny, swaying in the winds dependant on the forces of fate.'

'Yes, our story seems incomplete,' Himani agreed. She wiped the remaining tears with the back of her hand. 'So?'

'How about taking a bit of control? What do you think about giving us another chance?' Iqbal asked grinning.

'What do you mean?'

'Date? "Hang out", as the kids say these days?' Iqbal watched with relief as a wide smile broke through Himani's face.

'LOL, as the kids say these days?'

'IMHO, IDK why you think this idea is LOL-worthy. LMK when you figure it out,' Iqbal grinned, looking, Himani thought, utterly charming. 'Let's try and get to know each other better, small steps, just see where we get to?'

'Do you think it's a good idea?'

'I want us to share a life openly, Himani. No secret spots in gardens or the corner-most seats in the cinema or the bench farthest away from the gate. I want to love you the way you should be loved, honourably and with all my heart. If we can do that—*inshallah*—I think this is the best idea ever!'

Himani felt heat rise up her face.

'Is that a yes?' Iqbal leaned in, grinning and bringing his face closer to hers. 'Yes? Yes?'

'Yes!' Himani said loudly, laughing now, feeling the happiest she had felt in years. 'Let's get to know each other better.'

Iqbal's fist punched the air. 'Yes!' he shouted and then laughed, looking around. 'She said yes!'

'You're behaving like I said yes to marrying you!' Himani said, laughing.

Patrons on nearby tables looked at the handsome, older couple—the stylish man and his beautiful lady—and they ooh-ed and aah-ed and cheered and clapped. Himani glared at Iqbal, laughing and mouthed, 'Stop this!' as she blushed a deep red. She tried to say that they were not getting married, but the cheering refused to stop.

As she looked at the smiling faces of strangers beaming back at her, Himani realized that she could have never imagined getting another chance, or perhaps her first true chance at love in the seventh decade of her life. But here she was, feeling loved up like a twenty-year-old, butterflies fluttering in her stomach, ready to see where life took her with a handsome man she loved with all her heart.

Life. You live in constant fear of not knowing where the next bend will take you. But here was the thing, Himani realized as Iqbal got up and pulled Himani into a big embrace, the next bend could just be the beginning of the best part of the road trip called life—so why just fear the next? Why give up hope? Why think that just because life has not given you that one thing yet, it never will?

Life. How utterly amazing it can be, Himani thought, horrified in the nicest way as the waitress brought in 'celebratory cake' and congratulated them on the 'impending wedding'.

~

At that precise moment, halfway across London, behind firmly shut doors, Ika sat with Ellin in her office at HE HQ. Ellin was the only person in the world Ika could trust with the paper in her hand.

Ika looked on quietly as Ellin read the letter, swinging her chair around restlessly. When Ellin looked up, her usually expressionless face was distorted with a rare display of emotion. 'That bastard! That *fucking* bastard!' she said finally through gritted teeth, her eyes wide with anger.

'Now, Ellin, calm down,' Ika hurriedly said, putting a placating arm on her friend's shoulders. 'There's no time for anger—we need a plan.'

'Yes, I have one. We walk into that son-of-a-bitch's house and punch him hard in between his eyes and—'

'Ellin, stop. This isn't helping.'

Ellin let out a deep breath. 'What do you want me to do?' she asked a few minutes later when she felt calmer.

'Money is no problem—use whatever you need to use to get to the bottom of this,' she said, pointing towards the paper. 'Get me the truth. Just make sure no one knows what we are doing.'

Ellin, her face still red with anger, pushed her fisted hands into the pockets of her leather skirt and nodded.

'You and me,' Ika said gravely to Ellin, who nodded solemnly. 'And no one else. And certainly not Fredrick. Not Fredrick, no matter what.'

If this was true, thought Ika, breathing deep, the revelations would kill Fredrick.

Six months later…

33

Fredrick's Knightsbridge Penthouse, London

November 2019

Ika stared at Preston's Instagram update, shaking her head in disbelief.

'My elegant lady love,' the caption below a picture of him and Becca posing at Borough Market, mouldy-looking vegan bean wraps in their hands read. Since finding 'true love' with Preston, Becca had coloured her hair electric green and, in the picture, wore a matching green bralette and thick green eye shadow. 'How ye doin'? Awright, my followers? For the longest time, lavvy heid that I am, I thought I loved someone else. That love was funny, as in I didnae even know that I loved her,' the caption continued, and Ika winced, 'that 'love' sucked a lot of ma energy, leaving me breathless, bad breathless, like I was swimming against the tide. But loving this gentle soul,'—Becca had told Ika about how she regularly used to beat up boys in uni just because—'is easier. I swim with the tide for my Bikki.' Ika winced again at Bikki.

'True love, my dear followers, is easy. It flows. So, don't chase relentlessly after a love because if ye have to chase that much, that's yer clue right there to understand that the universe has not designed this love for ye. Yer true love awaits somewhere else, my followers, hidden at the moment, waiting for ye to discover it,' Preston preached to his forty-six Instagram 'followers'.

'Ika, love,' came Fredrick's voice and Ika looked up. He was leaning against the door of the living room, the sleeves of his white shirt rolled up, and arms crossed against his chest, looking scrumptious, 'do you think we can go to Paris?'

Ika felt a fuzzy, warm feeling wash over her as it did every time she saw Fredrick. 'Love someone who is kinder to you than you are,' Francesca had said to her earlier that day when she had popped over with baby Viv for brunch. Francesca, the mum, was both a revelation and a force of nature. Viv had not yet been allowed in a room with the telly on, was exclusively breastfed (obviously!), and consumed a healthy dose of classical music that was scientifically proven to increase her mental capacity. Party hopping Francesca now worked at a baby sling library in Wandsworth. She was already planning baby two, spoke a disturbing amount about baby poo and had still not slept a night since Viv's arrival. 'And Fredrick is that person for you, Ika. Love that you had not even thought possible is now yours. Forever,' she had gushed with hands clasped to her chest.

'Ika, darling? Paris?' came Fredrick's voice again, breaking her line of thought.

'Yes, sure—when?' she said, picking up her Smythson diary from her desk in the room in Fredrick's house that she liked to call her 'office'. 'Who are we meeting?' Ika asked, chewing the end of a pen.

Fredrick shook his head. 'No, not for work, just the three of us.'

'When?'

'Tonight.'

'Tonight?' Ika looked at Fredrick in surprise. 'What's going on?' she asked, narrowing her eyes and pushing away her new bangs. She tugged at her Zara shirt. Ika loved that Fredrick had not insisted she go full Prada when she started sharing a life with him. He was happy with her mad hair, pre-loved clothes and toys for Veer passed down from their friends with older kids. They make you, *you*, he'd said. Why would I want to change anything?

'I think it's time,' said Fredrick cryptically. 'A chopper is waiting for us.'

'Time for wha…?'

Just then, her phone rang, and she glanced at it. Ellin.

Ika took a deep, shaky breath. 'I need to take this, please,' she said with a nervous smile and got up, leaving a surprised Fredrick behind her.

Ika found herself crossing her fingers, unsure of what she was hoping Ellin would say.

'Hi, Ellin,' Ika said, picking up the call once she was in the living room far away from Fredrick, her heart beating fast. 'Yes, okay. Are you sure?' she asked after hearing Ellin out. Ika let out a deep breath, her heart sinking.

'Have you cross-checked everything?' Ika asked again, nodding as she listened to Ellin's response.

'Thanks, Ellin,' she said after a few minutes, exhaling loudly. 'You're a hundred per cent sure, aren't you?' asked Ika, pausing to listen. 'Okay, thanks very much, bye.'

Fredrick saw Ika stare distractedly at the phone. Her brow was furrowed, and she spread a hand over her head. Fredrick walked across the room littered with toy cars and fire engines to Ika. Veer was babbling a few feet away from them. 'Is everything okay, darling?' he asked, putting his hand on her shoulders.

She turned around slowly. 'Let's sit down, Fredrick.'

'Why, what's happened?' he asked, sitting down on the grey sofa next to her.

'Umm... I...' Ika faltered, spreading a hand across her forehead again, something Fredrick had realized she did only when she was very anxious. 'I need to tell you something.'

'What?' said Fredrick, 'you are making me nervous, Ika.'

'Ellin has found your birth parents,' she said finally.

Fredrick looked confused. 'What?' he asked, shaking his head. 'Valerie and... you mean... what?' he fumbled.

'I think you need to speak with Jacob, Fredrick,' said Ika, wetting her lips with her tongue.

'Why? What does he have to do with it?'

'Quite a lot, actually,' she said.

'What do you mean?'

'Can I hold you?'

'No,' he said defensively.

'Please?' Ika wrapped her arms around him and put her chin on his shoulders so that she could easily whisper in his ears. She didn't know if she could say it out loud. 'Valerie was not your mother, Fredrick.'

'*What*?' his voice was a whisper too.

Ika felt him snake his arms around her, and her heart broke for how Fredrick would feel once he heard what she had to say. But he deserved the truth, at the very least—the truth after all these years.

'Valerie was not your mother; a twenty-two-year-old named Isla, who lived in Texas, was your mother.'

Fredrick drew back, his beautiful face clouded with confusion. 'Was?' he asked slowly.

'Yes, was,' said Ika, her hands now ice cold, feeling the weight of every word coming out of her mouth.

'How do you know?'

'Isla was a bright college student who fell in love with a rich businessman who, it turns out, cheated on her. She left him and uni, got addicted to drugs, and it was during this time that she became friends with a prostitute called Valerie, whose name is on your birth certificate. Val was not your mum. Isla was.' Ika shrugged, her voice growing softer. 'Isla died by suicide after giving birth to you, and you went into foster care. Isla did not come looking for you, because she was…she was… gone the day after you were born…'

Fredrick drew back so that he was looking at Ika's face; his own was expressionless. 'What do you mean? How do you know all this?'

'Ellin—she has just finished tracking down the entire string of events leading to your birth.'

'And why do I need to speak with Jacob about this?' he asked slowly.

'Because,' said Ika, taking a deep breath, 'he was the rich businessman Isla fell in love with. He…' Ika fumbled, not quite believing the words coming out of her mouth, 'Jacob…is your biological father.'

34

Fredrick's Knightsbridge Penthouse

November 2019

At about 6.30 a.m., Ika, lying wide awake in bed, heard the door click open. The room was still dark, and Veer lay curled into her. Ikadashi saw Fredrick walk in and head straight for the bathroom. She sat up, her heart thudding.

Ika heard the sounds of water hitting the tiles. She followed him in. Fredrick had taken off his jacket and shirt and was standing in the shower, allowing hot water to run all over his bare back, scalding him. The steam condensed on the cool surfaces rapidly, giving the bathroom an eerie look.

Ika went to Fredrick and wordlessly wrapped her arms around his waist, her cheeks resting against his bare back. Ika let the water soak her too, her night clothes clinging to her body. A few moments later, Fredrick turned, wrapped his arms around her and buried his face in her shoulder. The noise of the shower drowned his muffled sobs, but the way his body heaved cut through Ika's heart. She held him tighter, somehow convinced that if she held him tight enough, she could save him from falling apart.

'I wanted answers, Ika,' he said finally, drawing back to look her in the eye, 'but not these answers.'

'I am so sorry, Fredrick,' Ika said, tears stinging her own eyes. 'James was your father then, and he is your father now. Nothing changes that. That is your truth.'

Fredrick rested his forehead against Ika's, the steamed-up glass around them mirroring the hazy, unclear thoughts in his head. 'I fired Jacob—and I almost hit him.'

Ika closed her eyes. 'What did he say?'

Fredrick exhaled audibly. 'He said he met Isla while he was still married and fell in love. Isla…' he paused, hesitating, 'found out about Florence and the kids and left Jacob. Jacob was apparently heartbroken. Very quickly, though, she started seeing someone else and no matter how much Jacob tried, she wouldn't speak to him. One day, she called him to tell him that she had had a baby with her boyfriend. She wanted to have nothing to do with Jacob, and he should never get in touch with her again.'

'And?

'Jacob then tried to forget all about Isla to get on with his life. However, when Valerie, Isla's best friend, was dying more than a decade later, she called Jacob to tell him that Isla died by suicide soon after my birth and Isla's boyfriend died soon after. So there was a parentless boy, aka me. Jacob could not imagine Isla's child living in an orphanage. He hunted me down and went to see me with Dad, who immediately wanted to adopt me. However, as time passed, Jacob could not ignore some things about me—apparently, I had his auntie's nose or something, and he got a paternity test done in secret a few years after the adoption. That's how he found out that I was his son. However, by this time, Dad was very attached to me and begged him to keep my paternity a secret.'

'Oh...' said Ika.

'So, he lied to me and kept on lying till you found out everything,' Fredrick paused. 'How *did* you find out?'

Ika breathed deeply. 'I chanced upon some letters written by Jacob. The one I got my hands on was addressed to Isla, and it spoke at length about,' Ika used her fingers to make air quotes, '"our son Frederick". The letter was dated—you were sixteen when it was written—and nothing about it seemed to make sense unless you indeed were Jacob and Isla's son. So, I got in touch with Ellin and asked her to investigate.'

'She has been helping me trace my parents for years.'

'And she has had this niggling doubt that Jacob blocked many lines of investigations.'

Fredrick shook his head in disbelief. 'Why did Isla lie to Jacob about me, Ika? Why could she not have told him straight away?'

'I don't know,' Ika shrugged. 'She must have felt very wronged, I imagine, when she found out about Jacob and Florence. She likely did not want Jacob to have anything to do with you?'

'Even when she was so fragile?'

Ika shrugged. 'Sometimes we don't know how fragile we are.'

'I wish I was there for her.'

Ika smiled. 'You were. I have no doubt that when she saw you, she was filled with love and her feelings for you must have tried to stop her.'

'But they were not big enough?' Fredrick asked softly.

'Maybe, Fredrick. Maybe her anger at the world was bigger? Maybe her heart was weaker. Maybe she looked for help and none came her way…there are a lot of maybes, but I have no doubt she loved you.'

'The way you love Veer?'

'Exactly the way I love Veer.' Ika shook her head. 'I wish I had found…' she said, looking around helplessly for the right word, 'easier answers, I suppose?'

'I wish that too,' said Fredrick, looking down. 'I don't even know who to trust anymore. Apparently, Isla lied even at the hospitals and checked in under Valerie's name—that's why my birth certificate had her name,' said Fredrick, shaking his head slowly, exhausted and spent. 'Isla betrayed me, Dad betrayed me, Jacob betrayed me.'

'Oh, my darling,' Ika whispered and pulled him back into an embrace. For a few moments, his body remained stiff with anger, but then he slumped into her, almost as if his own weight was too much for him.

'Help me, Ika,' he whispered. 'My heart hurts. Apart from you, everyone has betrayed me.'

'There is only one path to peace for you, Fredrick—forgiveness,' she whispered back, running a hand over his wet hair. 'Forgive everyone. For your own sake, forgive everyone.'

Startled, Fredrick stepped out of her embrace. 'Forgive Jacob too? Forgive the man who comforted me when I cried from the pain of not knowing who my father was, knowing full well that I was his son? I can think of no greater treachery.' Fredrick shook his head in disbelief. 'I will devote the rest of my life to making his life a misery.'

Ika put a hand on his arm, gently pulling him back towards her. 'Free yourself, Fredrick.'

'What do you mean?'

'These questions have haunted you for decades, and you have remained a prisoner of your past. If you do not forgive now, you will continue to remain imprisoned. You can't change what has happened. You have your answers—now push these chains away.'

'Isla and Dad are no longer alive, but I can't forgive Jacob.'

'Fredrick...'

'What if Jacob is lying about Isla and Dad? Jacob has taken both away from me—they are just two more people who also betrayed me. Apart from you and Veer, I now suddenly don't have *anyone*. Even my memories with Dad are now tainted.'

'The past won't change, Fredrick, and your future doesn't need to have anything to do with Jacob. This rage will destroy you too.'

For a few moments, the only sound in the bathroom was that of the water splattering on the floor. 'He is my father,' mumbled Fredrick, the awe in his voice unmistakable. 'You do realize, Ika... I have half-brothers and sisters I've known most of my life. Isla had siblings, and I'm sure some of them have kids. I have aunties and uncles and cousins...'

'I know, I know... and you will reach out to them. Fill your heart and their lives with love, Fredrick, and focus on this blessing instead.'

'What do I do? Just let Jacob be?'

'Parents are people too, Fredrick, as fallible as the rest of us. We now know that Jacob didn't even know of your existence until you were about twelve, but when he found out, he came immediately. Even though he did not know you were his.'

'But he let another man claim me, Ika!'

'Jacob did not know you were his. What was wrong in him letting one of the richest men in the world adopt the son of a woman he once loved?'

'Are you defending Jacob?'

'All I am trying to say, Fredrick, is that sometimes there is evil in good and good in evil. He did the best he could do. You know what this revelation also means?'

'What?'

'You once said to me that the thing you hated most about your mother was that she never came looking for you. Well, now you know—she didn't come looking for you because she was no longer alive.'

Fredrick nodded half-heartedly, thinking about what Ika was saying.

'And your dad,' Ika continued, 'if you have such immense love for him, I can only imagine the love he had for you. Maybe he asked Jacob to lie to you out of love? Maybe you were just beginning to settle into a life with him, and he didn't want your life turned upside down? Maybe he knew you were better off with him than with Jacob anyway?'

Fredrick stilled now, staring at Ika.

'Maybe what all these three people did comes not from their shortcomings but from their love for you?'

There was a lengthy pause after which Fredrick spoke. 'My heart breaks for Isla,' Fredrick said. 'She was *twenty-two*—just a kid.' He continued, his eyes sad. 'Perhaps she never wanted me, Ika.'

'Or perhaps she wanted you desperately and loved you more than you can ever imagine. Perhaps she hung on to you for far longer than her strength permitted her to? I am convinced, Fredrick, that every mother does *her* best for her child.'

'Perhaps, but we will never know.'

'Maybe we won't, Fredrick, and maybe that is okay?'

Fredrick seemed to think for a moment. 'Yes,' he said softly, 'maybe that is okay.' He reached for Ika again, and she put her hands on his face and rested her head against his chest.

'Do you know this is my favourite place to be?' she mumbled, jabbing a finger into his chest. 'This is home.'

'My chest?' Fredrick asked, surprised.

Ika smiled. 'You're home, Fredrick, for me and Veer,' she whispered.

Fredrick didn't take his eyes off her as he traced the shape of her face with the back of his finger. They slid to the floor, shoulders touching, holding hands, water falling around them in a curtain. 'I love you, Ika,' he said and looked sideways at her with a small smile, the first in what seemed like an eternity.

'Even though you can't see it, I *am* blushing,' Ika said in the darkness, and Fredrick's smile widened into a grin.

'Sometimes, I think that by putting you in my life, the universe is making up for all the love that I've missed out on. You're the answer to all my questions, you're who I belong to, you're my home, you're my faith—you're my everything.'

Tears, which Ika hoped were camouflaged by the water from the shower, streamed down her face, and she stared at the man she loved with all her heart.

'Before all of this happened, remember I was speaking to you about going away for a night? Well, this is what it was about.' Fredrick smiled and got up to fetch his jacket, water dripping off his trousers, his well-toned shoulders and back glistening in the light from the street. Once back, he pulled out a little jewellery box. He opened the box, and Ika saw a ring, the green of its emerald blazing at Ika as it caught the light from the moon that peeped in from the window.

'Oh gosh, no!' whispered Ika, with a little gasp, bringing her hands to cover her mouth in surprise.

'My plan was to do this with the Eiffel Tower in the background and not sitting on the bathroom floor, dripping wet and crying, but I don't think where I do this matters to you.'

In front of Ika's stunned eyes, Fredrick got onto one knee and said, 'I love you, Ikadashi Joshi. I love you with everything I have within me. I promise to look after you, love you and cherish you for all of our lives. Will you marry me?'

Ika hid her face in her hands as the emotions of the last few months found their way to the surface. As she crumbled, two strong hands grabbed her and pulled her into a tight hug. When her sobs subsided a few minutes later, she drew back from his chest and wiped the tears with the back of her hands.

'I am getting a bit worried here,' Fredrick said, grinning.

Ika giggled. 'Yes, Fredrick—a million times, yes!'

'I love you, darling,' Fredrick said as he took out the ring from the box and placed it on her finger. Her hands were shaking, and he held them tighter.

'I can't believe this,' Ika was mumbling to herself, looking a bit dazed. 'Have I just said yes to marrying you?'

'Yes. Is regret kicking in *already*, Ika?' he grinned, glancing at his watch. 'It has not been ten seconds!'

'No,' Ika laughed, 'no! no!'

'Silly!' he said, tapping Ika's head.

'Let's go and tell Veer!' Ika said, smiling and getting up. 'Everyone deserves some happy news!'

'Before we do, there's one more thing,' Fredrick said, tugging her back down. The two of them sat cross-legged, facing each other, as the water dripped around them.

'This is the biggest thing I've been meaning to talk to you about…'

'Bigger than Jacob being your dad and us getting married?'

'Yes,' said Fredrick with a gentle smile. 'Something I've been thinking of for a while. Veer,' he said simply, and Ika's heart skipped a beat.

'What about Veer?' Surely, he wasn't asking her to leave her baby boy? Or send him to India with Himani or to Vivaan?

'While I've had a very bad example for a birth father, I had an absolutely excellent example of an adoptive father,' his voice broke a little bit. 'If you would allow it, I don't want to just be Freddie to Veer. I want to be his father…it would mean the world to me if you would let me legally adopt Veer.'

Ika sat there, still, unmoving.

'He may not have my eyes or my smile, but he has my heart,' Fredrick said, 'as my father is supposed to have once said about me.'

Ika remained silent, looking intently at Fredrick.

When all Fredrick got was a blank stare, his heart began to sink. 'Ika? Have I upset you?' Fredrick asked, feeling very uncertain.

'I…' said Ika, biting the insides of her cheeks, '… have often thought that any child that has you as his father would be the luckiest kid in the world. And…' her voice broke, and tears started streaming down her face again, 'Veer would be delighted to call you what he probably already believes you are.'

Fredrick pulled Ika in and covered her face with kisses so tender that they made her cry harder.

'Veer Heisenberg then?' she asked, smiling, looking up.

'Veer Fredrick James Heisenberg, if you like the sound of that?' Fredrick quipped. 'Not that I've been thinking about this *at all*,' he said, grinning.

Veer. Fredrick. James, Ika thought to herself, mentally chewing on the name, *three men not connected by strands of DNA but by something far more powerful—love*. She smiled and rested her head on Fredrick's shoulders, wrapping her arms tighter around him and let out a deep, satisfied sigh.

'Veer Fredrick James Heisenberg is perfect,' she whispered.

~

A few months later, Mrs Pushpa Saxena, makeup-less and in an unflattering nightie, found herself staring at a photograph that had come to her from London via the post. She gasped when she recognized Sweety and Sammie. The *pretend* Sweety and Sammie, as she had found out about twenty minutes after the duo had escaped from the wedding. They were standing together, cheek to cheek, smiling, the man's arms around the girl.

> 'You were the first person to "see" us together, even before we saw it for ourselves. We thought you would like to know that we are getting married on the 15th of December this year. Thank you for your kindness that day and apologies for the lies.
>
> Kind Regards, Ika and Fredrick. (the Sweety and the Sammie)

A piece of paper fell down. Pushpa Saxena groaned as she bent to pick up the paper. And then she gasped again before her face broke into a wide smile.

It was a special £1000 voucher to be used across five years at any Waitrose Store when Pushpa Aunty travelled to the UK.

~

Thousands of miles away, in Washington DC, Harry Stiller stared at the note in his hands:

> *Inadvertently and as luck would have it, Harry, you played the biggest role in reuniting me with Ika. Despite all that has happened between the Heisenbergs and the Stillers, I'll never be able to thank you enough. Please consider this note as an olive branch. As a gesture of thank you, HE is pulling out of all bids where the Stilllers are keen contenders.*
>
> *Ika and I are getting married on the 15th of December this year and hope for your best wishes.*
>
> *Ika and Fredrick.*

'I always kinda liked this bugger,' Harry mumbled, running his fingers through his hair, fiddling with the note, perplexed at the unfamiliar warm and woozy honey-like thing that seemed to suddenly fill his heart. Was he having a heart attack, he wondered? He'd hated how Ika had spoken to him that day in the pub, hadn't he? But he had found himself thinking also about how she had stood up for Fredrick. It had, as they said, warmed his heart. What the hell was wrong with him, he wondered. 'You are made for each other. I guess I'm glad you found your way back,' Harry Stiller heard himself mumble, and then, much to his own shock his face broke into a very rare smile.

Fredrick was clearly Ika's one true love and for what it was worth, Harry was happy that she'd found him.

Epilogue

Houston Orphanage and Children's Centre, Texas
August 1992

Jacob watched as James turned around to look at Teddy for the third time.

James smiled. Teddy, his lanky frame making him look older than his twelve years, leaned against the entrance door of the centre awkwardly, unsure of how to respond to James. His eyes, the blue-grey ones that had captured Jacob's attention within seconds, didn't leave James' face. James waved. Teddy half raised his arm, hesitation written across his face.

Jacob looked at James. It was perhaps his frame—tall at six foot three, and broad—or perhaps his face, the blazing blue eyes and open smile or maybe it was the sheer goodness of his heart that shone through his face and his words—whatever it was, you could neither ignore James Heisenberg nor could you not be hypnotized by him.

Epilogue

Jacob jammed his hands in his pockets and looked at Teddy. My *son*, Teddy, thought Jacob incredulously. He took a deep breath. It was sweet, almost like a little present from God, that everything about Teddy was Isla. The blue-grey of the eyes, the almost imperceptible turn of the nose, the sharpness of his features—they all reminded Jacob of the woman he now knew he loved more than anyone else. Jacob's mind went to Isla's panic-stricken call from the hospital straight after giving birth. She was scared, sobbing as she asked him to help her bring up Teddy. Scared of a scandal, Jacob had refused point blank. A couple of hours later, he'd got the news that Isla had hurled herself on an oncoming truck. That Isla was dead.

Jacob still recalled with painful clarity the panic that consumed him in the coming weeks and months. That somehow this would come back to him, eating away all that he had worked so hard for—his job, his reputation, his family. He sent men to Austin to cover up anything that could connect the suicide to him. The baby's birth certificate was changed to reflect Valerie's name. The baby was sick, he was told and being put in foster care. No, he did not care, he had said.

All very good, till, a few years later, he allowed himself to acknowledge the deep chasm Isla's death had left behind. Antidepressants and never-ending sessions with therapists followed, but nothing seemed to help. In a cruel twist of fate, perhaps his punishment, half a decade after propelling Isla towards suicide, Jacob realized how much he loved her. Loved her and missed her. God, how much he missed her.

Sat in his den, in the darkness, he would play their story on loop in his head.

The day at the job fair when he had seen her first. That young, beautiful, lithe thing from a farm down south, about to start college at UT, looking for a job to fill her days. Her outdated clothes, the glasses, the stunning face: heart-shaped and angelic.

They'd spent hours listening to music at the Armadillo, eating ice cream on the Drag, walking around Seneca Falls, her co-op. She had, so sweetly, confessed her love for him. That night he had introduced Isla to cocaine in celebration. If only he knew.

Despite his truth, Jacob had not been able to help falling in love with Isla—more and more as the months passed. Till that fateful Christmas dinner on the UT campus when that stupid man had come up to him as he walked hand in hand with Isla and asked him about Florence and the kids. Every time he thought about that moment, his hands grew cold. If only he could go back in time and change that one moment.

Her slap still stung. Her tears still hurt. Her questions still haunted.

She dropped out of college, started doing drugs, became a mere shadow of her former glorious self. Unable to take any more of this, Jacob travelled to Austin one last time, his mind made up. He was going to leave Florence and set up life with Isla—he could not imagine being without her. He had been sure, hadn't he, that night, that he could make it work? They'd made love—make up sex, they called it now—one glorious night with her enervated, drug-riddled body. The next morning he had packed his bag and left Isla's little room before she woke up.

Such a dick.

Why? Why had he done that?

Honestly—he did not quite know. His best guess was that despite his resolution the night before, he felt petrified of losing everything—his career, family, reputation—for Isla's sake. When the time had come for the jump, he had not found in himself the

Epilogue

courage he had hoped for. She did not seem worth it all then. And how wrong he had been.

She tried to contact him, but he closed all doors. And then she told him about the baby—a result of their night together. And he told her he did not want to have anything to do with it.

His heart beat funny every time he thought about this. How alone his poor Isla must have felt. How had she coped? How? How? How?

And thus, he thought obsessively about Isla, the baby and what he had done to them, drowning himself further and further into depression. His therapist suggested he write a letter to Isla. That helped, pretending she was alive, far away but alive. It helped when nothing else did. And so, he wrote without stopping.

And then, just when it was all dark, dawn broke through in the form of a call from Valerie, Isla's best friend from her darkest days.

Val told Jacob about a baby, a baby she thought he did not know about. It was, Jacob felt, a new chance to undo some of his wrongs.

It took him a few months to gather both the courage and the information. The boy was twelve now he was called Teddy and he was in an orphanage in Houston. His son. His only son. Isla's son.

'I like Teddy,' James said, breaking into Jacob's thoughts. The two men were now both staring at the closed doors of the Children's Centre.

'I can see that,' Jacob remarked, raising a brow. 'What's going on in your head, James?' Jacob narrowed his eyes at his best friend and boss. 'Wait!' he slapped his thigh in mock surprise. 'Surely *you're* not thinking about doing it?'

'Doing what?'

'Adopting the boy?'

Epilogue

The night before, at an investor's party, finding James alone for a moment, Jacob had walked up to him, a plan forming in his head.

'I have to go to Houston for a day this Saturday,' he said, trying to sound casual.

'Why?'

'It's nothing—just an orphanage, charity, you know, the usual,' Jacob shrugged.

'An orphanage?' James asked. 'Do you mind if I come along?'

Jacob gulped; he had not foreseen this.

'Any problem?' James asked, one hand in his pocket, the other holding a glass of wine. He nodded at another investor who was walking up to them now.

'No, no.' Jacob hurriedly shook his head. 'Of course not—you are most welcome to join me.'

It's okay, Jacob had hurriedly reasoned with himself. *James can tag along.* Jacob only intended to see Teddy once before he went back to London and spoke to Florence about the affair. It was already giving him sleepless nights; Florence would leave, wouldn't she? The magazines would pick up on the news, wouldn't they? James would stop talking to him, wouldn't he? The price to keep Teddy in his life was going to be huge. Huge. But he was ready to pay it.

Was he?

For James, Teddy would just be a boy from an orphanage, Jacob told himself as the investor came up to them. There was no reason for James, even if he was with him, to suspect anything.

It was, thus, with a weird foreboding that Jacob had entered the Children's Centre that hot, humid afternoon in August, James in tow. He had stared unblinkingly at the beautiful, troubled boy who walked in, wearing an orange shirt and black shorts, both at least two sizes too big for him, clutching his rubiks cube like his life depended on it. And as he'd watched transfixed, his heart thudding, something unexpected had happened.

He saw James' eyes begin to shine the moment they fell on Teddy—a look he knew well. It meant James had seen something he wanted. Jacob saw Teddy stare at James, fascinated by the charismatic man, almost completely ignoring Jacob. He watched from the sidelines, the machinery in his brain working fast, as James and Teddy competed to solve the Rubik's cube. He smiled, proud, when Teddy won.

My boy. My son.

Fully aware of how desperately James wanted a child, an impossible plan began to take shape in Jacob's head. The plan was scary, atrocious and dangerous. But if things worked out, it would mean that he could always be by Teddy's side, never mind if it was not as his father. Teddy would have access to a world that James' huge wealth could easily grant, a world that Jacob may never be able to give Teddy. Florence wouldn't need to know anything—his marriage, friendship with James and reputation could all remain intact. And there was no doubt in Jacob's head that James would be a far better father to Teddy than he could ever be.

The downside was that there would be another string of lies. Could he do it? Live with this? Live in the continuous fear of being found out? Cover his tracks constantly? Keep looking over his shoulder? Keep lying to Teddy? Keep leading him astray as Teddy looked for his parents when he grew older?

Yes, came a voice from deep inside, *yes, you can*. He would if it meant a better life for his son. Yes, he would, if it meant he could still have Teddy in his life without having to lose his wife and kids.

Oh god, Jacob closed his eyes.

'What?' James asked, a look of annoyance passing across his face, bringing Jacob back to the stairs outside the Children's Centre.

'Are you thinking of adopting the boy?' Jacob repeated, making sure to arrange his face to register surprise.

'Why not?'

Jacob gave himself a mental high-five. There! He knew it—just knew it!

'Well,' Jacob rolled his eyes, 'Remember what Mike said? Teddy is a huge project!'

'He just needs love,' said James and the words hit Jacob like a bullet. 'How hard is it to love someone?'

'James... Teddy can't sleep without screaming through the night because of his nightmares. He doesn't read, has a history with the police—there are a million reasons to not adopt him. If you want to adopt a kid, let's find one that's more suitable.'

'His eyes...' James said, a faraway look on his face.

'Eh?' Jacob frowned.

'Jacob, Teddy's eyes are so sad. And they looked so trustingly at me.'

'James,' said Jacob, 'look at me. I am looking trustingly at you. Adopt me too, please?'

'Come on, mate!' James groaned, slapping his friend on the shoulder. 'Help me here.'

'You come on!'

'I've always wanted a child.'

'And you can have one whenever you want.'

'I am in the middle of a ridiculously expensive divorce, Jacob.'

'The entire world knows that,' Jacob chuckled, and James glared at him good-naturedly. 'Find another woman. There are enough exploding ovaries wherever you go. I can hear the sounds.'

'Sounds of what?'

'Ovaries. Exploding.'

James tried to suppress his laughter but failed, and a moment later, both men were laughing. 'I am,' said James, sobering up, 'only looking for true love now. I made far too many compromises with Diana.'

'We all make compromises in our marriages, James.'

'No, we don't have to—we should not have to.'

'You live in Utopia.'

'You're a cynic.'

'Marriage does that to a bloke.'

James grinned and said, 'I felt a very strong connection with the boy, Jacob. I… I don't think I can leave him here for any longer than is absolutely necessary.'

Jacob tried very hard to not smile.

'I know I am being impulsive, but… you know…' James left the sentence unfinished.

'Oh, come on, let's just get back to London, James, and think this through…' Jacob gently pushed James' elbow to nudge him towards their waiting car.

'I've been thinking so much about a kid, Jacob. Teddy may not have my face and eyes and smile, but he has my heart.'

Teddy has his heart. 'Okay,' said Jacob. 'Let me speak to Mike and figure out what needs to happen, should you decide to go ahead with adoption.'

James' face brightened at the words.

'Just getting details—that's *it*,' said Jacob. 'Then we go back to London and think it through.' And with that, Jacob began to climb the stairs leading to the main entrance of the Children's Centre.

'Jaco!' James called, and Jacob turned around. 'I don't think the boy is a Teddy,' said James, his brows furrowed in thought.

'Eh?'

'Can you also ask if we can change his name when we adopt?'

Jacob stopped and stared at James.

'Just ask?' implored James, grinning and raising his palms defensively.

'Any chance you have a name in mind?' Jacob narrowed his eyes at James.

'Fredrick,' said James. 'Fredrick James Heisenberg.'

Jacob, standing on the stairs, his body half-turned towards his friend, chewed his lower lip. Images of the intelligent, striking-looking boy came back to him. James was right. That boy was no Teddy. He was a Fredrick.

'Good choice, mate,' Jacob said out loud and continued to climb the stairs to go back to the Centre. The adoption would happen now. He knew it. He was going to make sure it did. The plan would work. It had to work. He was going to make sure it did.

Jacob let out a big breath and entered the Children's Centre once again.

Life is a gloriously mixed bag of things we deserve and those that we don't, thought Jacob. *Welcome, Fredrick James Heisenberg, welcome to a life you deserve and to lies you don't.*

Acknowledgements

Those who write will understand how a manuscript is not just a manuscript for an author. It is a real thing. Almost a person—sometimes more than a person. This book has been my companion for five years, my happy place in dark times, my peace in a sea of anxiousness. I held on to it during a terrible pregnancy, a global pandemic and through some difficult days as a working mother of two small children. With this, this little book starts its own journey and I stand at the doorway, sniffing away tears and waving goodbye. Thank you, my lovely fifth book for having been all that you've been to me in the past many years…

Priyanka Vardwaj, thank you for your patience and your time. You are my soul sister and also my unpaid shrink. I wouldn't know what I would do without you.

Katherine Clark, Jenna Walding, Anna Karin Conway and Andrea Edrupt, we are now that NCT group we used to talk wide-eyed about, the ones that survive the test of time, the ones that will be there, teary-eyed, at the boys' weddings. You girls are the best £350 I've ever spent.

Claire Higgon, Ankita Bhatia Dhawan and Catherine Martin, my best beta readers, for finding time to read my books and insisting faithfully that I write one wonderful story after another.

Gaurav Prakash for being the person that I turn to for help every single time.

Manasi Subramaniam because what you think of me as a writer is the wind beneath my wings. I dare to dream bigger because of you.

Prerna Gill for the unwavering faith you've had in this book.

Jon Vlassopulos for inspiring me in so many ways and for always seeing the good in me.

And finally, my most loyal readers who have waited patiently for half a decade for this book, you have my sincerest gratitude and love. Thank you for your emails and messages. You will never know how much every one of those messages has meant to me and how they egged me on when the road was most uphill.

To all of you very special people (and book), a heartfelt thank you.

About the Author

Ruchita is a best-selling, award-winning author of books on love and life. *Her One True Love* is her fifth novel. Originally from Lucknow, Ruchita is a triple gold medalist from IIFT Delhi and now works in music in London. She lives with her husband and two sons.

HarperCollins *Publishers* India

At HarperCollins India, we believe in telling the best stories and finding the widest readership for our books in every format possible. We started publishing in 1992; a great deal has changed since then, but what has remained constant is the passion with which our authors write their books, the love with which readers receive them, and the sheer joy and excitement that we as publishers feel in being a part of the publishing process.

Over the years, we've had the pleasure of publishing some of the finest writing from the subcontinent and around the world, including several award-winning titles and some of the biggest bestsellers in India's publishing history. But nothing has meant more to us than the fact that millions of people have read the books we published, and that somewhere, a book of ours might have made a difference.

As we look to the future, we go back to that one word— a word which has been a driving force for us all these years.

Read.

Harper Collins

4th

HARPER PERENNIAL

HARPER BUSINESS

HARPER **BLACK**

हार्पर हिन्दी

HarperCollins *Children'sBooks*

HARPER DESIGN

HARPER VANTAGE

Harper Sport